# Safe With You

**Faye Martin**

# Contents

# Prologue

A lice

When my mother told me to never trust a boy, I had taken her a bit too seriously. Well I always take whatever she says seriously, even though half the time she's just plain mocking me. Now you're probably wondering what type of mother she is but that's not the point -in case you're wondering she's an awesome mother with an annoying immature side. She even teased me once for dressing up like a nun. I think you get the picture.

The point is when my mother warned me about boys. I literally started keeping a ten feet distance from each, every one of those scary, loathsome creatures. My mind had been convinced thinking that boys are girl eating monsters. I'm pretty sure they are. I've seen so many girls cry over them. Girls say that boys break hearts. I don't know what it is that they do to 'break hearts' but anyways...

So you can imagine the terror I must be going through when I woke next to one. I have no idea how I ended up here next to this gorgeous looking creature with long lashes soundly shut and a long arm draped across my body.

For a moment, I felt safe when I should have been terrified but I wasn't. Maybe mother was really mocking me when she had said never trust a boy because I wanted to do nothing more than trust the creature lying next to me. Maybe he would be the medicine that could finally fix me. Maybe he would be the companion I've always missed.

Eyes fluttered open and I was swept away into an ocean of chocolaty brown eyes. I was drowning in the ocean. The waves were pulling me under. He stared at me half in daze, half in awe. I couldn't help but smile at him. "I can never get over the fact how beautiful you are,"

Everything was blurred into red. I pulled the white comforter over my face. "You're lying," I mumbled into the lenient comforter.

He pulled down the comforter from my face, the corners of his lips curling upwards into a breath-halting smile. "I'm not," His voice was pure and honest.

I bit on my lips, feeling somewhat insecure under his intense stare. "Damn, you're cheesy,"

A throaty laugh reverberated in his chest, I could his feel his laugh under my hands. It sent my heart into overdrive.

"I was trying to be romantic," He said in between laughs, wrapping his arms around my waist and pulling me closer to him.

I scoffed, wrinkling my nose upwards. "It doesn't suit you,"

"I guess it doesn't suit us, you know to do lovey-dovey things," He grinned. "I think I want to keep it simple,"

"Me too," I smiled, resting my head against his chest.

Maybe trusting a boy wouldn't be a bad idea afterall what could go wrong.

# Chapter 1

Alice

The skies were gray mixed with evening blues and the setting sun's orange. Rain cloud curtained the once shinning sun and its unreachable glow. A hazy, zigzag line of light separated the scenic sky, dividing into patchy portions. The colors were beginning to fade, smearing into the sky with long blue, orange steaks. The sun tried pushing the clouds away which only caused the skies to darken into a dark, blood red color.

As always my fingers were itching for a paint brush, I wanted to feel the cold wooden stick against my skin. I wanted feel the white canvas running under my hand. I wanted to watch colors come to life, I wanted white to fade. I wanted to stand in my room, next to the window and capture this scene with my very own hands but that won't be happening any time soon.

A loud, boom filled the air, the skies roared while the wind whipped wildly against me. The rain pelted against my back, fondling my bare skin, droplets of water slid down my face, past my eyelids occasionally few drops would fall into my eyes.

"Why am I such a cartoon?" I couldn't stop cursing myself.

You'd think by senior year I'd get used to high-school and everything about it but no, I had to act like a freaking freshman every single day of my pathetic life. As usual, I had missed the school bus because I was too busy helping our art teacher, Mrs. Clark set up for the art fair.

If my mother was here, she'd probably click her tongue and laugh at me to her hearts content. Then she would say "Ah, darling you should join the circus. I think they're missing you," I would give her my most annoyed stare and she would only pinch my cheeks in response.

None of this would have happened if my parsimonious father had gotten me a car. But hell no, he said that I'm a reckless driver and I'd probably kill someone with my 'terrible' driving skills not to mention he went far enough to add he would be guilty for the rest of his life since he'd be the root cause for the ending of an life. God, I cleared my driving test in the first try. I don't know in what dimension of space I'm a reckless driver.

This just proves he doesn't want to spend his precious, scraped up money on a car. He rather spend it on getting my little sister, Liza a make-over for her room. She has always been his favorite while I've always been the thorn in his eyes.

I kicked the empty coke can lying by the trash-can. It went rattling on the uneven side-walk stopping right in front of the automatic doors of a large, warehouse type store. There was a glowing green sign above the store with which the words 'Dollar Tree' had been written. The letter 'D' of the sign was flickering. It wavered a little bit before turning off completely.

Just then thunder boomed through the air muffling all other sounds-wait- I think that was stomach.  An empty stomach on a raining evening -What a magnificent combination! This combo surpasses all those pizza schemes the peeps at Domino's offer.

I hadn't had lunch today because someone thought it would be highly amusing to steal my hello-kitty tiffin box. I loved that tiffin box more than any plastic container I had in my kitchen. It had tiny, squishy-mushy hello-kitties on the front side and inside it's divided into three sections with three different hello kitty lids but that's not even the best part. It had a matching plastic hello kitty spoon which could transform into a fork with a push of a button.

Gah! Now I feel like crying on I'm going to miss that box- who so ever stole it may his/her soul burn in the never ending hole of hell.

Right now, I have an empty stomach to fuel. I stuffed my hands into the pockets of my green trousers hoping to find some money to spend. Come on, come on-there has to be something in here. I felt something hard hit the tips of my fingers, it was kind of sticking. I don't think I want to know what that was.

Nothing! I don't have a single penny on me. I wanted to smash my head against the brick wall.

"Why does the world hate me so much?" I huffed, letting my hands drop to the side.

Slouching my shoulders, I started walking past the store, trudging my feet along the pavement, the automatic doors flew open when I walked passed them. They sent a gust of air conditioning in my directions, stopping me in my tracks.

The store looked so tempting from here, I could see lanes filled gooey, icky junk food. I bet I'm drooling buckets loads of spit right now. Employees wearing green t-shirts stood idly behind the rows of empty counters, chatting animatedly with one another, occasionally one of them would burst into fits of laughter and the others would soon follow. Everyone was having a good time except for me.

A sigh left my lonesome mouth before could stop it. The eyes of the employees in snapped in my directions, well this is awkward. I better get moving before one of them mistakes me for a homeless plodder.

I picked up the empty can from the ground and threw it in the trash can nearby. HOLY Marconi and cheese! There was a dollar bill lying at the edge of the garbage bin. It lay totally unharmed by the wild rainstorm. I snatched it from the ground, straightening its edges.

Maybe, this isn't a bad day after all. With a dollar bill in my hand, I ran to the store, the straps of my backpack falling over my shoulders. I knew exactly what I wanted to buy.

A Chocolate Bar!!

Standing by the grey colored counter, a chubby guy with numerous puss filled zits covering his peachy face scanned my chocolate bar in a rich, purple wrapper. I could feel my mouth watering at the sight of it. I couldn't wait to have it my mouth. It sucks that could only have one bite because of my diabetes. I'll have to give the rest to Liza.

"That would one dollar and nine cents," And suddenly the world had lost its color, everything seemed so dull. It was like someone had taken a sledge hammer and ripped out my heart. 'One dollar and nine cents' I never knew those five words held so much power. It was enough cause a screeching sound to escape my throat.

I held up the crumpled up bill in my hand. "But I only have one dollar," I said meekly. The chubby guy rolled his eyes, chewing his gum more obnoxiously then before. I could see droplets of spit escaping his mouth and falling on his tight green t-shirt which showed his large belly.

"Do ya' have the money or not?" He replied, lazily.

"No but I can-"

I was interrupted by his bored voice. "Why are ya' wastin my time?"

He placed the chocolate bar on the other side of the counter above the cashier. My sweet, sweet love was now out of my life forever or so I thought temporary.

"Please, I'll pay you later,"  I pleaded.

"Sorry, can't" He shrugged his shoulders. "Rules are rules,"

"It's only nice cents," I groaned, resting my hands against the counter.

Mr. chubby let out an annoyed sigh. "Ma'am you're holdin up the line,"

"Just let me have the chocolate bar," I wasn't going to give up on my love without a good fight. No-way, you're going down chubby, pimple faced guy.

"Do I have to call the police?" He threatened, standing a bit straighter.

Okay, maybe I'll have to give up on my love. Good-bye, choc-bar -you and me shall meet in another life where we'll always be togeth-er for eternity (that is until I gobble you up). You'll always be the one that got away.

I was bidding my final farewell to the chocolate bar dressed in purple when a dime  appeared in-front of my eyes. I turned around to see a guy dressed in causal, plaid blue shirt hovering over my elf like frame.

He had his shirt rolled up, the sleeves neatly folded, and the shirt was tucked into his brown pants.  Strands of straight black hair covered half of his forehead while his chocolate like brown irises were hidden behind a pair of thick, black framed glasses stared at me in annoyance.

I bet he'd make a pretty girl. I mean look at this guy. He had a long, perfectly straight nose and thin, lean figure plus his clean shaved face just confirmed my idea of him being a pretty girl. If he'd just put on a wig and fake bra, I bet all those guys in my class would fall to his feet.

"You'd make a pretty girl," I breathed out, not listening to a word he was saying.

His eyes widened as he scrunched his nose upwards. "What did you say?" He raised the tone of his voice, bringing me out of my la-la land.

"Noth-nothing," I felt color rush to my cheeks.

He stuck the coin in my face, it sparkled in the light. "If I give you this dime, will you leave?" He spoke through his gritted teeth.

Without waiting for my answer, he gave Mr. Chubby the dime, his chest brushing against my nose, the trivial smell of his cologne surrounding me.

There goes my rule about keeping boys at a ten-foot distance. He took my hand and placed the receipt & chocolate bar in my hand.

"That's the thing about you girls," He grunted, looking at me as if I were some disgusting rat or cockroach. "They can't get one thing right,"

I bundled my eyebrows up, my mouth slightly agape. "Excuse me?"

He rolled his eyes in the most obnoxious manner possible. "Whatever," He sneered, standing back in the line behind the lady with her child in the shopping cart.

He leaned against the counter's black belt, picking up the basket from the ground. He stared past me, outside- at the store's display window.

"Jerk," I muttered under my breath. I would have picked-up a fight with him but I was feeling too weary from the empty stomach.Stupid stomach!

Gripping the chocolate bar in my hand I began dragging my sneakers against the tiled floors of the store, each step seemingly getting harder and harder to take with every passing second.

A gust of nausea shook my body violently, everything blurred, things were tumbling to the side maybe it me who was actually tumbling. I felt the cold, wet floors underneath me. There was a loud shouting noise.

I could sense people gathering around me, none of them bothering to help me. A warm hand lifted me upwards, cradling my back. I felt the hand snap to my wrist.

"Low pulse," A deep, rustic voice broke through the haziness, I lifted myself upwards, the throbbing in my head refusing to leave me.

I peeled my eyes open to find myself lying in the lap of the jerk from earlier. I got full-view of his brown eyes, I could see flecks of gold dancing through them, mixing in the deep, browns. I think he's eyes were more beautiful than any chocolate bar I've ever seen. I wanted to paint his eyes, I wanted to capture the strange, awe-striking quality about them. He readjusted his glasses, frowning slightly.

"Chocolate," I mumbled, pointing to the fallen bar. He picked it up and handed me the bar.

Peeling the wrapper, I bit into the bar, the instant the chocolate melted in my mouth, all weariness abandoned me. The crowd scuttled away seeing that I was okay.

"You alright?" he asked, helping me sitting upwards, he had his hand on my back and his long,  gaunt fingers wrapped around my small ones. His brown eyes were looking at me critically. "You're diabetic, aren't you?"

I nodded, untagling myself from him, I scooted away. Must keep the ten feet rule in my mind.  "Yah I had a low sugar attack," I stuffed the chocolate bar in the pocket of my green, military trousers.

"You should eat something every four hours,"

"I know," I sighed, closing my eyes for a slight second. "I usually do, today being a rare exception,"

"You're a rare exception, aren't you?" He gave me a crooked smile, the sides of his thin lips looping upwards, he leaned towards me, his slow, hot breath tricking down my neck. I tried moving away but he kept on moving his face closer "and by the way I think we'd make pretty girls-together,"I just stared at him. What did he just say? I felt my mouth fall open, did he just imply that......jerk! bastard!

He got up from the floor not waiting for an reply, dusting himself, he picked up the grocery bags and walked away.

I couldn't breathe. My ten-foot rule had been broken not once but thrice. I could still feel his breath on my neck. My skin was literally on flames.

I bet that chocolate-eyed jerk did that on purpose.

The door knob clicked open. I walked on into the house, the place I once called home. It didn't feel right to call it 'home' now that the one who had made this place a home was long gone. Tossing my wet backpack on the floor, I walked into the living room. Heavy, golden draperies, toffee colored sofas, glass center table, and out-dated side lamps decorated our small, gaudy living room.

Everything lay the same way since I left it this morning. The heart-shaped pillows on the sofa were still scrunched up on the ground, the carpet was still covered with the popcorn from last night, the T.V. was on, family albums were scattered on the glass, center-table.

There was a photo sticking out of the album, carefully sliding the picture out of the album, I held it in between my fingers.

It was a picture of my mother on Liza's birthday, she was standing next to Liza with a piece of cake in her hand, and she was stuffing the piece into Liza's mouth. Liza was wearing a short-black skirt. Her blonde hair had been styled into a tight bun.  My mother's brown hairs were perfectly straightened, tied into a ponytail with a blue ribbon while her bright green eyes stared into the camera, smiling broadly without sparing an ounce of happiness. People claimed that I looked like her, that I had her soft, tender features. They were wrong.  I was nothing like my mother. She was loving, brave, and confident. On the other hand I was a scaredy cat, a freak, an outcast.

Tears fell out of my eyes, landing onto the photograph. I missed her. I missed her so badly.

I wish she could come back. I wish she would come back call me a baby for crying all the time. I wish I could her laughter one more time. I wish she would tease me and laugh at my silly mistakes. I wish she would braid my hair. I wish she would hug me for the last time. I wish I had obeyed her maybe she would have been alive today.

I wish I wasn't the idiot who had let her mother die in front of her very own eyes. I wish I wasn't the girl with whom no-one talks. I wish I wasn't the daughter whose father can't look her in the eye. I wish I wasn't the sister who couldn't lend a shoulder to cry or provide comforting words.

I really wish I wasn't Alice Brown.

# Chapter 2

The ocean whisked me away from the palling surroundings, its blue waters, saline smell, glimmering waves alluring me, tempting me to run away. Seagulls soared through the sky, dancing with the warm rays of the sun. Fragments of sand sparkled in the light, twinkling like those proud diamonds in the sky.

Oh my, what I'd give to paint this mesmerizing scene. My fingers were itching for a brush. I could hear my soul cry for paint.

"Listen up," The beautiful scene in my mind was blurred by a voice, it was fading away leaving me with nothing other than memories.

"Children!" Mrs. Oswald shrieked like a parrot in a cage as her unflattering petunia colored dress ridded up her hideous, scrawny legs veiled by black stockings. She clasped her hands, together holding her breath ready for the revelation of today's torture. "There will be no classes today,"

A series relieved sighs escaped through the small communication application class. I too couldn't help but release a relieved sigh. You have no idea how torturesome this class is, the only reason I signed up for it because I needed the extra-credit since I wasn't too far behind from flunking high-school.

Now you're probably thinking "It's impossible to flunk American high-school, this chick must really be dumb," Firstly, American education system is not that easy you have to actually work to get good grades, shocker, I know right. Secondly, I'm not dumb, I just have a really, really bad habit of day-dreaming in class. It's not my fault though; the artistic part of my brain won't let me rest in peace.

Sandy, my friend, who was conveniently sitting right beside me, started bouncing in her seat, her red pigtails went flying off her shoulders. I couldn't blame her though. A day off in this class is just a really big deal. Mrs. Oswald makes us worker harder those experimental lab monkeys, by the end of her class you can't help but feel like a drugged monkey.

Sandy turned to face me, her freckled cheeks fraught down with a wide grin. "This is a miracle Alice, Now you can finally have some time to go to wonderland," By wonderland, she meant the day-dreaming land in which I always get lost.

"And you can finally finish reading your SpongeBob comic," It's safe to say Sandy is obsessed with SpongeBob hence her pet name Sandy. She practically forced everyone to address her as Sandy instead of Emily which was the name her parents had bestowed upon on her.

"Actually, I was going to finish my SpongeBob and Sandy fanfic," She replied after a moment of biting her nail. Okay, maybe she's more than obsessed with SpongeBob. It's kinda creepy if you ask me.

"That sounds great!" I tried smiling but failed miserably. Thankfully, she didn't notice this. She was too busy planning on how Sandy and SpongeBob would perform the act of copulation. Curse, my corrupted mind! This was all Liza's (my little sister) fault. She had forced me to read fifty shades of grey. I used to be an innocent, little dame-poor me, the price I had to pay for the loss of innocence.

"Class, I didn't say you have a free period," Mrs. Oswald smiled cheerily, leaning against the podium while her skull shaped earring began spinning. Those skulls looked real, maybe they belonged to one of her ex-students. "We're heading out to the science hall to meet the career counselors,"

And I thought I would get to go to wonderland. Chocolate Fudge!

Dazedly, I entered the science hall with Sandy walking besides me. Mrs. Oswald was leading our class, marching about like a Elf in Santa Clause's toy factory, her short height and  slippers with a cotton balls at the tip made her look more Elf like.

The science hall was large, around the size of one football field. There were several rounded tables placed against the walls with small, blue plastic chairs at their fronts. The light fell from the fiber-glass ceiling, covering the floor with an irregular green pattern. The hall was filled with teens and teachers chatting animatedly with one another. It was quite noisy in here.

Mrs. Oswald came to an abrupt; turning on her heals to face our class. She opened up the attendance roster. "Alice, Sandy and, Oliver go to table number one," She dictated the order faster than a military commander.

"Come on, let's go" I breathed out, feeling somewhat suffocated in the over-crowed hall.

"Aye-aye Captain," Oliver spoke, popping up in front of me. I narrowed my eyes at him. Oliver Stale, a guy staler than that chewy French bread they sell at Wal-Mart. Fastest swimmer on the swimming team, all A-student, and an amazing cotemporary painter were one of the few reasons I hated him. Fine, I admit it, I'm jealous of him, how can one person have so many talents? I could barely handle my passion for painting and yet here he was managing three.

"While you're at, sweep the deck, it's gotten dirty with stale bread," I scoffed wrinkling my nose upwards.

"Ouch, that must've hurt," Sandy pitched in, laughing.

Instead of getting offended, Oliver brushed it off with a lazy smile. He came started walking along me, the strong smell of chlorine escaping from his body almost choked me to death. I moved away him and closer to Sandy -must keep that ten-feet rule in mind.

His stormy blue eyes looked at me, amused. "I don't get why you hate me so much?"

I rolled my eyes. "Oh, please," I held my hand. "I just don't bother sucking up to you,"

"Nah, I'm pretty sure you hate me," He laughed, running a hand through his curly, blond hair, making them look dirtier than before. "Enough to push me into bucket of Fluoroantimonic acid which is the strongest acid known to man," Show-off using fancy, smansy words to mock me.

"I'd rather you tell that tooth-fairies don't exist," Chocolate Fingers! That didn't make any sense, I speed walked away from him, tugging Sandy along, I pushed my way through the crowd towards table number Uno.

"That didn't make any sense," Sandy hissed in my ear.

I shrugged my shoulders. "Patrick would laugh at that," Patrick as in SpongeBob's best-friend.

She furrowed her eyebrows together. "He's not that dumb,"

"Well, guess what? I am," I grinned, sarcastically.

"Sheesh woman, stop PMSing all the time makes me think you're on period-"

I held up my hands surrender. "Gawd, I get it, I get it," Talk about embarrassing the lady counselor on table number duos was giving me strange looks.

We stopped by table number one; there were three vacant chairs, two for me and Sandy and one for Oliver who was probably trying to find his way through the crowd.

There was a man sitting on the other end of the table, his head buried into some bulky looking book. I squinted my eyes to look at the title of the book he was reading with so much interest Medical Terminology: Language of Doctors and I thought he was reading some new novel or something.

Sandy and I took a seat, the chairs made odd squeaking sounds. I hope their structurally sound creatures.

The counselor didn't even bother looking up from that fat book of his, he kept on reading like there's no tomorrow. I didn't mind him reading and stuff but I was getting bored. Sandy stifled a yawn with both hands.

Oliver reached table Uno all out of breath. He was huffing and puffing faster than the big bad wolf and I thought he was swimmer. Aren't swimmers supposed to be good at breathing? His cheeks were tinted red and so was his nose. He placed a lanky hand on the side of his waist.

"I thought...you had gone to other end...of the hall," He said in between breaths, gripping the edge of the chair. "I went to table ten and then...I had to rush to other side,"

"Well we were supposed to go to table one," Sandy stated the obvious. I had an urge roll my eyes at her stupidity.

"No-duh, I know. At-least you guys could have warned me before running off like that. You know I had to push myself through stinky people who couldn't have bothered to put on deo-"

"If you're done with your hissy fit," He was interrupted by a cold, strict voice.  "I would like to start the counseling session," I turned around in my chair, only to be startled by a familiar pair of eyes.

"The chocolate eyed jerk"- How could this be? I think I called him a jerk out loud, thankfully no-one heard me.

He had closed the book he was reading earlier, setting it by his elbow. He looked different today, maybe because of the absence of glasses. His black hair was out of order, ruffled up in every direction. A slight subtle traced the edge of his jaw. He was wearing blue scrubs; the color really suited his complexion, making him look gorgeously flawless. There was a stethoscope clinging to his neck.

He caught me staring; recognition glinted in his mesmerizing brown eyes as he flashed a haughty smirk in my direction.

I averted my eyes from him towards Sandy who was fan-girling like there's no tomorrow. "I'd so replace SpongeBob for him," She tried whispering in my ear but she ended up half-screaming it.

Oliver grunted in response, wrinkling his nose upwards.

"No-one can replace SpongeBob, Sandy, No-one," Which only earned me a peculiar stare from the chocolate-eyed jerk.

I felt color rise to my cheeks as everything blurred into different shades of red. He wasn't supposed to hear that.

Grudgingly Oliver took a seat next to me, making a big show out of it by pulling the chair out far behind the table then sitting on it whilst strutting his legs outwards to cover the maximum amount of space. What bit into his butt?

"Well I'm supposed to help ya 'all pick a career," The chocolate eyed jerk started out, in a thick Texan accent. What was with the accent? He didn't have one when I met him the other day. "I'm going start it out by introducing myself," He spoke this without an accent. I think he had intended the accent to be some sort of joke. I don't know.

He placed his elbows on the table and leaned forward. "I'm Devlin Hutchins, a medical student at Johns Hopkins and I will be your career counselor for today," Johns Hopkins is the most prestigious medical college in the world. It was ranked number three in the top ten medical colleges last year. How do I know? It was my mom's dream to study in that college. Sadly, her dream never came true.

He held out a hand in Oliver's directions. "Why don't you introduce yourself as well?"

Oliver crossed his arms over his chest. "Oliver's thy name, a swimming beast and I'm gonna compete in the Olympics,"

Devlin, nah- I'm going to stick to chocolate eyed jerk raised an eyebrow in Oliver's direction but didn't say anything about his intro. "And you?" He stared at me with an expressionless face.

"Um," I felt my heart-beat increase. I hadn't really thought about this but here goes nothing. "Alice Hutchins,-" Wait!, did I just say Hutchins? Why did I just call myself Hutchins? I wasn't trying to imply anything like that? Gawd! Could I die out of humiliation?

"Aren't you Brown?" Sandy jutted in, making a weird face.

I blinked a couple times, "Yah, sorry about that. It's Alice Brown, painter, and I want to," I caught Devlin trying to suppress a laugh. I wanted to rip his head off. With great difficulty, I controlled my sudden urge to growl at him like a street dog and continued speaking. "I want to be an interior designer,"

"Interesting," He smiled slightly with edges of his lips lifting upwards. "Okay, now it's your turn," He turned towards Sandy.

"Name's Sandy Bottom, math's genius and I want to be a computer engineer," She spoke looking proud of herself; I would be too if I were a math's genius.

Devlin looked impressed by Sandy's choice which made me want to hide in a burrow and die with cute bunnies. Sniff yup that's life.

"Okay, I see you guys have your future's planned out so there isn't much left for me to do,"

"Free period?" Oliver jumped up from his chair, almost pouncing on Devlin.

Devlin shook his head, "But there are few words of wisdom I'd like to share with you guys-"

"Nah, I'm good so can I have a free period?" I wanted to laugh at the pleading expression Oliver was giving. I almost did but then I was reminded of the mortifying incident from few minutes ago so I bit down on my tongue instead.

"No and shut up with that free period crap," Devlin lashed out, looking awfully annoyed. I could literally see smoke escaping from his ears.

"Whatever," Oliver muttered under his breath before leaning back into the chair.

"I would like to give you guys some advice, keep a second career options ready like in-case you aren't able to compete in the Olympics, you should have another career option,"

This earned Devlin a loud grunt from Oliver.

"Or if you're unable to become an interior designer you should be prepared to change fields and stuff like that. Just imagine if you're unable to succeed in the field of your choice there should be another place you could run into so won't end like that homeless guy on highway i10," He sounded really bitter, almost pessimistic to me.

It was like he was putting our dreams down, squashing the rays of hope igniting inside of each one of us.

"That's not true. If we believe in our dreams and put everything into them then there is no-way we won't succeed,"

"Yah, I'm with her," Oliver pushed himself forward.

"Sometimes things don't work out you know because of-"He challenged my statement.

"Because of a negative attitude," I retorted.

"No, because of destiny," He stated, there was a rigid expression on face. Nothing I was going to say would change his thought process.

I pounded my fist against the table. "I don't believe in Destiny. It's all about hard-work,"

He shrugged his shoulders, calmingly, not affected by my angry mood. From the corner of my eye, I could see Oliver getting all worked up as well. On the other hand, Sandy sat their awkwardly watching us argue with bobbing her head back and forth.

"Sometime you are forced to believe in the existence of such things," Devlin smiled wistfully, as his brown eyes became a bit misty.

"Pft, Destiny," Oliver scoffed.

"I'm just stating the reality of life," He sighed, picking up his book and opening it to where he had left off.

"I think you have a distorted sense of reality-"I was cut-off by the bell. Finally! I got up from the chair without turning back to look at Devlin once and I got the hell out of there.

I wasn't going to miss the bus today. Not in a million years shall I miss the bus. The sole purpose of my life was to get on that yellow machine before it ran away.

I rushed out of the classroom, swiftly packing my bags in the process. I tumbled into the overly crowded hall. The incoming body of students shoved me towards the exit. I moved along the crowd like a wave slipping niftily through the packed hall. There is no freaking way I was going to miss the bus.

A little opening was visible, little rays of light and hope danced in front of me and boom I was out of school. I took in a deep breath of air, happy with my feat. Now all I had to do was go to the parking-lot and find bus no. 21.

My fellow schoolmates, who had cars, walked away in the other direction while I head towards the bus parking-lot aka loser zone. I spotted it, eight rows of buses neatly parked against the side-walk.

I rushed towards bus no. 303, the black paint of the bus sparking under the direct sunlight. Boom! There was clash. My body had crashed into another alien body. I fell down on the hot road, a heavy weight on-top of me as my vision blurred.

"Ow," I groaned when I felt an elbow dig into my mouth. Disgusting! I think I can taste the persons sweat inside my mouth.

"My elbow is covered in spit," a familiar voice spoke, my eyes adjusted to the surroundings; soon a face entered my vision. The chocolate-eyed jerk! Gah! My ten feet rule was now buried in the ground with RIP sign above it.

The smell of lavenders drifted through the air, our school territory was filled with lavender bushes, no wonder I was smelling lavender in the middle of the day.

"And your sweat is inside my mouth," I nearly gagged, wriggling beneath him.

Devlin wasn't making a move to get up. He just kept on staring at me in very, very weird manner, the one which involves someone continuously staring at your face.

"Is there something on my face?" I snapped.

In response, he smiled to himself, shaking his head slightly.

I didn't like being this close to him. I could see every single detail of his face. I could see golden specks of light dancing in his brown iris which stared right back at me. His eyes were almost magical, I could see stars sparkle and waves of mystical brown hues collide over one another. Then there was that mysterious edge to them where you want do nothing more than to dive into the mystery and let its blackness sweep over you. I could feel Goosebumps rise on my skin. His eyes were really something.

Screw the bus, I wanted to paint his eyes. "Can I paint your eyes?" I was hoping for a yes but in the back of my mind I knew he'd refuse, after-all I was nothing more than a stranger.

But then again, he surprised me by nodding his head.

I felt really happy, after a long time, I felt happiness soar through me and pulse along my heart. Just the thought of getting to paint those two eyes was blissful.

# Chapter 3

D evlin cautiously strode behind me, he had his white-doctoral coat resting on one arm, while his other hand held onto a loosely, strapped leather bag. I twisted the silver handle of the art room, stepping inside the room with him following me.

Incandescent lights lit the spacious room; panels of sceneries were displayed on the white walls while neat rows of desk were placed in horizontal series. In the back, there were worn-out wooden shelves filled with art supplies. Paints and brushes of all sizes and shapes lined the shelves.

Mrs. Clark was no-where to be seen. Even though, I had full-permission to use the art room, it felt as though as I was intruding into forbidden territory

I set my backpack on the front-desk. Turning my head, I saw Devlin standing there awkwardly, his long, gaunt fingers curling and uncurling themselves around the leather strap of his bag. I was surprised that he wasn't freaked out by the idea of someone randomly asking him to paint his eyes. I'm the one who came up with idea and even I felt kind-of weird about it.

"Stay here," I ordered afraid that he might run away or something. It's still hard to believe he's going to let me paint his eyes. Maybe he'll go all freak-show on me and tell me that I'm a creep. "I'll go grab the supplies,"

He smiled at me, the corner of his lips lifting upwards. "Yah, sure"

I quickly set up the panel and my painting stand. Pulling out my pencil, I roughly sketched the edges of his eyes on the small, square panel.

Devlin was sitting in-front of me; his legs propped up the metal stool while his eyes bore into mine. It was quite nerve-wreaking; it was like they could see right through me and my thoughts. I felt my pulse radiated and coarse painfully against my rib-cage. Everything was blurring into blue, pink, and grays.

"Stop it," I snapped, setting the pencil on the table, it rolled off the table, falling onto the ground with a hollow clicking sound.

He furrowed his eyebrows together, a crease dividing them. "Stop what?"

I massaged my temple as a sigh escaped my lips. Chocolate Syrup! What's wrong with me? It's official, I'm going insane. I was about to tell him to stop looking at me when I need to him to look directly at me. I shook my head, my teeth biting down on my lips. "Nothing,"

He frowned, in one swift move he hoped off the stool. "You did have lunch today?" It almost warmed my heart to see that he cared. But why should it matter, if he cared or not, damn those butterflies. Now I understand, why all those Disney princesses sang those sappy songs. I wanted to break out into my own little tune which would go along lines of-

If you can see chocolates in the sky,

Then you can dream about chocolate eyed jerks,

Wish made upon a chocolate bar,

Colors found in his chocolaty eyes,

If you can dream about chocolate eyed jerks,

Then you've must lost your mind.

I found myself, inches away from him. He stood beside me, his fingers pressed against my wrist while his eyes were glued to the wall-clock above the white-board. You know, I can literally see the ghost of my ten-foot rule standing in front of me.

"Your pulse is normal," He spoke after a moment, his hand slipping away from my wrist.

"I'm fine. Just go sit,"

He held up his hands. "I'm going woman, no need to be pushy,"

He mounted the black stool, placed at the front of the class. His hands rested on his thighs as he stared at me; once-again I felt my heart beat erratically.

I picked up a thin bristled brush and swished it into the cold glass of water. Let the magic begin.

Three colors, three shades of paint were all I needed to paint his eyes. Dirt brown, metallic yellow and coal black pellets of acrylics lined my tray; I dipped my brush into the brown, its tip sinking into the dab.

White was fading away; brown was covering the panel fizzling with gold then black. My green eyes met his brown ones, again I was rendered breathless. In his eyes danced the light that had filtered through them like golden specks.

I felt a grin build up inside of me, I couldn't bite it down. It rose, higher and higher, enclosing my lips in joy. It's been a long since I've been this happy, this content.

It was like I was back homes, I had returned to my tiny escape known as wonderland.

With a tilt of the brush, I made the lashes framing his eyes.

On the panel, the dull sketch was beginning to come to life, it wasn't as beautiful as the eyes of the owner but they still held some of the magic, some of that intangible charisma.

"Can I ask you something?" He spoke, the voice shattering the silence. He looked at me in a strange way like someone caught in the middle of admiration and sorrow.

I nodded, not being able to avert my eyes from his face. I still think he'd make a pretty girl.

"Why do you want to paint my eyes? Other than obvious fact that you enjoy painting,"

I bit down on the corners of my lips, the brush dangling from my fingers in mid-air, waiting to be stroked against the panel. "Because I'm weird like that," I shrugged, striking the panel, filling the eyes with light.

"Other than that,"

"Your eyes are really beautiful," I replied honestly, I bet that just inflated his ego.

He smiled wistfully as though remember some distant memory. "I get them from my mother,"

A pang of pain surged through me- mother. "Me too," I smiled.

"Really? That's cool,"

"I guess," I murmured, feeling a strange lump form in my throat. I lowered my eyes to the panel, not wanting someone to see the tears welling up in them.

"She must be really beautiful, just like you," He continued speaking with enthusiasm.

She was really beautiful both on the inside and outside unlike me...

I took a quick breath in and out, "Sorry for taking up so much of your," I tried changing the topic, not wanting to break down in-front of him.

I added the final touches to the painting.

He waved it off, grinning like there's no tomorrow. "No worries. I was free anyways plus I needed some time off my studies,"

"You must study a-lot since you're a doctor in training,"

He wrinkled his nose upwards, slightly. "Yah, I get sick of it some-times,"

"Seriously?"  I wonder how one gets sick of studying. I avoid studying; only picking the book up when I need to prepare for exams and all.

"We have to study about eight to twelve hours day,"

I felt my eyes widen. He must be kidding me, probably showing off. "No way,"

"Some days it's like sixteen hours," He stated, as though talking about the weather.

"Dang," I breathed out. "How are you even alive? If I were you, I probably would have turned into a zombie by now,"

"But you aren't me," He replied, rather coldly. Maybe my comment had offended him.

"True, what gives you the strength to torture yourself so much?"

"It may seem like torture," He straightened his back. "But it's not when you're passionate about medical science and have an actual interest in it,"

I thought about it moment before replying. "I can understand that," In some way or another, my passion for painting, resembled his passion for science.

"Sure you-"He was cut short by the entrance of Mrs. Clark.

She skipped inside the art room, her plump cheeks tainted slightly red. Behind her, she was rolling a small, red cart filled with large plastic tubs-probably clay for the crafts class. Mrs. Clark was dressed in red jumper, which made her look like a tomato. Her blond hairs with streaks of white were pinned up in a river braid.

She dropped the handle of the trolley by her desk. This is when she caught the sight of me. "Alice, what are you doing here?" I couldn't tell if she was pleased or annoyed.

"Um, well I was just finishing up a painting,"

Mrs. Clark turned to look at Devlin. Her eyes widened slightly. "Mr. Hutchins, you're here as well? Weren't you supposed to leave for an important lecture?"

My head snapped towards him. He lied to me. Why?

His face contorted into uncomfortable expression like that of a deer caught in the headlights. "Something came up so," He left his words hanging in the air.

Mrs. Clark came to my side and observed my painting. "You were painting Mr. Hutchins eyes," She finally concluded, a knowing smile graced her lips as she glanced in between Devlin and me.

"Y-yes," I stuttered unsure on what to say.

She stared at the roughly sketched eyes filled with different shades. There was a pair of eyes in the center, the iris were painted brown with slits of metallic yellow fused along them. Black had been used to highlights the edge of his eyes in the hope making them look more realistic.

"This is a masterpiece," She let go of a piece of air. "Ah-Alice you sure have a way with colors,"

I could feel color rise towards my cheeks. "Thank you," It's all because his eyes are so memorizing I wanted to add but decided against it.

"Oh, look I forget the clay downstairs," Mrs. Clark slapped her head lightly. "Silly old me, you guys carry on,"

She quickly rushed out the room whilst humming to herself; she was lying about the clay though. There were tubs of clay in her trolley right there. I wonder why she had excused herself so quickly.

"Can I see the painting? If you're done with it," Devlin spoke up, genuine curiosity lacing through his voice.

"Sure,"

I stepped aside. He strode to the panel, his eyes carefully studying the painting. I felt somewhat scared on what he'd think of it. I could feel my hands getting clammy.

"Are these really my eyes?" Awe was painted on his face.

I bit the corner of my lips. "Not half as good as them but yah,"

"Wow," He smiled, breathlessly. "Amazing,"

I let go of the piece of breath, I didn't know I was holding. "You like it?"

"Of-course, it's bloody brilliant," He grinned, flashing his two rows of perfectly aligned teeth.

I could hide my smile. "Thank you," It felt so good to hear him say that. I felt my smile waver as I recalled something. "Why did you lie?"

He titled his head to one side. "About what?"

"You didn't tell me that you had a lecture to attend."

"You didn't ask," He shrugged, picking up his coat and bag from the front-desk. "Are you keeping that painting? If you don't want it then I'll have it,"

"Don't change the topic," I snapped. "Yes, I'm keeping the painting since I painted it,"

"But they're my eyes," he protested.

"I'll give you photocopy," I sighed. "Now tell me why did you miss your class for me?" since you barely know me.

He smiled-why? I don't know. "I was trying to save you,"

"From what?"

He slung his leather bag over one shoulder. His gaze met mine, fiercely. "From yourself,"

Not waiting for a reply, he brusquely strode out the room, leaving a meddling confusion behind.

....It's scary to think-he had understood something about me that skimmed above everyone's vision.

In just three meeting, he had caught a glimpse of the war raging inside me -the guilt of my mother's death sinking me, pulling me into an ocean of black. I was drowning, sinking deeper and deeper, failing to swim above, I was falling down instead. There was no-one to save me here. There is no-one that can save me. I won't let anyone save me because I deserve this. I deserve this suffocation. I deserve this silence. I deserve all the cold stares. I deserve all the hatred. I certainly don't want a savior to keep me from all that I deserve.

I reached the doorstep of my house, feeling worn-out and tired. The sun had set behind the horizon, suspending this part of the world in darkness. It's a tiresome thirty minute walk from high-school to my neighborhood, Winterville.

The warm air from the heaters greeted me when I stepped inside. I walked into the small, cramped living room. It smelled like moldy popcorn in here.

I was surprised (shocked) to find my dad sitting on the toffee colored couch, the remote in his hand, he flipped through the channels. He never came back from office this early. Liza sat on the leather armchair, her knees curled up to her chest; she munched away on a bowl filled with butter popcorn. Her blonde hair had been scrunched up in a messy bun.

How does that girl manage to keep up with her weight when she eats like a freaking pig? It probably has to do with the amount of gymnastics she has to do in her middle-school cheer team. Yah, she's a cheerleader, in-fact she's the cheer team's captain. She's loves gymnastics as much as I love paint (and let me tell you I love my colors more than life).

"You're late," My dad spoke, readjusting himself on the couch; he turned to face me so his gray eyes would be directly staring at me. Ever since mom left us, he has become so strict and cold. It wasn't like this. He used to be the one who used to save me from my mother's scolding's, he used to take Liza and I for shopping and he would never yell at me for getting bad grades at school instead he'd just laugh it off but now....

"Um I missed the bus," I scratched the back of head. Liza was giving me pleading look, it was like her green eyes were trying to warn me about something.

"Again? What happened this time?" His gray eyes were beginning to stir with anger.

"Art class-"

"You and stupid art," He ran a hand through his blonde hair before abruptly getting up from the sofa. "Art ain't getting you anywhere. I rather have you focus on your studies," He didn't understand. He never did.

There's no point in explaining anything to him. We'll only get into an unwanted fight.

I started walking towards the staircase, not wanting to start another fight. I didn't have the strength to go on.

"I'm not done talking to you," He thundered.

A sigh escaped my lips. He won't let me rest in peace.

"What?" I groaned, turning to face him.

"I got a letter from your school," This isn't good. God, please no.

I dreaded the next few words. "What did it say?"

"If you keep up this darn thing with your art and paint, you're going have to repeat senior year," It should have made a difference. Those words should have scared me but they didn't. It didn't matter. Nothing did now. I just couldn't force myself to care.

"You better clear your final exams or else-"

"Or else what?" I barked.

The coldness of his face didn't waver for a minute. "Look just focus on your studies and forgot about all the other useless crap,"

"I'm not letting go of art, not now, not ever," My voice was firm.

He raised his hand high above in the air, I shut my eyes tightly, waiting for the impact of his hand to hit my cheek but it never did.

I opened my eyes to find Liza holding onto dad's arm. Her face looked so fear-stricken. She trembled ever so slightly, standing in-between us.

The expression on his face softened, he averted his eyes to the floor. "Please, Alice please I beg of you- just stop ruining your life,"

Broke sobs shook his body as he crumbled onto the floor. I have never seen him break down in-front of me. Liza tried calming him down while he cried.

I couldn't take it anymore. I rushed towards the stairs. Tears choking my throat, they burned a trail down my cheeks. It was getting harder and harder to breathe. The weight on my chest was increasing by the minute.

I don't how much more I can take.

# Chapter 4

"I'm a blonde," Liza stated the obvious, pushing the shopping cart through the over-crowded Target store. The glittery red Target logo stamped on the floors made them look all too glossy. There were small circle cut-outs scattered in the bakery isle, hanging from the ceiling.

I felt my mouth water at the various sweet delicacies lining the display counters. There were yummy cupcakes glazed with chocolate icing. I couldn't take my eyes off those large chocolate doughnuts. Chocolate Heaven, I wanted one so badly.

There were several sugar-free cupcakes and doughnuts but they were too expensive to be bought by a poor, student like me-sigh. Not in million years am I paying fifty dollars for box of doughnuts when I could buy an entire shelf of chocolates with that much money.

Liza agitatedly flipped a strand of hair off her shoulder. "If I'm a blonde doesn't mean I'm dumb,"

I have no idea what she was talking about. I usually zone out on half of our conversations. The only reason I tagged along on this early-morning shopping spree was so I could buy my trusted monthly partner, Whisper aka ultra comfortable sanitary napkins. I find tampons way too creepy and weird to be used. Chocolate Fudge! Don't even get me started on why tampons are my nightmares.

"Exactly," I muttered, trailing behind her. Liza tossed a loaf of bread into the cart. She kept up with all the groceries. I kind-of felt bad for making her take up all the responsibilities of our house. After all she's only fourteen and she has to acts like a grown, responsible woman. From cooking to laundry to cleaning, she did everything. I occasionally helped her with laundry and cleaning but it wasn't enough. I wish could be a better sister, I really wish...

"I'm a straight A student and yet everyone stereotypes me for a dump blonde. It's just not fair," She groaned, stomping her foot. Yes, at even this age, my little sister acts like a toddler-sometimes.

"That's so not cool," I responded with another generic response.

She frowned as usual she noticed my lack of attention. "You aren't listening,"

I guilt fled me. I bit down on my tongue. She needed me to listen that's what family was for. "Sorry, I was trying to"

She gave a resigned sigh. "Forget it. I wasn't making any sense anyways,"

She forgave me so easily. From where had she obtained such a magnanimous heart? I think I knew the answer. Mum. Liza had many of mum's qualities inside of her like her bravery, kindness, her ability to understand me, to speak out without being afraid to doing so and most of all her ability to love others unconditionally.

I felt my eyes go moist with unshed tears. "Thank you for yesterday, it was really brave of you to stand up to dad,"

She rolled her eyes in exaggerated manner. "Sometimes I feel like we're total strangers or something. Come on, it was my duty to protect my sister,"

With flick of the wrist, she toiled the cart forward-towards the frozen food isle.

"And it's my duty to be there when you need me. I admit that I totally suck at it,"

"No, you don't," she contradicted, shaking her head ferociously, sending strands of hair dwindling out her bun.

I raised an eyebrow. "Stop lying,"

"Okay, maybe a tiny, winy bit," Her face was so guilt ridden when she said that. God, it was damn amusing.

A bubble of laughter escaped my lips before I could stop it.

Liza gave me peculiar look, and then a slow smile drawled on her lips as she watched me laugh like a crazy buffoon.

"What?" I snapped, having caught my breath.

She shrugged. "You've never really laughed so freely since..." She left her words hanging in the air. "It's just so new,"

"You're face looked funny," I tried defending my actions. I don't know why but it felt like I needed to.

She carefully observed my face, her emerald eyes squinting together. A strange joy lit her eyes. "You're changing," she exclaimed in glee.

I made a face. "What are talking you about? I'm still the same old Alice with diabetes and an undying love of chocolate,"

"You're so stupid,"

"I'm not," I mumbled half unsure. Okay, Maybe I'm a bit stupid. I bet Patrick is smarter than me and he lives under a rock.

She clasped her hands together, jumping up and down. "Who is it?"

"What? What are you talking about it?"

Her fingers randomly started jabbing my stomach. I squirmed under her hands; biting down on my lips I tried controlling the laughter about to burst out.

"Stop it, people are watching," I tried pushing her away but she was way too strong. Damn, my skimpy, nerdy arms. "I don't have a clue about what you're talking about,"

"Tell me the boy's name," She demanded.

"There is no boy, what-ouch!" She kept on probing me like hungry piranha. "You know that I like to stay away from the unknown male race,"

"Lies," She poked harder than before.

"Will you stop it? I'm on my period for Chocolates sake!" I screamed. All the heads in the store snapped in my directions. Kill me, now! Why won't the earth divide into two and swallow me?

Liza withdrew her hands, wrinkling her nose upwards in disgust. "Eww, why didn't you tell me before?"

"I'm go-going to grab some pads," I rushed towards the other side of the store, in the hopes of avoiding all the amused stares. "Meet me by the check-out counter,"

Why do I always end up embarrassing myself? I swear I'm an embarrassing machine on two feet. If mom was here, she would laugh and say "Honey, are sure you don't want to join the circus?" "It's a natural talent you have- to amuse others," "Aw don't be so glum, not many people can make others laugh" "You don't like being laughed at? Then laugh with them,"  "Darling you're spreading joy.

You give them a reason to smile." "You're lifting their spirits, in a way you're like a silent blessing working your magic in a different way,"

A smile made its way up my lips; she always knew how to cheer me up. Oh how dearly I missed her.

My eyes raked the rows packaged pads. I don't really get why these companies wrap pads in colorful, intricate coverings. Worst of all is that they manufacture scented pads and not just any random smells for example: strawberry, floral, vanilla and many more smells. Gross, I think I've lost my appetite.

I pulled out a green pack from the shelf and then 'it' happened. All the packs came tumbling down one after another. I tumbled backwards, tripping on my shoes laces.

Boom, I collapsed onto the cold, germ-filled floors. I was buried inside a mountain of packages; they were beginning to suffocate me. I tried worming my way out, throwing the packages off my chest. This is not the position I would want anyone to catch me in. Just as thought entered my mind, yes -you guessed it right-a masculine voice echoed through the air above me.

"Um... hey? Are you alright there?" The 'guy' spoke. Double chocolate fudge, that voice sounded familiar. Maybe I should join the circus. They need me. Ekks yes, of course I'm packing my bags and hitting the road. Circus here comes the biggest clown of the century –no, not the century- the biggest clown in the history of clowns, yah that's more like it.

My little wonderland moment was rudely interrupted by a hand digging its way through the heap above me. The hand grasped my arm and pulled me upwards all the packages fell to the side. Just don't, please don't mention my ten feet rule, it died a long time ago. Its ghost haunts me at night.

Last night the chocolate-eyed jerk (though I don't consider him a jerk anymore) consumed all my dreams. It was quite rude of him if you ask me. He was invading my sleep without my permission.

My worst nightmare was about to come to life. Mother of all things chocolate! Oliver held me by the arm, his face as red as the Target employee apron he was wearing.

I felt my face go all hot and prickly. This is definitely going under the top-ten most awkward moments of the measly seventeen years of life I have managed to live.

He stared intently at his shoes, as if they were more interesting than the girl found under a pile of pads. Let me tell you, nothing is more interesting than that.

"Stuff knee- needed to be bought so chocolate then fairies died when ate chocolate," Oh, did I tell you that I tend ramble when I'm mortified? Yah, well guys I ramble faster than the girl whose writing this book. No-offence but she rambles like hiccupping hippo and I know that doesn't make any sense.

"Chocolate strawberries brought them back to life. Real fingers are not chocolate fingers. Yummy in my tummy when I eat chocolate," I carried on and on. Why wouldn't my mouth shut up?

"You really like chocolate. Huh?" Oliver gave me timid smile, the blue in his eyes sparkled under incandescent lights. His cheeks were tainted pink.

I had feeling my cheeks were worse than his, they probably were burning with red. "Yup, I love chocolate makes me happy like goblin,"

"Remind me get you some when we're at school," He stuffed his hands into the pockets of his apron, still smiling.

His blonde hair unlike in school, they were perfectly combed to one side, making him look a bit mature.  An apron with a white logo was tied perfectly around his slim waist, why wasn't my waist so thin? This is not fair.

"Sure," I hesitated before asking him. "You work here?"

"Yah, on the weekends, I substitute for the regular employees,"

I bobbed my head up and down, in amazement. "Cool," I've never had a real job. It must be fun to have one.

"It's not cool," He grimaced slightly. "Actually they make work so hard. It's not worth the pay,"

"That sucks,"

He sighed tiredly, his eyelids almost dropping over his eyes. "It does,"

I hadn't noticed that Oliver was still holding onto my arm. Panic began taking control of me. My ten-feet rule, no! It lay in ashes. I reached for the green package on the floor; automatically Oliver's hand left my arm. I almost released a sigh of relief.

"Came for these," I spoke, my fingers wrapped around the green packet. Well, this is awkward.

Oliver blushed as he bit the inside of cheeks. "I can see that," Even his ears were tinted red.

I could feel my own cheeks burn with heat. "Ya-yah, period troubles," I did not just say that. Chocolate Triple Fudge! Why? Why do I embarrass myself so much?

He made a face. "That must be hard,"

"Yah, especially the cramps,"

"There are some pain-killers that help with cramps," He scratched the back of his head, blushing like a girl caught picking her nose. "Um, my sister keeps some with her,"

"You have a sister?" I said in the hope of getting off the period topic.

A fond smile drawled on his lips. "Yah, she's in college,"

"That's nice," I tried forcing out a smile.

Just then my sister came skidding down the aisle, zooming on the cart. God bless her for coming at the most stupidest hour.

"Sis, you done?" She stopped beside me; her eyes flickered to Oliver then to heap of pads under my feet. I bet our red faces didn't miss her sight. "Did I interrupt something?"

"No, you didn't" I grabbed her arm, and began dragging her away from there before she says something utterly mortifying. "I'll see you at school," I yelled back to Oliver.

He gave me a small wave. "Yah, see you on Monday,"

Once we were a safe distance away from the pad isle, I let go of her arm.  Liza kept on staring at me, looking gleer than the entire glee cast combined.

Liza nudged her shoulder with mine. "Who was that?" She wagged her eyebrows up and down.

"A friend from school," I groaned. Curse her wild, imaginative mind!

"Oh really?" She smiled that annoying, sly smile. "I thought you like to stay from- let me repeat 'unknown male race',"

"Don't ask," I sighed. "Just don't ask,"

Seriously, what was happening with me? The more I tried staying away from those girl eating monsters, the closer I got to them.

I think I spotted Devlin running towards the check-out counter with his hands filled with packets of frozen peas but that's probably my imagination.

Liza piped about Oliver and how cute he looked. I think I'm going to throw up.

This was going to be one long weekend.

# Chapter 5

One Month Later

Sometimes it feels like you're standing on the edge of a cliff. Every small action pushing you closer and closer to the edge, the tiniest of winds feeling like gigantic storms. One wrong move, one wrong word and you are sent tumbling down the cliff into an ocean made of tears. This is when you've reached your breaking point.

It is the time when vulnerability is at its peak. You're heart is naked, unarmed. You're walls are down and someone might just sneak past them, right into your heart.

It felt no different today, seeing that it was my eighteen birthday. A lazy Sunday sun greeted me, its light filtering through the blinds. I jumped out of my bed, pulling the blinds upwards.

"Good morning world," I spoke to no-one in particular. In response the sun, shone brighter, its warm rays muzzling across our cozy neighbored. The roads were empty; cars were parked by the front while people slept soundly in their beds dreaming about better futures, shiny cars, lustrous money, and some –maybe- dreamt about hopeful loves.

I, on the other hand, didn't dream of anything. Dreams abandoned me a long time ago, the more I try to grasp for one, the faster they slip away, blurring my thoughts.

Make a wish they would say when I blow the candles on the cake.

But what should I wish for? I would ask.

Whatever your heart desires they would reply.

I would end up with a muddle of thoughts. What should I wish for? Should I wish to be better at painting? Or studies? Should I wish to be a interior designer? Or how about to become a famous painter?

But my heart didn't desire any of that.

The only thing it wanted was happiness and its happiness lay in one certain person. It longed to bring that person from the gates of death. It longed for mom.

Silently, I approached the breakfast table, dad sat in the furthest corner his head buried into the newspaper. Liza ate her favorite strawberry cereal, grimly, the shape of mouth turned downwards as she stared intently at the framed picture of our family hanging from the wall opposite the table.

My stomach grumbled, I placed a hand on it-in the hope of hushing it. Just few more minutes before I shut your mouth, stomach pal, keep quite till then.

"Err...good morning?" I greeted, standing at the head of the table, my hands resting on the chairs edge.

"Morning sis," Liza smiled that forced smile which would even make Barbie cringe. "I made some pancakes for yo-"

She was cut-off by an icy, cold voice. "So you finally decide to grace us with your presence," Dad gave me a bitter look, his face was burning with a harsh red color. I could literally feel my heart jump out of my mouth.

He tossed the newspaper on the floor, his hand finding a yellow envelope and throwing it towards my face. I caught the envelope in time before it could poke me in the eye.

My hands trembled slightly as I lifted the flap; a crisp, white sheet came into my view. It had my high school's watermark.

To the parent/guardian of Alice Brown,

Subject: Final Exam result

This is the principal, Mark Smith, informing you that Alice Brown has not cleared her final exam in the following subjects:

1.   Human Health Science [Compulsory course for all students]

2.   Communication Application [optional subject]

3.   Botany [compulsory subject]

We are sorry to inform that Alice will not be promoted hence her gradation certificate has been withheld until and unless she is able to clear the retest for the following subjects.

Mark Smith

The Principal

Winterville High school

The piece of paper fell out of my hands, landing on the table. I couldn't meet his eyes. I tried. I really had tried to clear my exams for his sake.

All of the sudden, I felt so helpless and so vulnerable. Everything was crumbling, beginning to fall apart, I wanted to scream. I wanted to scream so badly.

It did matter now that I failed. Gradation did matter now that it was almost unattainable. Funny, isn't it? How you realize the importance of something once you trash it.

"You failed," He spoke through gritted teeth, his hands slamming on the table as he got up from his chair. I had failed, not just these exams but in almost every aspect in my life, this just added on to the ever so long list.

"Thanks for stating the obvious," I muttered under my breath.

Liza dreadfully stared in between us. I hated for her to witness this. If I had just tried harder then maybe this wouldn't have happened. She didn't deserve this. She wasn't supposed to pay for the mistakes I made. Why is life so unfair? I'm supposed to shield her from this hurt but here I am bringing the pain.

"You were supposed to clear these God damn!" His fingers ran agitatedly through his hair. "What am I supposed to do with you?"

I didn't say anything.

He advanced towards me; I held my spot, not afraid of my impending doom.

"This is not you, Alice," He breathed out; his hands coiled in a fist, resting to the sides of his thighs, veins protruding out his arms. The hurt, the anger, the disappointment was tangible. It was choking me as its chains wound around my neck.

"Where is my brilliant daughter? What have you done to her?"

"She died," I heard my mouth say. "A long time ago,"

I wasn't here, my mind was far away, lost in distant memories I wished to forget. My mother's laugh echoed through my ears, deafening me.

"The past is past. Just get over it," Liza spoke this time. "We all have," She was trending a dangerous territory by bringing up the past.

"I'm trying-"I began.

"You're not," Dad was fast to cut me off. "You have a whole life ahead of you. If you don't work hard now, then when will you? How

will you survive in this world?  I can't feed you for the rest your life,
"

"Then don't," I laughed. A hollow realization settled itself in the
nest of my chest. He considered me to be a burden, a heavy boulder
on his shoulders that he had to pull, unwilling. "I'm leaving and I'm
never coming back. Good for you! This burden is leaving you," I
rushed towards my room.

"Wait!" Liza screamed her face void of color. "Dad didn't mean
that-"

"No," He placed a hand on her shoulder, his ancient eyes looking
dolefully at me. He looked so old, the wrinkle on the side of his eyes
deepened, it seemed like he hadn't slept for years. All of the sudden,
my bitterness towards him fazed, he didn't deserve a daughter like
me. "Maybe this is what she needs so she can finally realize her
mistake,"

Words didn't find when I needed them the most. I wish there was
a way I could tell him how sorry I was for everything, how dearly I
loved him, and how I still considered him the world's best father.

I think it's best if I leave and take this heart-ache with me. Liza and
Dad deserved to be happy; they didn't deserve someone like me.
Maybe if I left, happiness would return to this house. Maybe finally,
they could sleep in peace without having to worry about me.

"We'll be here for Alice, if you ever wish to return," Dad finally
spoke when I didn't say anything.  "We'll welcome you with open
arms,"

I couldn't reply. I couldn't even turn to look back. I feared to see
tears in the eyes of my father and sister.

The river rushed past the jaggedly cut rocks, flowing towards the
edge of the cliff. The freezing late summer air bit my bare arms, the

slight breeze picking up strands of my brown hair and tossing them off my shoulders. My bags lay few feet away from me while I sat here by the bank of river, contemplating on where I should go.

The moss of grass felt nice under me, I leaned back and lied down on its maze, my eyes finding a way to the sky. Five sparrows soared through the sky, free and unafraid. They flapped their wing finding a way back home.

Where should I go?  I asked the dark, blue horizon.

There is no place I could go. I truly felt alone today.

There was no-one here, this early-no-one bothers to visit the Creek valley cliff. A perfect hour to be here. I was standing at the edge of the cliff, an empty stomach and chaotic thoughts raging through my head.

Below the steep cliff, the river gushed by, filling the air with a swoosh sound.

Left foot past right foot, the gravel crumbled beneath me, falling into the river.

I was tired of living. I didn't want to live anymore. I didn't need to. What should I live for?

Just one more step, everything will over. No more pain, no more tears, just peace an everlasting amount of peace. The curtains of life were slowly falling; I wanted nothing more than to sleep forever.

I closed my eyes and jumped. The wind rushed by me. It was one those moments where everything happens in slow motion. The river was getting closer, cliff was going farther. My life was slipping out of my fingertips.  Everything was fading into blackness.

My body hit the water, that one impact was enough to dwindle away all consciousness.

# Chapter 6

------------------------------------------------------------

Warm, soft lips were forcefully planted on mine, bringing me to life, breathing air into my lungs, returning the breaths I had just lost. My muscles were sore; my sight was hazy-though even in the mist of confusion- I could make out those eyes-those warm golden brown eyes. He was trying to bring me back but I didn't want to come back. I had no reason to.

But he wasn't letting me go, damn his stupid stubbornness, his gaunt fingers held onto my hand tightly-it made my heart contort, twisting achingly- it was more agonizing than my half dead state. Again, another ounce of air entered my mouth, again my chest rose; again his chest fell but this time my lungs took the air in on their own.

I pushed him, away from myself once I found the strength, once I calmed the rapid beating of my heart. His lips parted from my mine, leaving a lingering taste of their presence. This time I didn't bother to open my eyes, my eyes lids were tightly shut. I wasn't ready to face the world.

"Are you alright?" He asked, I don't know if he accepted the typical answer 'yes, I'm fine,' or if he wanted me to answer honestly but people usually don't want an honest answer, no-one wants to deal with someone else's problem or listen to them.

I didn't answer him-because I didn't know what to say, I wasn't in the state to lie again. The silent sound of the river filled the awfully empty air. It was cold outside and dark on the inside but I didn't mind. I felt nice.

Strangely-I never thought I would use that word to describe any-one other than myself- he started laughing, the loud, hearty sound of his laugh caused me to open my eyes, my head lay still on the ground beside the river, peeking through my lids I saw him gripping his stomach and laughing to his heart's content like tomorrow's sun would never rise through the horizon. His back fell onto the blanket of moss, he rolled to my side, six tears (yes, I counted them) falling out of his eyes. He was facing me, laying on one side, one laugh after another left his mouth.

Out of curiosity, I couldn't help but ask. "What's so funny?"

He smiled, that charming smile- prince charming would give to Cinderella. Unfortunately, I wasn't Cinderella and he was definitely not my prince charming.

"Things that I have to do to make you talk," That smile wasn't leaving his face and it was beginning to scare me because I liked the way he smiled way too much. I liked how a small dimple would form on his left cheek, how the side of his eyes became crinkly, and how his lips would stretch perfectly like two red strokes of paint.

"You're weird," I muttered. I tried getting up from the ground into a sitting position, partially because I felt uncomfortable lying next to him with his breath falling on the side of my face. "Very Weird,"

He didn't make a move to get up from the ground. He placed his hands behind his head; laying his head on top of the nest of hands- I noticed that he too like me was drenched in the saline, river water. His brown checkered shirt, slickly stuck to his slim chest. I didn't want to think about how my transparent white tee looked, I crossed my arms over my chest-saving the scraps of dignity I had left.

"All of us are weird in our own weird way,"

"I guess,"

"You know," He spoke slow, dragging each syllable. "The sunrise looks beautiful from the here," Just as those words escaped his mouth, my head turned in the direction of his wistful stare. A startled gasp escaped my mouth as I almost fell back on onto the ground.

From the edges of the jagged cliff- the one from which I had tried to end my life- a golden sun radiating a warm, satisfying glow illuminated the entire sky-darkness was fading- the color was rising-no, not in the sky but on my cheeks. Devlin, yes, he was the reason why my cheeks were painted the color of a stop sign- he was staring at me, his eyes watching-with more warmth than the sun, basking in the morning light, each and every contour of his face was brightened.

"There are few things that make life worth living," He smiled, almost invitingly. It was an open invitation for me to trust him. "And this happens to be one of them,"

I honestly did not know if was talking about the sun-rise or.....me.

"I slipped err I kinda tripped on the edge of the cliff. It was not like I did it on purpose," I let my damp hair fall in-front of my face, suddenly I felt ashamed of what I had done.

"But I didn't ask you that," He replied, nonchalantly.

"You were implying-"

He stood up abruptly, brushing off the dust. "Words are words. You can twist them in any way you want,"

I don't want you to judge me for what I did.  I wanted to say but couldn't. I didn't have the courage.

"After all who am I to question what you did? It's your life. It's your choice to do whatever you want with it,"

There has to more to his words. He definitely didn't mean that. "Why did you save me?"

He shrugged. "I wanted to play hero,"

And like before, he walked away, and like before I was left with unsaid words, dissolving in my mouth.

# Chapter 7

-------------------------------------------------

Tip-plop-tip-plop the droplets from my drenched clothes slid onto the plastic doormat. I don't know if I should be doing this. Since my mother's death, I haven't spoken to my aunt once-not even on the phone-not a single word had been exchanged between us -then what gave me the right to stand at her doorstep now? I didn't try to apologize for ending her sister's-(my mother's) life. I didn't offer consoling words when she silently cried by my mother's grave. I didn't even thank her for taking all the blame.

I turned my back towards the door, picking up my bags and slinging them across my shoulder. Just then, the door flung open, all breaths were caught in my throat. Aunt Julie was standing few feet away from me, a delicate floral dress clung to her bones, she wore one of her bright smiles, the green in her eyes sparkled in way that reminded me of mom.

"Alice!" She stepped out into the cold morning air. "Oh my," Before I could process all that was happening, she encased me into her famous chocolate melting hugs.

"It's nice to see you Auntie," I mumbled into her shoulder, for moment, it felt as though was mom here, hugging me, holding me in her arms. "I was just passing by..."

She pulled away- looked really happy. "God, I didn't think you'd visit me before I left for Manchester," She was leaving? How come no-one told me about this.

"You're leaving?"

The smile on her face dimmed. "Yah, I'm moving in with Charlie," Charlie as in Aunt Julie's boyfriend who lived in London.

"Oh," I smiled, trying to look cheery. "Congratulations. I hope you two have wonderful life,"

"Thank you dear," She patted my cheek. "Come in. I'll make you some of your favorite chocolate shake,"

"No, it's alright. I'm kinda in a rush," I lied, whilst staring at the welcome sign on the doormat.

"I won't force you," Aunt Julie replied, laughing. "I'm really busy myself," A breaking sound came from the inside of the house, "Oh my," She gasped before scrambling towards the sound. "Charlie, I told you not to touch the flower vase!" I heard her yell. "Now look at what you've done..."

I didn't wait for her to return and walked out of the wooden patio of her house. A dreadful realization set itself inside my chest. I was officially homeless.

Lights were lighted. Small, blue feather birds were rising out of their nest, flapping their wings they flew away into the lighted azure sky. Few of them pecked each other, stretching their feathers to provide warmth to the other.

Strangely, as always, I felt lonely. This time haunting freedom was trailing along my side. What was use of this freedom when nothing felt right enough to be free?

Drenched in the rivers water with an aching stomach, and watery eyes I walked and walked through the empty streets.

"You're not supposed to cry about it, darling," A beautiful lady with plum red hair said to a small boy wearing bright yellow, boat shoes.  I watched them from a distance, standing on the sidewalk, just past the lamppost.

The little boy was in tears as he stood at the door of their apartment, his small arms reaching out for her. "Mommy, don't leave me please,"

"I have to go," The beautiful lady picked up the boy in her arms, stroking his cheek with her free hand. "I would stay if I had choice,"

"I don't like being alone," The boy threw his arms around the lady.

The lady stood tall and firm. "Be brave, my dear, bad times won't last long. There needs to be rain before a rainbow can come,"

I wanted to believe the lady. I truly wanted to believe her.

Cypress Creak Library Sandy said she would meet here once she could get out of her house.  The warmth of the library provided solace to my cold bones. Few early birds walked past me, giving me peculiar stares and some stifling their laughter.

"Looks like someone had a cold shower," A guy with the baseball cap snickered when he walked past me.

I didn't reply and quietly went to the washrooms.

"You can still go back you know," Sandy spoke, sitting across me at the circular table-her red pigtail would flip back and forth whenever she moved her head. "I'm sure your dad will forgive you,"

This was the last thing I expected her to say since when did she become the sensible one. I shrugged my shoulders, with my free hand I tucked wet strands of my hair into the blue hoodie that I had just changed into.

"I'm not going back," I sighed, my head falling down onto the cold, table's surface. "I can't go back,"

"Where will you go? You don't have enough money with you to rent an apartment,"

"I don't know,"

"I would take you to my place but," Sandy's skin turned into the color of her orange freckles. "My parents can't you know,"

"Hey, It's alright," I patted her hand.  Her family wasn't really financially strong so they couldn't afford to feed another mouth. "I can understand,"

"I'm really sorry, Alice" Sandy sniffled, rumpling her nose upwards. "I'm not of much help,"

"No, Sandy don't be sorry. You're an amazing friend. I'm really lucky to have you,"

She gave me a shy smile, biting down the corner of lips. "Thanks,"

"I'll figure something out," I didn't want to stress her with my problems. She already had enough to deal with. Maybe calling her to meet me here wasn't a good idea. Why I do always drag people into my problems? I needed to learn to deal with my own problems. Mother of all things chocolate, I can be so selfish sometimes.

Sandy squeezed my shoulder tightly; I guess she was trying to comfort me. "Don't worry. Only good things happen to good people,"

"I'm not necessarily a good person,"

She gave me a closed lipped smile, the one when she usually gave me when I failed to understand a math problem. "You are good. You just don't realize it,"

Sandy had long left me. The sun was beginning to fall behind the horizon, the Liberian came up to me and informed me that it was closing time. I picked up my bags and books, my legs sore from siting in the library all day, and walked out of the library.

The cold evening air hit me with surprise; it was colder than I thought it would be. The streetlights were beginning to flicker to life. I walked along the sidewalk of the library. People were laughing, chattering-their arms filled with books and their eyes lit with joy. Some people like me, walked alone, their hands tucked safely instead their pockets and their eyes lost in some thought.

A light breeze picked up the dead, autumns leaves and blew them across the street. I too felt like the leaves, light enough to blown in any direction by the life's winds.

I still didn't have a place to go.

If mom was here, we would be celebrating my birthday right now. I still remember how she used make me my favorite chocolate truffles and in the evening she would sit with me by the fireplace. She would hand me a plain cup of milk and a truffle then sing me a soft birthday melody. I remember smiling the whole time she would sing.

Suddenly a sharp pain jolt of pain shook my body; it started from my head and soared till my toes. I think I bumped into someone as I lost balance. Of course it had to be him-Delvin was smiling at me- his brown eyes boring into mine. A white coat was neatly folded on his arm while a stethoscope clung to his neck. Just then, I blacked out for a second, stumbling forward, landing right into his arms. Great-this is exactly what I need-another Chocolate

Emergency (please with great attention note heavy use of sarcasm) And I thought my day couldn't get any worse.

"Whoa," He breathed out, his breath cascading down my neck. "Steady there," He held my hand; his gaunt fingers were tightly wrapped around my hand.

"Why do I keep bumping into you?" I groaned, removing myself from his grasp-my ten feet rule is dead so please don't mention it. "Were you following me or something?"

He gave me a lopsided grin before shrugging his shoulders. "It's called destiny, love,"

Love- a strange firework show erupted in my stomach- it was probably because of my low sugar. I was about to reply when another wave of black fell over my eyes; before I knew it- I was drowning in black water but this time I wanted to swim...

# Chapter 8

There was fire, everywhere I went. Reddish, yellow flames rose and fell blazing through the office. Everything was my fault. I had left the cylinders open, the gas was leaking catching fire the instant it came in contact with the air.

There were screams; petrifying screams that made my heartbeats halt. I ran, deeper and deeper into the fire. My breaths were raspy, the soot was chocking me. I couldn't breathe. My feet were bleeding but no I had to be strong. I have to save her.

The smoke was burning tears down my cheeks, I couldn't see anything. She must be here, somewhere here. A door collapsed, burning the skin on my back, I could feel the fire scorching my skin but it didn't hurt. It was as if someone had poured a bucket of icy water on top of me.

Then there was a scream but unlike the other screams I recognized the voice. Dread choked my throat. I felt my body go numb. A woman emerged through the door. Her entire body was lighted by the fire. She was screaming. All I could hear was her screams, nothing else-not even the voice calling out my name, not even the sound of the building collapsing.

The flames weren't letting go, they were stubborn. The women stopped fighting. She stood still, the fire eating her away, the red flames swallowing her whole. She reached out for me, I backed away. My head dizzy, everything was fading into white.

The women didn't move, her body collapsed- the fire had burned her down. But before she collapsed, she raised her hand in farewell. All that was left of the woman was a charred body of black. She was dead. My mother was dead.

I could have saved her but I didn't.

I woke up, drenched in sweat and fear. The same dream, the dream that had become my reality- never left my eyelids.  During the day, I pushed back the memories of her demise but at night they came back, haunting me, stealing all the peace and calm I had gathered.

If she was here, she would smile- that reassuring smile- her lips drawn together into a small smile; she would place her hand on my head. 'It'll be alright, Alice, it'll be alright,' she would whisper.

When the tears wouldn't stop, she would get angry. 'Oh, be strong now. You're a brave girl,'

I felt my eyes water, this isn't the best time to cry.  I pulled my strings together, like always, piece by piece I put myself back together. Like every other time I broke- this time too I lost another piece of my once whole self.

Where was I? My body was sprawled across a small bed. A colorful quilt with teddy bears was draped over me. I blinked a couple of time- the darkness of the room making everything seem fainter.

The moon lit its way through the window-the curtains were parted letting in the ghastly night sky.

I noticed there was a SpongeBob bandage on my left hand. Strange, I don't remember getting hurt. Tossing the quilt aside, I walked towards the door- the slight amounts of light falling through it. I tripped few times-over things unknown to me before reaching the door.

The light blinded me when I walked past the door. Shelves filled with numerous books greeted me- the walls were covered with a light cream color. Everything was so organized- not a page was out of line.

In the corner sat Delvin, his back hunched over the book, his legs crossed on the chair placed near a wooden table. A blue study lamp was placed on the desk, its light lighted the whole room in a serene oceanic blue color.

He wasn't lying when he said he studied sixteen hours a day.

"Err...Hey," I breathed out, tucking a stray strand away from my face.

He turned away from the chair to face me; a pair of thick-framed glasses covered his eyes. He looked quite tired, there were lines running across his forehead. Even in his tired state, he managed to pull out an inviting smile. "How are you feeling now?"

I shuffled my feet, feeling a bit out of place, standing by the door, in a room filled with books, and a boy who had yet again saved me. "I'm feeling great,"  The lie slipped off my tongue, easily. I even add my own smile to compliment my lie.

"How are you feeling now?" he repeated with the same inviting smile.

"I'm fine," I spoke a bit louder this time, maybe he hadn't heard me.

But that was not the case. "How are you feeling?"

"I already told you, I'm feeling fine," Is he deaf or something?

"How are you feeling?"  Mother of all things chocolate, this guy may be a chocolate treat for the eyes but there is definitely a bolt missing in his brain.

"I'm fine," I sighed.

Again, he asked me the same question but this time I snapped.

"I swear there is something wrong your brain. Chocolate Fudge! Are you deaf or something? Sheesh you're annoying me," I burst out before I could stop myself.

"Finally!" He exclaimed, hoping off his chair. Yes, he literally hoped off his chair like the white rabbit from Alice in wonderland. "You're finally speaking the truth,"

Is it me or this guy is on a chocolate overdose?  "So you're deaf? I swear you had normal hearing powers the last time I met you,"

He laughed, shaking his head. "God, you're so funny,"

"Um, I'm not joking," I replied, in all seriousness. "So you're not deaf?"

"Why would I be? I don't close off the world around me," He stared at me, his eyes never leaving mine. Everything seemingly blurring into different shades of pink.  He was talking about me.  "Things would be a-lot more easier if you spoke your mind,"

"You're not supposed speak your mind,"

He scoffed. "Who said that?"

"Your words can hurt others,"

In long strides, he advanced towards me, I didn't back away. The subtle smell of his cologne filled my sense. "If you keep them inside, the only person you're hurting is yourself,"

I hated it when he spoke about things like these. Each and every word he said made me want to believe that things could be fixed, that I could be fixed. Hope can be a wicked thing-it can manage to grow in the bleakest of circumstances. Hope is the one thing I did not want.

I remained silent.

He let go of a piece of air. "You're really stubborn. You know that?" He closed the distances between us, step by step. Right when I was about to move back, he angled himself towards the door. "Come on. You need to eat something and I'm not letting you go anywhere without having food,"

For a medical student, he sure had a nice place. I sat on the tall metal stool placed by the granite counters of the small, warm kitchen. Devlin skipped between the microwave and the sink. I watched flip through the teak cabinets before pulling out a jar.

"Do you need my help?" I asked, biting down my lips.

"Nah, it's okay," He quickly popped a bowl filled with god knows what and turned on the microwave. "I've got it,"

"Um...okay,"

He sat down on the stool beside me, after wiping his hands with a red towel; he twisted he body so he would be directly staring at me. "So in the morning you were trying to kill yourself and then in the evening you faint because of low sugar. You know I'm really curious to know your story,"

I was caught off guard by his bluntness. Of-course, anyone would want to know the reason behind my current state- he wasn't an exception. "I don't want to talk about it,"

"Ah, I see," He laughed. "But I would love to talk about it,"

He's so damn annoying. Chocolate Flipping Fudge. "I'm not comfortable with sharing my problems,"

"Trust me," He smiled, that same inviting smile, the way his eyes shone in the faint light of the bulb- made me feel like home-maybe it was because his apartment smelled like apples and cinnamon. I think the piranhas in my stomach just growled at the thought of apples and I hated apples. Chocolate Fudge, I seriously needed food.

I wrinkled my nose upwards, the thought of trusting a stranger seemed foreign to me. "Why should I?"

"Because," He spoke slowly, almost like a song. "It is easier to trust a stranger. Because there's no fear of being judged,"

"I don't know," I muttered looking down at my SpongeBob bandage. It was really cute. It had SpongeBob and Patrick blowing bubbles while they tried to catch jellyfishes. I still don't remember getting hurt.

"I gave you a glucagon injection," Devlin stated, almost as if he had read my mind. "Hence the bandage,"

I raised an eyebrow. "Are you allowed to do that?"

"Do what?" He asked, his eyebrows were bundled up in a confused expression.

"Administer medicine,"

He scratched the back of his neck, looking somewhat flustered. "Well I am a doctor," That came out as a question.

"Well?" I urged him to continue.

"Okay, I confess," He held up his hands.  "I'm not allowed to do that and I could get into shit loads of trouble if someone finds out,"

"Then why did you do it?'

"Duh? I needed to save you," He spoke as though he had done nothing but loan me a pen.  I felt flabbergasted at his modesty.

"Bu-but you're risking your career,"

He smiled- oh my and his smile made my heart melt faster than any chocolate bar. "Some people are worth risking their careers for," My surroundings were fusing with different shades of reds, fluffy bunnies, elf's with open toed shoes all seemed so lovable.

"You stole that from Frozen," Yup, that's all I could say after he said such endearing words. "I bet that snowman is going to feel sad,"

He laughed, clutching his stomach, his glasses nearly falling off the crook of his nose. I couldn't help but join. Ah, it felt good to have air filling my lungs as quick it left.

I don't know when he stopped laughing and I was the only one left making fool out of herself.

I soon realized that I was the only one laughing. This so darn embarrassing- but as you know me, I had to make things worse. "The snowman with a large carrot said 'that some people are worth melting for,' so yah it's not the same but yah," I shrugged my shoulders, my cheeks were burning hot from mortification.

"So you want me to melt for you," I could tell he was trying not to laugh at that and that's pretty impossible- you know to not laugh at Alice. Sigh, mom was right. I should really join the circus. They could use a clown like me. I bet they could paint an amazing smile on face so I wouldn't have to fake it anymore.

"No," I muttered, dryly- feeling somewhat weary. "I don't,"

"You know I would melt for you if I could but I'm not really a snowman," I felt my cheeks burn more brightly then before. I tucked a strand of brown hair from face, looking down at my empty lap.

"I figured,"

Saving grace of microwaves and all things with beeping sounds! The loud sound beep-bleep of the microwave made Devlin hop off the stool and rush towards it. Silently, I thanked the god of electronic appliances for saving me from yet another clown worthy fall.

He quickly brought out the blue bowl from the microwave- balancing it on a plate- he placed it in front of me. From the drawer, he took out a plastic spoon and set next to the bowl. I looked down at the bowls contents. Steam rose and created swirls in the air.

So there was a grey, bubbling mixture in the bowl and it certainly did not look appetizing.  I wonder if there is brain puree in this.

"I know it looks.... well ...like vomit," He started out. Great, he just ruined my appetite.  "But it tastes pretty good,"

"Um...what is this exactly?" So I might be on the verge of starving and I should probably stuff whatever I get into my mouth but....this is just so grey.

His face got knotted into a muddled expression. "There's like rice bran, oats and some other things that I don't know,"

I hesitantly picked up the spoon and placed a small amount on the tip of tongue. It was quite hot, but soon the heat melted away leaving a vanilla flavor behind. Before I knew it, spoonful after another the entire bowl vanished-this tasted like heaven-maybe because I was so hungry.

"Thank you," I set the empty bowl on the counter. "I hadn't eaten anything since dinner yesterday,"

"How come?" He picked up the empty bowl, turning his back towards me. He set it in the sink before coming to sit next to me.

I placed my hands on the counter. "I left my house,"

"Oh, like the big move out thing," He concluded, leaning on his elbow. "'I'm eighteen and I'm going to move'" He spoke in a squeaky voice.

I shook my head, chuckling. "No, not that one,"

"Then?"

A long, resigned sigh left my mouth. My head fell onto the maze of my arms, lying right above the cold counter as its coldness slowly sunk in. "I don't know. I was bringing my family down so I thought that if I left things would get better,"

He titled his head to one side, a strange bleakness in his eyes. "So you gave up on them?"

"No, I gave up on myself,"

"Why?"

Slowly, steadily webs were untangling inside of me- words that had been corroding me were being heard by someone else. The gentle hum of two voices were mixing-one being of my heart and the other being his.

# Chapter 9

The faint light of the bulb flickered off the wall.  Our shadows were sitting close, it almost looked like we were caught in a embrace, the way his shadow fell over mine making it seem as if he were the gentle shed and I was the lost bird.

"Why?" he asked.

I never realized how much I wanted speak out- those things. Out of all people, I had to confess my deepest secrets to a stranger, a stranger who was becoming so much more.

"Why did I give up on myself?" I hummed. "Why?"

He was waiting, his lips drawn into a mute line; brown eyes watched me with warmth causing a strange ghastly sensation to enter my body.

I took in a deep breath. I couldn't say it.

My lids fell down and my head sunk into the granite counter. Tears landed on the counter before I could order them to stop.

There was a hand on my shoulder. "Don't worry about it," He whispered, his hand lay still on my shoulders.

Before I knew it, I rose, my arms fell- right around his shoulder. He didn't flinch away; instead he opened up into an embrace. I breathed in, my head buried in his Kashmiri sweater.

He held me, tightly. "Are you okay?"

And this time I replied honestly. "No,"

I unwrapped myself from him, my cheeks beet red. Chocolate Fudge, I shouldn't have done that.

Devlin didn't seem to mind- a blank expression covered his face.

"I'm sorry," I spoke, drying my cheeks with the back of my hand. "I should leave,"

"Do have a place to go?"

I bit down on my lips, shaking my head.

"You should stay here,"   I was surprised by his offer. I stared at him for a moment. His eyes looked sincere and so did his intentions. But I wouldn't take advantage of that. I couldn't.

"No, it's alright. I'll manage," I got up from the stool, straitening my hoodie. "You've done too much for me,"

"Are you sure I did this for you?" a strange smile overtook his lips; I started at him in confusion.  What was he talking about?

"What do you mean?"

"I mean a-lot of things it depends on what you think of them," In one swift motion he got off the stool, standing- uncomfortably close to me. I had to crane my neck to look up at him. "Maybe I did this for myself,"

"I don't get you,"

He shrugged his shoulders. "You should stay here,"

"But I can't," I replied unsure. My mother had warned me about this. She told me to never trust a stranger no matter how friendly he may seem to be.

"Why?"

"Because I can't trust you,"

"Do you have a reason to not to trust me?"

He did have a point. He had saved my life...twice.

I chewed the inside of cheeks. I can't trust him. I shouldn't be trusting him.  "No," I finally replied.

"Great!" He grinned. "I've set your bags in the other room. My roommate left a month ago and I was feeling really lonely-"

"I can't stay," I spoke, wearily.  "I can't stay with you for free,"

"Then don't. You can pay me rent,"

"I don't have money with me,"

He ran a hand through his hair, looking slightly annoyed. "What's the problem with you girls? If I let you stay here for free then that's a problem. If I ask for rent then that's a problem,"

I narrowed my eyes at him. "I'm not asking for a favor that's all,"

"Oh, it hurts your winey, little ego," He puffed up his cheeks like a three year old.

"Yes!" I replied without thinking when I realized what I said, it had me cursing myself for being a clown.

"Wait," I groaned, mortified beyond every chocolate cookie. "I didn't mean that,"

Devlin started laughing, his glasses almost falling off the crook of his nose. I wanted to punch his perfectly carved face- even though that might be considered a crime for ruining a perfect piece of chocolate candy but still I'm willing to take the risk.

"Forget about the rent," He said in between laughs. "You'll be a good source of entertainment,"

I stopped on him foot, yes- I don't since when I've acquired that trait from Liza. A startled yelp escaped his mouth. I was about to do a victory dance – when the chocolate eyed jerk (yes, the name's back) thought it would save him from the fall if he grabbed my hoodie.

Both of us began falling towards each other. It was one of those moments when everything happens in slow motion. I was advancing towards him and he was falling backwards, his arms failing outwards.

I groaned in pain as I fell on top of him. "Oof, why do we always end up like this?"

"Ow, my head hurts," He grumbled under me. "And you're heavy,"

I slammed my elbow into his stomach. "Opps my bad,"

He gave me an aggravated stare. "You did that on purpose,"

I sighed in a dramatic manner. "The kind of things people conjure up in their minds. It's absolutely ridiculous,"

"Will you get off me?" He grunted.

"No thank you. I love lying on top of you," I muttered, sarcastically.

"Well, that's fine with me. I'm enjoying having you here," A smirk crawled up his lips. I realized how close we were- our legs tangled up in an awkward manner, my arms across his chest- his face so close to mine. Goosebumps rose on my skin as I felt myself getting lost in his eyes. Damn, those eyes-they'll be the end of me.

"You're really pretty," He breathed out, half in awe, half in daze. "My kind of pretty,"

I felt my face grow hot and prickly. Triple chocolate, damn those piranhas in my stomach- they make feel gooey like a melted chocolate bar.

I quickly got off him, tugging my hoodie down my waist. "Chocolate bears taste really good and I love dark chocolate. I mean it's so perfect. It goes all melty and yummy in my mouth. Once I had a chocolate bear. I'm so evil I ate him,"

Devlin got up from the ground, giving me a peculiar stare. "Is melty even a word?"

"Uh?" I scratched the side of my head. "I don't know. But I feel like melty all the time. Yah, so once there was unicorn with purple fairies who like dancing and I don't like dancing you know I have two left feet- figuratively speaking,"

He cocked his eyebrow. "Unicorn? Purple fairies?"

"Sorry, I tend to ramble ...sometimes when I'm nervous,"

He gave me a lopsided grin that made my heart melt like dark chocolate. "So you're nervous?"

I shook my head, violently-sending strands of brown hair in all different directions.

He advanced towards me- I moved back-my back slamming into to the counter. There was teasing smile on his face as his eyes bore into my green ones.

"Why are you nervous?" He asked, his breath washing over my face.

I gulped. "I'm not,"

Suddenly he let out a loud roar, throwing him head backwards. I screamed, pushing his chest for my bloody dear life.

"I'm a zombie, be scared," He chased after me. I ran through the living room, my legs nearly getting caught in the Prussian rug. There was grubby, orange couch and large LCD screen pinned up the wall.

I screamed. "Devlin, I'm warming you stay away from me,"

"No," He howled, carrying his arms like a dead weight. "I'm zombie, I like eating girls for dinner,"

"Mama!" I cried. "I shouldn't haven't trusted a stranger,"

I ran behind the sofa, chucking the colorful cushions at him.  He dodged them easily, a smile playing on his lips. He jump onto the sofa as a loud yelp escaped my mouth.

He laughed, falling onto the sofa. "You're so stupid,"

"Jerk," I muttered my breath. I'm so stupid for buying that.

He sat up on the sofa, clutching his stomach- tiny tears left the side of his tear ducts. "I can't believe that someone can be so stupid,"

"You're such a jerk," I felt my face heat up from anger. "Chocolate eyed jerk,"

"What?" He stopped chuckling like a man bit by an ape. "Chocolate eyed?"

I opened my mouth to reply but he cut me off.

"Never mind that," He grinned, flashing his perfect rows of teeth. "You should definitely stay here. God, you're so darn funny,"

I should have been offended but I don't know why I was biting off a smile. "Dang, thanks meanie,"

He propped his arms on the sofa hedge. "No, I mean it. Stay here until you don't figure out your life,"

"I can't do that," I breathed out. "I don't want to be a burden,"

"I think it's time you stopped thinking about others," There was firm expression on his face- the kind that made me avert my eyes to look in another direction. "You need to live for yourself,"

Now, tell me- how are you supposed to say no to something like that. "Fine," I clenched the side of my arm.  "Only until I figure out what I'm supposed to do," I hesitated -I don't why- before adding the next part. "Then I'll leave," I finished, slightly shaken.

A wistful smile dawned his lips- his eyes were lost somewhere- somewhere far from here.  "Like all the others,"

I furrowed my eyebrows together in confusion. "What?"

"Nothing," He gazed at me for a moment before staring at a vacant wall. "Nothing at all,"

I sat cross-legged in the room next to Devlin's. The room was slightly cramped but it was more than enough for me. There was an empty wooden closet in the corner. It creaked every time you opened it. A small bed-with white linens and checkered comforter-pushed against the shady, brown wall and a large, glass bulb hung from the ceiling. There was wall clock which would click noisily reminding me of every second that passed by.

My bags were scattered on the soft, carpeted floors.

In my hand lay the yellow envelope that had created a ruckus through my already hellish life. What am I supposed to do now?

School opens again tomorrow. Everyone will probably gush about their amazing scores and how they couldn't wait for graduation day and prom. What will I do? What will I say? That I'm supposed to spend the next month preparing for the exams while they shop and party.

I closed my eyes.

I have to clear these exams. For dad who never blamed me for all that I did, for Liza who stood strong for my sake and for mom who never failed to understand me.

Once I clear these exams, I'll go back home. I could already envision the proud smile on my dad's face and Liza's outstretched grin.

After that I'll apply for Infinto University of Arts and finally pursue my dream to become an interior designer.

Maybe Devlin was right, it's about time I started to live for myself.

My head fell onto the cotton filled pillow. A content sigh escaped my lips "It's about time I change," And with new hope, I soon escaped into dreamland and this time not a single nightmare haunted me.

# Chapter 10

--------------------------------------------------------------

The light gale below the late autumn leaves through the busy Winterville High school's streets. Seniors and juniors parked away their shiny cars in the respective lots while I sat here Devlin's red 1996 Toyota Camry. He had out of kind courtesy decided to drop me off today claiming that I wouldn't be able to find my way from his apartment complex to school- a bland lie- his apartment was on the same street as my high school.

"Thank you," I spoke up, clutching my backpack close to my chest.

"It's alright," He smiled, warmly. A bright, clean pair of scrubs clung to his slender body.

I quickly opened the front pocket of my backpack, pulling out a white envelope. It had about hundred dollars in it. I had saved them from my lunch money. I was going to buy myself a new kit of paints and brushes from the money but now I don't think I could afford such a luxury.

With a heavy heart, I handed the envelope to Devlin. To conceal my emotions, I stretched my lips into a thin smile.

He gave me a questioning look. After hesitating for a moment he took it from my outstretched fingers. "What is this?" He asked, his gaunt fingers lifting the pale flap.

"It's not much," I bit down on my lips, a red blush settling on my cheeks out of embarrassment. "But I figured I needed to give you this. I promise once I'll pay the rest later,"

A frown made its way to his face. He shook his head. "No, you keep this," He grabbed my hand, the warmth from his skin sunk into mine, and placed the envelope into my palm. "I can't keep this. You need the money,"

"Devlin, please." I held his hand, forcing the money back into his hands. "For my sake just keep the money, please,"

He stared at me. Tensed lines ran across his jaw "I can't,"

"For me, please. You've done so much for me. This is the least I can do,"

"I get it," He smiled, almost bitterly. "You feel burdened by all that I did. But you don't understand. I didn't do this because I pitied you,"

"Then why are you helping me?" I nearly yelled, gripping my backpack tightly.

"I have my reasons," He looked away, not meeting my eyes.

"And I have mine," I whispered. "So please respect that,"

Grudgingly, he tucked the enveloped into his pocket. "Happy?"

"Very,"

To my surprise, I found Liza standing outside Mrs. Oswald's class. Oliver patted her back. It looked as if he was trying to comfort my sister. My heart warmed at gesture. Bless thy swimming beast for being a kind soul.

I approached them, feeling strangely anxious. My chest felt heavy like someone had placed a huge boulder on it. The instant Liza's watery green eyes found mine, she rushed into my arms, nearly knocking me off my feet.

"Sis, thank god you're alright," She cried, burring her head on my shoulder, her blonde hair falling over my face. Oliver looked at me. His stormy eyes watched me with caution as if he expected me to burst into tears as well. He didn't give me his usual teasing smirk instead his mouth was turned downwards in way that my heart fall to the pit of my stomach. The concern on his face was almost palpable. I averted my eyes, focusing them on Liza.

"Liza, stop crying. I'm perfectly fine," I pulled away from her, gripping her shoulders. Just for her sake, I smiled. "Look, not a scratch,"

She sniffed- with the back of her hand she quickly wiped the stray tears. "Come back home, Sis. Dad is sorry for everything. I know he misses you even though he won't admit it. It's killing him,"

My entire body stiffened. I couldn't hurt her. "I will" I lied. Each passing breath was becoming harder and harder. "After I clear the exams, I promise I will come back,"

"You won't," Fresh tears fell down her angel like face. The way her voice broke pained my heart. This was for the best. I did this for their happiness. She'll be alright...eventually. "I know you. You're just like dad- stubborn. You won't turn back. I know you won't,"

"I will Liza. Trust me. Once I get into a good college, I will come back. I want to show Dad that I'm still the old Alice. Anyways," I quickly changed the topic, hoping to get Liza's mind off my problems. "Aren't you supposed to be at cheer practice? And how did you find me?"

Liza shrugged her shoulders. "I'm skipping on practice,"

I feigned a gasp. "Liza Brown skipping cheer practice. Impossible!"

She laughed at my expression. "And the dude from target helped me find you,"

"I have a name," Oliver snickered from the door of Mrs. Oswald's class. I had completely forgotten that he was still here.

I gave him a thankful smile which he didn't return.

"Liza meet Oliver aka the swimming beast," I grinned, motioning towards Oliver.

"Nice to meet you Oliver" Liza smiled, winking at him. He gave her a baffled stare before pulling out his quirky smirk.

"Pleasure is mine,"

But as you see my sister is not easily distracted, her focus was back on my problems. "Sis, where are you staying? How's your diabetes? I hope you're taking your meds,"

"Chocolate Fudge, Easy with the questions girl," I laughed easily, feeling flustered by her sudden attack.

She looked at me expectantly.

"I'm living with a friend," I stared out. A friend? Devlin? Lord of Chocolate forgive me for lying all the time. Hopefully I won't end up in hell for doing that.

Oliver gave me a dubious look. Something was off. The way he was staring at me it seemed like he didn't believe me one bit. "Friend? Which one?" He asked.

Triple Chocolate Fudge!

"She doesn't go to this school actually. So you wouldn't know about her," I replied calmly. "Actually she has her own apartment so I'm sharing with her," Why was I lying about this?

Liza breathed a sigh of relief. "That's good. I was worried that you wouldn't have a place to go,"

She was so right. If it weren't for Devlin, I wouldn't probably be a dead body flowing with the river's current.

Oliver didn't look convinced. He made an odd face. Whatever was on his mind, I'm sure it wasn't good. Literally, this was the first time I felt so scared. More than that I began questioning my decision- why was I scared of telling Liza about Devlin? Am I doing something wrong by staying with an unknown man?

Sandy and I sat on our lunch table. Sandy munched away on a peanut butter and jelly sandwich as her red pigtails jumped around her shoulder.

During our communication application class, I told her that I was living with Devlin because I needed someone to tell me that I did the right thing.

She was quick to give her consent saying that she would exchange SpongeBob for him any day.

I couldn't help but laugh at her silly crush on the chocolate-eyed boy.

"I bet his apartment is better than a pineapple,"

I rolled my eyes "He isn't SpongeBob, you know?"

"No duh?" She stuck out her tongue causing the freckles on her cheeks to stretch out. "He's so much better,"

I stuffed another spoonful of plain yogurt.

"Sandy, you're bonkers,"

"Tell me something I don't know,"

"You're-"

Our conservation was rudely interrupted by a rough tug on my hand. I turned around to find Oliver standing behind me, holding my wrist.

I jerked my hand away from him, angrily. "What are you doing?"

"I want to talk to you," He spoke through gritted teeth. His hair was damp and he reeked of chlorine- obviously he had rushed here from his swim class.

"Okay?" I shrugged my shoulders. "Speak up,"

"No, not here," He gave Sandy a pointed look. I stole a quick glimpse of her.

Sandy chewed the insides of her cheeks- her face red and guilt-ridden. "I'm sorry Alice,"

"Oh, no!" I gasped, clasping a tight hand across my mouth, quickly understanding what she meant. She told him about Devlin. "But why would you tell him? Out of all the people? Why?"

"I-I.." She stuttered. "He gave me a good reason,"

"What was the reason?" I narrowed my eyes at her.

She didn't meet my eyes. "It's best if Oliver says it himself,"

"Come on, Oliver," I got up from my seat. Mustering all my anger, I scowled at him. "You better start talking,"

We stood outside by the dirty bleacher with the football team giving us wacked up stares. For whatever reason Oliver had gotten Sandy to spill the beans it must be fudging good.

I wasn't liking this the least bit. I wasn't like the way Oliver was watching me like I had committed some sort of horrendous crime.

"Don't even think of blackmailing with this info," I spit out, pulling out a nasty glare.

His eyes widened. "What the heck? I'm not going to blackmail you,"

"Then? What do you want?"

He groaned. "Alice," His face became bloodshot red. "You really don't get this, do you?"

"Get what?"

"How can you live with that freak? I mean come on. Seriously,"

The nerve! How could he call Devlin freak? He was such a good guy with a heart of gold. He's the only person on this earth who cared for me when no-one dared to.

"Shut up! He's not a freak. Don't you dare call him that or else"

"Or what? Huh?" Oliver grabbed my arms, his eyes burning a hole through me. He was scaring me. "He does one bloody thing for you and you-you go all defensive for him,"

"You have no idea what he has done for me," I breathed out, my pulse racing away. I could feel my hands get clammy.

"He gave you a place to live, Right?  So what? I could have done that,"

I furrowed my eyebrows together- nausea tightening its reigns over me. "Where are you heading with this?"

He ignored my words. "Stay away from him. You don't know the kind of guy he is. He uses girls and throws them away like pieces of garbage,"

I felt something twist instead me, blinking a couple of times, I stared at Oliver horrified.

"Ho-how do you know this?" I stammered- not noticing how Oliver kept on removing the space between us.

Droplets of water from his hair slid down my cheek. I bit down on my lip to stop them from trembling.

"He's the guy who ruined my sister," He finished in a low voice- pain was etched deeply into his features.

I could feel my lungs burst with the news. Breaths were leaving me faster than before. "No, you're lying," I gasped. No, Delvin he can't be the bad guy. I pushed myself away from Oliver.

'He was lying. I don't why would Oliver was lying. Devlin was just trying to help me, right?

"Maybe I did this for myself,"   His words from earlier came back in a rush, slapping me in the face.

"I would never lie to you," Oliver's voice cut through the webs I had been trapped in.

My eyes shifted to his meet his. The waves of emotions in his eyes rendered me speechless. Suddenly I dreaded the words that lay on the tip of his tongue. My mouth felt dry-words were trapped inside my throat.

"I like you way too much Alice,"

And I really hoped he meant that in a friendly way but who was I kidding?

# Chapter 11

T he football team had left the field, leaving me and Oliver in the cold air outside, alone. The bleachers squeaked as I shifted my weight from one foot to another.

Oliver watched me, expectantly, as if he expected me to confess my undying love for him but that wasn't going to happen. I never saw him in that way. Yah, sure he was everything I wanted to be but that didn't mean I liked him.

"I-I Oliver you and me no, I can't" I was one hot mess. My face felt all hot and prickly. I couldn't even look Oliver in the eye.

"Save it," He said, his face too a light shade of pink. "Pretend you never heard me,"

"I can't do that," I bit on my lip to stop it from trembling. This was too much for me to handle. All I wanted do was run away from here and bury myself in a castle dreams. I blinked my eyes several times to stop the tears from coming out. They left my eyes nevertheless.

He noticed this; his stormy blue eyes were drawled together in confusion. "Why are you crying? I'm the one who got rejected,"

"I didn't reject you stupid," I shoved his shoulder. He almost tripped from the stairs but he caught himself quickly. "It's just I'm not ready for this and I think you know the reason,"

He laughed, wrapping his arms around me. I rested my head against his shoulder, chuckling to myself. "This isn't the first time you've told me that,"

"And this isn't the first time you've confessed. Darn, but it gets to me every time," I bit back, the smell of his chlorinated hair sinking into me.

"Well, I can't help wishing you'd finally give in,"

I pulled away from him, a frown settling into my features. "I can't Oliver. I'm so sorry," Yes, I've known that Oliver liked me for a long time. It all started in our art class when we were in middle school back then I wasn't the outcast I'm today.

Things were different then. Oliver and I were literally joined at the hip that's how much we stuck together. I used to be an all 'A' student while he was an average one. He confessed his feelings for me at our eighth grade dance but I told him I wasn't ready for all of that because it didn't feel right. I don't know why my heart always got panicked whenever I saw him. It's like it was pushing me away from him. I liked him yes but only as much as I liked Sandy. I figured that I wasn't ready for any of this love business.

Things changed after we came to High-School. A tragedy in my life pulled me apart from Oliver. I began distancing myself from him. I no longer could bear to see him. He was everything I was not. He shone like a star while I fell apart like a comet. The main reason why the distances grew was because I was scared. After mom's death, I changed. Guilt consumed everything I had. I could no-longer be around people without vainly wishing that could be me if I weren't so messed up.

The reason I was surprised  today was because I never expected Oliver to still have feelings for me. I was an outcast. He was a star. We simply didn't gel together anymore.

"I can't believe you still like me," I whispered, tugging the sleeves of my sweater.

He shrugged. I had a feeling he didn't want to talk about this. "The feelings kinda came back after Sandy told me that you're staying with that freak,"

He's not a freak I wanted to say but I bit back on my tongue.

"You know after..." I trailed off, not wanting to complete my sentence by saying my mother's death.  "I just don't want to have any sort of relationship,"

"I can understand," He replied, after a moment of staring at me. "That must have been tough,"

"It was," I sighed.

The bell rang loudly through the field, signaling the end of lunch break. Oliver took my hands in his; I couldn't help notice the way his hands trembled when he held mine. His skin felt strangely rough under mine.

"Just promise me one thing. You'll stay away from him,"

"Why?" I asked. "What did he do to your sister?"

He glanced nervously at the field around himself, his stormy eyes looking so terribly scared.

"He made my sister abort her child,"

I gasped, nearly collapsing on the floor. "Why would he do that?"

"He didn't want the kid," Oliver face contorted into a disgusted expression. I could tell that Oliver would do anything to get his hands on him.

"But why?" It wasn't making any sense. "Unless it was his child," The pieces seemed to fit together in my mind, I looked at Oliver wanting him to shake his head and tell me that I was wrong.

But he didn't. He simply stared at me with a solemn expression. "Yah, it was. He was the father,"

I don't know why I started crying. Everything I had done so far seemed so wrong. I had trusted the wrong the person. I wish mom was here. I wish she could hold me in her arms and tell me that everything would be alright.

I tried controlling the colossal hysteria about to break upon me as I made my way to the Devlin's apartment. Oliver had left alone on the bleachers to cry my heart. He didn't bother to pick me up while I broke apart. I didn't want him to either. I could tell he was having a hard time as well. He rushed away. I saw his shoulder shake terribly while he walked away. My heart hurt for him. Afterall a long time ago, he used to be my best-friend.

The leaves rustled through the empty sidewalk, paling bright yellows and orange leaves shed off the trees whirled in the air, dancing there like fairies. Usually I would stop and stare, trying to memorize the beauty so I could paint it later. But not today, my eyes were blurry I could barely walk without tripping on every other step. The sound of my footsteps echoed along me.

I trusted someone after so long. I trusted a stranger even though my mom always told me not to. Here I am, torn apart like I had been hit by a hurricane. Why was crying like this? I shouldn't be this hurt by a mere stranger. Yet I was. Obviously Devlin wasn't just a stranger for me. He was so much more and that was really scary. Maybe it's not my fault- he had saved my life- maybe that's why I felt like this.

I stopped in front the blocks of tall brick buildings with straight, metal black frames. Welcome to Oak Apartment Complex a sign said that had been hanging off the hinges of a green wooden frame. I paced up the iron stairs, my heart beating a thousand times a minute.

An old lady with white hair holding a small girl in her arms walked passed me. "Are you okay dear?" She called after me.

I nodded, not having the strength to speak.

I tumbled into a stop in front of Apartment number 303. A wooden door painted maroon greeted me. I pulled my backpack off my shoulder, rummaging through it for the spare keys he had given to me. Something cold hit my fingers, I quickly pulled it. I stared at the golden keys dangling from fingers. Why did he do this to me?

Coughing, spluttering on the tears, I jammed the keys into the lock and unbolted the door to an open. The apartment's warmth swept me out the cold state I had been in. The seating area was neatly organized- in the same way we had left it.  The orange, floral sofa sat in-front the television. A heavily intricate Prussian rug lay underneath it. It was dark inside- the floor-length window had its pale, creams curtains pulled over it.

I tossed my bag on the floor at the entrance, near the foot matt that said sweet home. Not wasting any time, I ran past the seating area into the small lobby that led to the small kitchen and two independent rooms.  I flung the pale blue door to my room open. Its shady brown wall greeted me -sadly enough- this place was beginning to feel like home a day ago.

My empty sport bag lay beside the frame of the twin bed- I picked it, throwing it on the bed. Foolishly, I had unpacked everything and had arranged my belongings into that hoary wooden closet. The closets doors creaked nosily when I opened them. I filled my arms with the clothes, silent tears still streaming down my face. It was crazy of me to trust him like that. I threw in the clothes into my bag. I have to get out of here before he comes back.

In all the haze, I didn't notice when the clock struck six. Gathering my books and notebooks, I placed them inside the bag. I was to zip my bag and toss it over my shoulder when it was flung out of reach.

Devlin stood there beside me, his hands holding onto to the straps of my bag. He was dressed in his all too blue scrubs with a stethoscope clinging to his throat. My heart fluttered in my chest. I felt terrified as more tears left my eyes. He placed my bag on the floor out of my reach.

"What are you doing?" He asked, confused, frazzled. I don't why in his brown eyes which shone like golden stars I saw concern for me.

He hovered over me, stepping forward when I didn't say anything.

His striking features didn't really help my situation. I gulped as the smell of his cologne mixed with the smell of the hospital antiseptics filled my senses.

"I trusted the wrong guy," Why wouldn't these tears stop? Chocolate Fudge Alice! Get a grip on your stupid eyes.

"Care to explain," He titled his head on side, strands of his black hair moved out of his eyes. Again, before I could lose myself in his eyes, I averted my gaze.

"Let me go," I snapped, trying to reach out for my bag.

"No," He grabbed my arm before my fingers could grasp the bag's straps.

I felt Goosebumps rise on my skin. This isn't good. I want to get out of here. I want get away from him. How heartless can someone be? He forced his girlfriend or whatever she was to abort their child. How could he do that? He had saved my life. Then how could he take away an unborn life.

A sob left my mouth before I could stop it. "How could've I trusted you? I knew I shouldn't have a trusted a stranger,"

"What did I do? Tell me. Why are you upset?" He groaned, pulling both of my arms into his hands. "Just stop crying. Will you? I can't see you like this!" He nearly yelled I could his eyes were beginning to redden from anger. The usual straight contours of his faces were now distressed.

I bit down on my lips and closed the lids over my eyes. My breaths slowly began returning to normal. Why overreacting about this? Why was I crying so hard? This is not me. I don't express my emotions so freely. I never cry in front of anyone. Why do I always end up crying in front of him? Why?

When I opened my eyes, I saw Devlin still wearing that stressed expression on his face. "What happened?" He asked- his voice was stiff and strained. I knew that I wouldn't get away without telling him. The look of pure determination on his face told me so.

"Oliver said-"Was all I needed to say. Understanding dawned on his face- he shook his head regrettably before muttering something under his breath along the lines of. "That ...stupid kid,"

"Come on," His hands left my arms to hold onto my hands. I bit back the blush on my face. Oliver holding me was different thing because we've been friends for long it hardly mattered but Delvin he's.... I don't know.

"I'm not going anywhere with you," I retorted, trying to be angry. I guess I didn't look that angry because it had Devlin rolling his eyes.

"Come on drama queen. I'm not giving you a choice," He was acting like whatever Oliver had said wasn't a big deal. Maybe it wasn't. Maybe it was.

I stuck out my tongue. "Fine, I'll give you one chance to explain yourself," That was the least I could do after he had saved my life and turned it all around to the brighter side. Okay, you got me- I wanted to stay with Devlin a little bit longer even if that meant my heart could be broken in a way that couldn't be fixed.

We sat on the concrete roof-top, the floor felt strangely cold under my legs but it was alright because he was here, sitting next to me- his head thrown back to look at the darkening sky. Our legs were touching and the heat sunk in. All I could feel was nausea and my rapid heartbeats- Good Chocolate Heaven- the effect he had on me was terrifying.

"The kid wasn't mine," He began, I shifted my eyes to watch him- I found my heart sinking when I saw the expression on his face. Streaks of crumbling sorrow clung to the side of his eyes. I didn't like it one bit.

His eyes looked lost as he stared at the stars that burned brightly. "Maria as in Oliver's sister had few classes in grad school with me. She was dating my best friend, Aaron so naturally I became friends with her. Slowly, without realizing it I began liking her. I mean she was really something- sweet, kind, bold, and really strong-headed. It was kind of hard to not like her. She was perfect,"

Why did I feel this strange pang of pain when he said that?

"It was wrong of me to have feelings for her. She belonged to someone else and that to my best friend. Eventually, I pushed away the stupid crush.  One day, Aaron came up to me- he was nervous and tensed as hell. I asked him what was going on. He told me that Maria was pregnant with his child. He didn't want the baby. I should have known Aaron was always such a coward when it came to taking responsibility.  He told Maria to get an abortion and I was beyond horrified. How could he say such a thing?"

"I went to Maria. Honestly, I was angry at Aaron and at his stupidity. When I found Maria, she looked so damn scared like there was nothing that could save her. Instantly, I figured that she wasn't ready to be a mother. I did what I thought was for her best. I helped her get an abortion.  I signed all the papers that needed the consent of the father. After the abortion, Maria was really weak. She could barely stand on her feet. I brought her to the apartment that Aaron and I shared and kept here until she got better. Aaron didn't want her to stay with us so he packed his bags and left,"

It looked like Devlin was talking to himself rather than me. I placed my hand on his shoulder in the hope of easing his pain. The fabric under my hands slumped. I could feel his muscles relax to some extent.

"Once Maria got better, she left. Later when Maria's parents found about the abortion and they wanted to know who did the child belonged to, she begged and begged for me to take the responsibility of Aaron's action. I did because I loved her.  I took all the blame. That's why that kid- Oliver hates me,"

"Do still meet up with her?"

Devlin shook his head, resting it on the maze of his hands.  "I haven't heard from her since we graduated. All I know she's across the country getting a Bachelor's Degree in Nursing,"

"But how could she do that to you? How could she just leave you like after you did so much for her?" I didn't realize that I was literally yelling at Devlin until I noticed that he began cringing at my loud tone. "If someone did so many things for me, I would probably have never left their side. Chocolate Fudge, I'd probably love the life out of them,"

I didn't realize what I was saying. The words left my mouth before I could even stop them. The swirling stars in the night sky thankfully hide the massive plum red that was shading the sides of my face.

"Love the life out of them, huh?" Devlin asked in a playful tone, a smirk crawling up his lips.

I had an urge to bury my face in my hands. I bit down on my lips, trying not to blurt something utterly mortifying. "Uh..." I trailed off.

He leaned closer to me, his lips grazing at the edge of my ear as his hot breath fanned my face. "I'd like to know what that feels like,"

I gaped at him, feeling like a fish out of water. Flustered, embarrassed, nervous all the emotions at once never did much good to me.

He leaned back- turning his head to once again stare at the sky- thankfully that gave me time to gather myself. Breathe in, breathe out I reminded myself.

I looked up at the sky as well. What I saw stole my breath. Spiraling star shone brightly in the sky. There were so many stars in the sky, filling every edge of the sky. It felt like Devlin and I sat under a blanket with small pores of stars through which the light fell inside.

"It's beautiful," I whispered, half in awe, half in daze.

"It is," He replied, his eyes finding mine- there was a slight smile on his face. The pain from earlier seemed to have dissipated from his striking features. I could feel my stomach turn into a pool of fluttering butterflies. The way he always looked at me, I don't know- it always made me feel so special.

A strange yet comforting silence fell upon us as we watched the denizens of the night. We stayed there for what seemed like could have been an eternity when it could have been seconds or few hours. The silent gust of winds flowed in the empty space between us. I don't why my fingers were itching to hold his hands to know that he was here, to know that I had actually found someone as softhearted as him.

"I'm sorry for earlier. I kind of jumped to conclusions-"

"No, it's alright. I would have done the same thing," I doubt he would have done what I did. "Though I'm not sure about the crying part," He finished with a teasing grin.

I punched his shoulder. "Dang, you're mean," The argument was invalid after what he told me I doubt he was anything but that.

"Yah, sure like you believe that,"

I shoved him. "Jerk, just because I took your side one time doesn't I'm going to change my views about you,"

"I'm not asking you to either,"

"Whatever," I replied, running out of witty comebacks.

A fond smile was on his lips, the side of his eyes crinkled while a small dimple formed on his left cheeks. He looked so darn cute- very irresistible. Gah! Chocolate Fudge what's going on? "Thank you," He spoke with so much sincerity that it had be blushing like a drugged pig in seconds.

I coughed, trying to hide that awkward blush. "For what?"

"For just being here,"

And I don't think anyone has made me smile this wildly. I literally could feel my cheeks hurt with the smile. I found myself averting my eyes to looking at the stars.

He reached for my hands. Gallons of warmth melted inside me, making a pool at me feet. His fingers wove through mine, tangling them. Slowly, He lifted our hands up into the sky.

"You know whenever we look at stars we're actually looking into our past,"

My eyes widened in amazement. "How is that?"

He stretched our finger so in between the gaps we could see the glittery stars, twinkling in our hands. It felt like the universe was in our hands. We were the ones who were controlling them, controlling our destiny. "The light we seen now began its journey millions of years ago,"

"The same way the person we know today is actually someone shaped by their past," I breathed out, everything seemingly fitting into a perfect beaded chain of stars.

"Precisely,"

# Chapter 12

-----------------------------------------------------------------

The night danced past us. Each second glided away with articulated peace. Devlin chatted with me, his voice sounding like a calm wandering song. Occasionally in between silence would fall upon us and we wouldn't dare to interrupt it.

Just knowing that there was a presence, a person other than myself here, listening to my silly thoughts and ideas was a fulfilling feeling. After years, I felt whole. This wholly goodness seeped through my chest and flowed till my toes.

The lively spark in his warm eyes told me that he felt the same.

"Would you rather have a night filled with stars or just the full moon?" He asked, smiling, his eyes not leaving the night sky for a minute.

I smiled to myself, unable to tear my eyes away from him. "I used to like it with the full moon,"

"And now?" His eyes found mine for a breathing halting moment. I felt Goosebumps rise on my skin as my heart sped faster than any clock.

There was a small teasing smirk on his lips.

"A sky filled with stars"

"How come?" He turned his shoulders slightly so I would have his full attention.

I shrugged. All of the sudden I felt strangely flustered. "I don't know," My voice was barely above a whisper. "The moon looks so lonesome. Just floating through the empty sky. While the stars, they look so-"

I stopped, trying to find the right word to describe my thoughts.

Devlin's hand found mine, hesitation flickering on his face like an open flame. I don't know what made me weave my fingers through his. He took in a small piece of air, his chest falling slowly. Clear surprise scrawled on his face.

Suddenly I found the word to say and for the first time they didn't fail me. "They look so happy because they have someone by their side,"

Something about what I had said caught him off-guard. Delvin looked at a loss of words. He averted his gaze but his hands didn't leave mine.  Maybe I had said the wrong thing. Maybe I shouldn't have said that. Why did I even say that?

I wasn't trying to imply anything when I said those words.

"Let's go," He said after a while. There was a torn expression on his face. His eyes- they looked so lost. I felt his hand leave mine as he got up from the cold terrace.

Had something I said upset him? "What?" I asked, confused.

He snapped out of whatever daze he had been in and smiled, half-heartedly at me.

"I'm pretty sure you have school tomorrow,"

"Yah, so what about it?"

He rolled his eyes while shaking his head. "It's late, Madame and as your personal caretaker I think it's time for dinner,"

"Pft," I huffed, crossing my arms over my chest. "Who made you my caretaker?"

"Destiny did," My mind reverted back to the time Devlin had visited our school for career counseling then too he had said. "...because of destiny,"

I frowned. "Why do you believe in destiny so much?"

Again, that same lost look flashed in his eyes. He quickly rearranged his features into a smirk. "No more dilly-dallying. Come on we need to get something inside your stomach before you get another low sugar attack,"

"You sound like my mom," For the first time, I said mom without having a wave of guilt and pain pull me under.

He gave me teasing smile. "You must annoy her like you're annoying me,"

I gasped, feigning hurt. "You think I'm annoying. "I placed a hand on my head and let out a dramatic sigh. "All this time I've been under the illusion that the chocolate-eyed jerk enjoyed my company,"

He raised an eyebrow. "Chocolate-eyed jerk, seriously?"

I shrugged. "Suits you,"

"Are my eyes made out of chocolate? Wait! you think I'm a jerk,"

I bit back a laugh and got up from my spot because I was sure the thing I was about to say was going to have him going livid with anger.

Placing my right foot past the left, I got into racing position. "I also think that you'd make a very pretty girl,"

"You what?" He screeched, his face red from a mixture of anger and embarrassment.

"Like if you wear a dress you'd look more beautiful than me," I laughed.

Oh chocolate fudge! Literally, there was smoke erupting through his nostrils.

"That's what you said at the Dollar store," A slow realization dawned on his face. I watched his skin turn into darker shade of red. "That I'd make a pretty girl and I though you said-"

Before he could come to anymore conclusions, I dashed across the rooftop, carefully avoiding the empty cans.

I could hear Devlin screaming like a outraged tiger. "Alice Brown you're so dead,"

I laughed louder than I had in a long time. My lungs felt like they were going to burst open with joy. Truly, I felt alive.

Devlin was still sour about me telling him that he'd make a pretty girl. He whisked the cream in the glass bowl, his lips pressed into a thin line. I was sitting on the metal stool placed beside the granite kitchen counter. My revision assignments for the upcoming exams were scattered on the counter.

Intermittently, I would glance at Devlin and see him wearing that same sour expression as he cooked dinner. He paced between the rows of white cabinets in the small lobby like kitchen and placed a pan on the stove. After tossing some onions into it, turned around towards the counter I was sitting at and wiped his hands with the red towel.

I sighed again. Seriously, he's acting like a little boy about this whole thing. I'm pretty sure he still believes that girls have cooties.

After we had come downstairs, I had changed into my comfortable Alice in wonderland jumper. I felt a bit wary about wearing it but then again I didn't have anything else to wear. All of my other clothes need some serious washing. I'll probably stop by the Laundromat tomorrow and get them cleaned. When I walked out of my room wearing the jumper, I could saw Devlin's eyes nearly pop out of their sockets. He coughed a couple of time to cover his laughter. I heard it nevertheless.

I stared, shamelessly as Devlin added the boiled pasta into the pan. He looked quite handsome in those checkered pajamas and loosely fitted blue jersey. I wish I could look as good as him.

Another sigh left my mouth.

Devlin's eyes shot in my direction. He caught me staring. I quickly averted my eyes to the assignments pretending to be deeply engrossed in human health science. Then I noticed what assignment it was and felt color flee to my cheeks. Male Reproductive System.

I didn't even have any other book to cover it up. All I had was my pencil box and a stupid wooden ruler Why do I even a have ruler with me? I don't even need to study maths anymore. I passed the subject with flying colors.

Devlin placed a glass lid on the pan and let it simmer on low heat. He dragged his long legs and took a seat on my other side.

Please don't look down. Please don't look down.

"I still can't believe you would think that," Devlin grumbled, propping his elbows on the counter. "Talk about a hard blow to my masculinity,"

Keep your eyes on my face. Don't look down. For chocolate's sake don't you dare look down.

"Think of it as compliment," I bit down on the corner of my lips. Gawd, he looked like a cute five year old boy.

"No," He huffed, angrily. "How in the world 'you'd make a pretty girl' a compliment,"

"Well, it means that you're so good-looking that could pass as a girl,"

I did not just say that.

A large grin erupted on his face. "You think I'm good-looking?"

"Well," I dragged the word, enjoying myself as I teased him. "In a girly way,"

Instantly, the grin dropped from his face. "Gee thanks, you just killed all my manliness,"

"I was kidding,"

He scowled "I knew that,"

"Come on," I punched his shoulder, playfully. "I think you're very, very handsome,"

There something seriously wrong with my mouth. I swear on chocolate I'm going to kill my mouth if I utter something like this again.

An obnoxious smirk crept to his lips. "Oh really?"

"Whatever. I still think you'd make a pretty girl," I muttered under my breath as I fidgeted with my pen's cap.

"You think I'm-"He shot up from the metal stool and stretched his arms to both sides. He began flexing both of his arms. I don't think there was any muscle there. All I saw was skinny pricks of arms. "Wait for it, wait for it,"

And then he posed like some Greek god and placed a hand under his chin. "Very, very handsome,"

I rolled my eyes. "Talk about no muscles,"

"Hey, I have muscle," He flexed his arm to show me his invisible biceps.

"Oh my Gawd, Devlin," I squeaked in a high pitched voice. "You're so ripped. Those muscles, Gah. Those toned arms. I think I'm dreaming,"

He narrowed his eyes. "Ha-ha very funny,"

"I'm glad I could amuse you," I turned my attention back to the assignment. Bad move.

"What are you working on?" Devlin leaned forward to examine my assignment. Chocolate Fudge, I just hope he doesn't see anything. Maybe he won't, afterall he wasn't wearing his glasses.

"Mhm," He muttered, thoughtfully. "I hated this chapter back in high-school. Never really understood it until I got into collage,"

I was pretty sure there was hideous blush covering my cheeks.

"If you need any help with it, let me know," He looked up from the paper and smiled at me.

I thought he was teasing me but there was sincere smile on his face. He didn't look the least bit bothered or embarrassed by the fact I was studying the freaking male reproductive system.

Noting my blush, he buckled up over his knees and laughed till tears left his eyes.

"You'd be a terrible doctor," He said in between breaths.

I wanted to strangle the life out of him yet at the same time I never wanted him to stop laughing.

A stupid smile erupted on face. "I can't help it. I'm just not doctor material,"

He huffed. With the back of his hands, he wiped the stray tears. "Neither was I,"

Furrowed my eyes together, confused on what he meant by that?

I was about to ask when he cleverly declared. "Dinner is ready!"

The gentle sound of shuffling of paper and scribbling of pen was all I heard through the night. After tossing and turning for few minutes, I finally shot up in bed.

Silently, I crept into Devlin's room. A pale blue door with chipped painted greeted me. The door was slightly ajar, letting small amounts of light peek through it.

When we had dinner, it was like around elven thirty and I think I've been asleep for few hours so that probably means it's like two or three o'clock in the morning.

What was Devlin doing up so early in the morning? I don't think he slept last night. Straight after dinner, he retired to his room saying that he was way behind on his study schedule. I even apologized feeling like I was the reason for it but he lightly told me it's was no big deal. Obviously it was a big deal if he's still awake.

Chocolate Fudge, I feel guilty.

The door creaked open, I stepped inside. There was small bed with a colorful teddy bear quilt over it and a large wooden closet in a one corner. Pale cream colored French windows opened up to a small patio.

His bed was empty, not a single crease on the mattress or the pillow. It seemed like no-one had slept on it for ages.

There were two doors- one small door that led to the bathroom (I suppose though I've never seen it) and another large one which had blue light falling through it led to his study room.

Should I check on him? I don't why I felt strangely worried. What if I disturb him? No, I'll just see how he's doing.

I peeked in through the small opening. The last time I saw this room everything was so organized. Every book was perfectly arranged in neat rows on the teak wood shelves. His desk was perfectly organized all the pens and pins in their respective boxes. But today, the room looked like one hell of a mess.

Stacks of books were scattered through the room. Devlin sat in the middle of the room on the floor instead on his desk which was cluttered with torn pages. A pair of thick-framed glasses covered his eyes. His neck was craned over some bulky book. To be honest, he looked frazzled and confused.

His black hair which usually were neatly combed to one side were now a dismantled mess.

Rapidly he would flip through the pages and scribble words onto his notebook that lay on his lap.

This is my fault. I always screw things up. Back home, I was burdening dad and now Devlin. He wouldn't be caught in this mess if I hadn't freaked out about the Oliver incident.

There was nothing I could do to help him. All this time Devlin made sure I was alright. What am I to him? Nothing. Just a girl he's helping out of pity.

He makes sure I'm fed on time so wouldn't I have a sugar attack. He placed his own troubles aside to mend things with me. Despite having a mountain of work to do, he spent half of the night with me.

If he does so many things for a complete stranger, I really wonder what he'll do for someone who has gained his affection.

The mere thought of having a small portion of his love made all breaths halt inside the cage of my ribs. The usual slow, steady beat of my heart changed into something completely erratic and wild.

Devlin Hutchins -the girl, who will receive your love, honestly is the luckiest girl to ever walk this earth. You have no idea what I'd give to be that girl.

# Chapter 13

-------------------------------------------------------------

I t's often the little things that win someone's heart. Mom always used to tell me 'everything coming straight from the heart is far valuable more than any gift money can buy,' how come? I would ask her. Her green eyes would light up with this strange warmth, she would smile to herself, her slim back bent over the pot of boiling beans and then what after some quiet seconds, she'd reply. 'Alice, a lifeless object can't give us happiness. Happiness is inside us. A piece entitled from one to heart to another always strikes happiness because it hits right on our heart," I'd shake my head, confused. 'I don't understand,'

The sound of her laughter filled my mind. 'One day you will, my silly clown,'

I bit down on the side of my lips, my hair pulled back into a tight braid as I stood dressed perfectly into a neat pair of plaid trousers and  a red tee.

My eyes shifted to the timber wall-clock. Five o'clock it read while the black second needle swept away.

"Straight from the heart." I whispered to the narrow kitchen draw-ers.

The cabinets creaked nosily when I opened them. The white paint chipped off into my hands, sticking to my clean and nicely scrubbed hands.

I spotted a large container filled oats and a box of raisins. Right then I knew what I was going to make for Devlin.  The minute I checked on Devlin last night ( or early morning whatever you want to call it), I knew I had to do something for him. It's not fair that he's the one who gets to play the nice guy all the time.

Now it's my turn to be one to him.

I smiled and set right to work. Even though I may or may not be a good cook but for his sake I had to try. With each passing second, it was getting harder and harder to control the massive burst of happiness erupting inside me. I couldn't wait to surprise him.

After exactly one hour and eighteen minutes I had the accom-plished the impossible feat of baking a batch of fresh oatmeal and raisin cookies. Not to mention, the kitchen was absolutely perfect-all the dishes were clean and the granite counters were spotless.

Liza would be so proud. She probably wouldn't believe me if I told her that I, Alice Brown had baked cookies without tearing down the kitchen.

Carefully, I balanced a warm cup of milk in my left hand while the other gripped tightly to the plastic tray filled with cookies. My cheeks were beginning to hurt from the wide grin on face but I couldn't care less.

I walked to Devlin's room and was greeted by a closed pale blue door. Should I knock?  Yah, Alice how are you going to manage to do that. Both of your hands are filled with food. Maybe I should try using my foot.

No, I won't do that.  What if Devlin opens the door and finds standing looking a freaking one legged rabbit. Never mind.

"Devlin," I quietly spoke up.

No reply.

"Devlin," I tried a bit louder.

"Oof" A grunt resounded through the other side of the door. Sounds like someone fell off the bed. Maybe I startled him. Yikes.

"The door's open," Devlin replied, his voice tried and gruff.

"Um," I shuffled my feet, staring at my SpongeBob socks- the ones Sandy had gotten me for my birthday. "My hands are kinda occupied,"

"Coming," He sighed loudly.

He stepped out, his black hair in disarrayed mess while these hideous purplish, grey bags were under his striking brown eyes. A loose white undershirt clung stubbornly to his olive colored skin.

He let me into his room, an amused smile on his lips. "So is this some sort of sorry for thinking I'd make a pretty girl,"

I stuck out my tongue. "No, doofus it's a thank you for staying-"I caught myself in time. There is no-way I'm telling him that I checked on him last night. He'll think I'm some sort of creep.

"For?" Devlin urged me to continue, a teasing spark in his gorgeous brown eyes. Mother of all things chocolate, his eyes- waves of comforting warmth filled them, golden-browns and black streaks lighted their way through his eyes. I swear they'll be the death of me.

"For everything," I shrugged causally, placing the plate on the messy bed and milk on the bedside table.

Devlin's teddy bear quilt was sprawled across the floor and so was his pillow. "Were you sleeping on the floor?" I asked- trying bit down the laughter stuck in my throat.

He came up to me and wrapped the quilt around his arms whilst dragging the pillow onto the bed. Quickly, he placed them on the small bed.

There was faint red tint in his cheeks. It was barely visible but it was definitely there.

"No. I wasn't," His eyes briefly flickered to my face before turning to fix the quilts.

"Really?" I grinned, crossing my arms over my chest.

"I fell," He smiled -all to himself. For a silent second, our eyes met. "I fell hard," He finished in a quiet voice. Strangely enough, I felt heat rush to my face. With an awkward hand, I tucked away the loose strands of hair behind my ear.

Is he implying that he fell for someone? For me?

What in the world are you thinking Alice? Get grip over idiotic brain. He probably doesn't look at you in that way. Or does he?

"Mhm," I averted my eyes to look outside the elegant French windows. The sun was beginning peak through the clouds, shadows of the previous night began disappearing from the sky.

"So cookies, huh?" Devlin picked one up and bit it into it. I watched his face, my heart beating wildly with anticipation.

Finger's crossed, I hope he likes them.

His face twisted into a wide grin as he stuffed the entire thing into his mouth. "They're really good," He mumbled, his cheeks filled with cookies.

I never thought a compliment would make me this happy. "Seriously? I've never baked before. Lisa always told me I'm a terrible cook," I clasped my hands by my chest.

He furrowed his eyebrows together. "Lisa?"

"My little sister. You know I met her yesterday."

"She must really miss you," The side of his cheek was caught in a small dimple as he smiled wistfully.

"Yah, she does. I told her I'll come back after I pass the exams,"

His smiled dimmed. "What exams are you talking about? Aren't the semester finals over?"

Embarrassment covered my face. I didn't want to tell him about this. What if he thinks I'm a dumb girl? I don't want him to think that. I'm not dumb. Well I used to be somewhat brainy back in middle school. One thing was suddenly confusing me- why do I care what he thinks of me? Why does it matter? It shouldn't matter but it does. It does matter. Why? I don't want to know.

In a minute, understanding dawned upon on Devlin's face- the thin contours of his face were arranged into sympathetic expression. "Re-test, right? You flunked your exams. Is that why you left your place?"

I chewed the insides of my cheeks, not really wanting to reply. I'm not dumb. I'm not stupid. I'm just lost. I lost myself. That's why I couldn't clear those exams. That's why I couldn't clear any test life threw at me. I wanted to scream on top of my lungs but I couldn't.

His eyes took my silence in, the expression on his features softened. With large steps, he strode to where I stood, his long, gaunt fingers finding mine. "Hey, it's alright. There's nothing to be ashamed of,"

My eyes closed on their own accord. The gentle warmth from his fingers sunk into my aching bones. I wanted to cry yet I wanted laugh out of joy at the exact same time.

"Look all of us mess up at times. Even I did,"

I opened my eyes, shaking my head angrily. "You're lying just to make me happy,"

"I'm not," He smiled. "I flunked the first year of grad-school. Man, seriously I couldn't mind to focus on those stupid books. But then I realized something-"He pointed to his chest. "I blamed my heart all that time- for falling in love with wrong person, for giving everything to a girl who didn't deserve it.  When the poor thing did nothing, I was the one who choose not to pay attention to my education. I didn't realize it at the time my degree may not make me happy but the happiness of all the people around me lay in it,"

"Is that why you choose to become a doctor? For your family,"

The smile disappeared from his face, a condemning look took reign.  "Not just for my family but for a better life as well. I wanted to help the people around me in my some way,"

"Oh," I mumbled, looking away from him. "So I should have tried for my family's sake,"

"No, that's not what I meant,"

"Then?" I asked, tears brimming in my eyes. Devlin thinks I'm selfish for not trying. He thinks I like making my family miserable. Not everyone can be like him.

He brought his hands to my arms, gripping them tightly. His eyes refused to leave mine, they stubbornly held my gaze. "For yourself, Alice, do this for your own sake. This may sound vain but education matters. You may not realize this now but in the future all of us need money and these books I so dauntingly called stupid always stay by our side. They never betray us. When everything in the world abandons us, knowledge stays. Wiser is the man who learns from his mistakes. The past is done and over with. All we can do is pave a better future,"

"You sure know how to talk," I breathed out. "Are you sure you don't want to run for the next presidential election? I'd vote for you"

"Alice," He sighed.

"Okay, okay. I promise I'll try my best and I'm going to clear those exams with flying colors,"

He shook his head slightly, laughing. His hands still hadn't left my arms. I don't think he realized how close we stood. I could feel his peppermint breath fan over my face. After a while a wave of silence fell over us, a blank look covered his face.

His fingers tucked away a stray strand away from my face, leaving a trail of fire behind. My heart hiked up to my throat. I didn't dare to breathe- afraid a small move might shatter the thin glass of air between us.

The tips of his fingers lingered on my skin for a second longer before leaving them in a subtle gist. A ray of light from the morning sun flittered through his eyes, making them glow with a golden hue of warmth.  The sharp counters of his angular jaw were fitted into a thin line. He drew his lips together, pressing them together until color drained them.

Even I don't know where this confidence came from as I lifted my hand to his cheek.  The stressed lines on his face relaxed under my hands. I could feel his rough stubble brush against my skin. Goosebumps rose on my skin. The beats of my heart were growing louder- they were so loud that I was afraid he might hear them.

"Alice," Devlin spoke in a straitened voice, shattering the tender moment in a quick second. My hand left his face. I watched as a painful piece of air left his parted thin lips.  A mortifying blush covered my face.

Dishearteningly, I noticed Devlin put some distance between us. He stepped back, his hands leaving my arms. What was I doing a minute ago?

I blinked a couple of times to hide the tears in my eyes. Did he just reject me? No, there was nothing in the first place to be rejected.

"Thank you for the cookies. I really liked them," The polite nature of his tone caught me off-guard.

"You don't have to thank me. I should be the one-"

"Alice, look um-"Devlin pressed a hand against his head. "I have a-lot of work to do," He wanted me to leave. Of-course, he wouldn't want to be around someone like me. Alice, Stop being so dramatic. He probably has a ton of work since I wasted his time yesterday.

I didn't reply. I don't think I could.  Quickly, I left him in the room. Despite what I told myself, the stupid ache inside my chest wouldn't lessen.

"Are you okay?" Sandy asked, a frown making an appearance on her freckled cheeks. She tied her pigtails into a bun, standing next to me in the gym lockers. I hated P.E. (physical education/ gym class). Actually it wasn't Coach Stockens hard drills and exercises that made me hate this class. I enjoyed running till my lungs began burning and my pulse hiking upwards painfully. There were other reasons why I abhorred gym, reason I didn't want to think of right now in my current terrible mood.

I shrugged, my gym shorts hiking up my legs as I placed my leg on the bench to tie my laces. Sandy sat down on the bench, her eyes scrunched up in a perceiving way. "I swear on SpongeBob and Sandy's love that I won't tell Oliver anything ever again no matter what he says,"

She had gotten the wrong idea. I wasn't mad at her. I was upset because of a chocolate eyed boy. If I were in her spot, I would have done the same. Come on, Oliver told her that he had feelings for me. He pulled out the love card on her and according the invisible friendship manual love comes before everything.

"Sandy-"I began, only to be interrupted.

"Oliver told me he'd tell your dad you're dating Devlin. He saw you come to school in Devlin's car,"

"He what?" I screeched -my blood boiling as a feverish blush rose to my cheeks. Oliver, how could he even say that? Chocolate quadruple fudge!

"I'm sorry. I'm sorry," She chanted, frantically, her reddish orange hair falling out of the white hair clips. "Oliver looked so mean. He told me if I didn't tell him who you're living with. He'd get Liza to tell your dad about Devlin. I was scared. I didn't want you to get into trouble,"

I honestly couldn't believe Oliver would do that. Why didn't Oliver tell Sandy the real reason? Why didn't he tell her that he liked me? - Not that I wanted him to but still why did he lie?

I placed a hand on Sandy's shoulder. "Calm down Sandy, it's okay. I'm not mad at you. Oliver is a jerk,"

"He is," She sniffled, rubbing her nose with the back of her hand. "We're good?"

I gave her a quick hug. "Of-course, you're the best friend I've had. I could never be mad at you,"

"You're awesome," She smiled. "But maybe not as much as SpongeBob, "Her face looked so guilt ridden when she said that I couldn't help but laugh.

"Silly Sandy,"

"Girls," Coach Stockens shrill voice rang through the soccer field, halting the intense match between the senior and junior girls.  All of us were dripping with perspiration. Our cleats were covered in mud and grass. I wiped a hand across my face, trying to block the mid-afternoon bright sunlight.

Sandy jogged back to my goalie position. She looked ready to past out at any moment. Her skin was burning with red patches. Good thing, I didn't get sunburned as easily as she did.

"You okay?" I whispered, getting out of my stiff stance.

She fanned her burning face.  "I could throw up,"

"Err, that's not good,"

She coughed in agreement.

"Two laps around the ground now," Coach barked from under the shed by the bleachers. "All of you," All the girls started heading towards the edges, wearily- their movement sluggish and slow. No-one in our class treated gym seriously. Everyone was here just because gym was a compulsory subject and an easy A.

Sandy groaned. "Is she trying to kill us?"

I started running to the corner of the field, ready to use up every last ounce of energy I had left. "Come on, the faster we get this done the better,"

I heard her steps behind me. "Yah, yah you just want to be the first one to finish as usual,"

"I do not," Okay, maybe I did. Reason one, being it looks really cool to be the first in the lockers. Secondly, I wanted to get the hell out of here before any of the other girls get a chance to catch up with me.

"Slow down," I heard Sandy yell. Never. Today is the one day I didn't have the strength to face them.

I ran as fast my feet would carry me. My P.E. tee ruffled with the wind, leaving gentle cool trailing along the sweat. One more lap to go.

"Alice," I heard the voice I despised the most call for me. Beatrice. She jogged freely next to me, her dirty blond hair in a neat ponytail. An overly sweet smile was fitted on her perfectly craved face as her brown-black eyes stared at me in pure disgust.

My strength seemed to be failing me now. I tried running faster but it was of no-use. This is as fast as my empty stomach would allow me to go. Beatrice had far more stamina than me. She may not be fast but could run for miles and miles without breaking into sweat.

I would admire her if she weren't so nasty to me.

"I was doing this project where I have to survey people-"She ran in perfect synch with me, her feet not in a step ahead of mine. "And ask them how many time do they shower in a week and if they use deo," She spoke loud enough for the girls running behind us to hear.

A few snickers left the group while some of them laughed. I turned around to find Sandy staring in a different direction. She was too afraid of them, afraid that if she stood up for me they might turn against her as well. I didn't want Sandy suffer with me anyways.

Everyone had stopped running. All the junior and senior girls with their faces covered in sneers made a loosely-tied circle around Beatrice and me. Carmen another junior from Beatrice's group walked right up to me- her messy curly hair in a tight bun. "Yah, tell her how many times do you shower in week. I bet the answers zero,"

"You stink," Amanda hollered, her petty figure standing in front of the group of senior.

I'm pretty sure I don't stink. They just need a reason to pick on me. Why did I ever do to them? Why do they hate me?

"Haven't you heard of a thing called deodorant?" Carmen wrinkled her nose upwards.

I bit down on my lips, not in the mood to reply, knowing that if I spoke back they'd make my life a living hell.

"I heard she failed her exams," Jessica, the tall one, shouted as she approached the group. "Looks like the loser ain't going to prom,"

"Omg," Beatrice cheered and did a fist pump. "Prom won't stink. Phew,"

Everyone hollered in agreement- their face lit up in haunting grins. Beatrice beamed at the response, twirling in her spot. "Prom's gonna be purr-fect,"

I ran, tears prinking my eyes. It still hurt. No-matter how many times I go through this. I will never get used to it. Every time a lump formed inside my throat wanting me to rip myself apart. Each and every thing they said still cut through my thick armor.

Their words tore my flesh, gnawing the soul inside- my heart believed whatever they say. It's stupid but my insecurities always got the best of me. I am Alice Brown and I am a loser. I am Alice Brown the outcast, the girl who was never accepted by her own father, the girl who will never fit in no-matter how hard she tries.

I didn't ask for the world to be at my feet. I just wanted a small place in this big wide world. Did I ask for too much?

River of tears was threatening to break lose. I bit down on my lips until I could taste the rusty taste of blood. I won't let them see my cry. They want to see me break apart and fall down but I won't. Not in-front of them.

The Cafeteria was filled with different, tempting aromas. All the students were chattering animatedly- few were standing on top of the lunch tables and instantly got down when they spotted the principles or teachers. The environment here was chaotic and so vibrant. Everyone was excited for Prom. Girls chatted about their dresses and dates. The guys were too busy coming with news ways to propose to their girls. Long lines enthusiastic teenagers filled the left wing- that's where the prom tickets were being sold.

Turning my attention back to our table, I opened the lid of my Tupperware lunch box. I had packed few of the oatmeal cookies I had kept aside before I gave them to Devlin. Sandy clicked her pen noisily as she tried finishing her brand-new math book which she bought from the money she was 'supposed' to spend on her prom dress.

She looked up from the bulky book, a guilty look on her face. "Sorry about gym class,"

I sighed. "Don't start on that again. Like I said before I don't care about them,"

"I should have said something but I get so scared,"

I tried giving her a comforting smile. It's always hard for me to smile when I'm down. Your lips bleed when you smile, the pain is almost unbearable but I had to nevertheless. "I don't want you to say anything. It's bad enough that they're miserable to me. I don't want them to pick on you as well,"

"It's not fair. You should tell coach about this,"

I rolled my eyes. I'll tell Coach Stockens about them when a steam roller runs over my dead body. She will probably make fun of me and tell me to man up. I remember when Martha Tucker, the freshman, was balling her eyes out during a basketball practice because she someone stole her science fair project. Coach Stockens specifically told us to not to help her. She told us that Martha need to learn few things about life. All of us watched Martha cry her heart out, no-one daring to help her.

"Coach probably knows about it,"

"She doesn't-"

"No, she does. Sandy, she was standing literally ten feet away from us when they made fun of me. She doesn't give a damn,"

Angrily, I stuffed an oatmeal cookie in my mouth. The minute the cookie dissolved I had to spit out. Coughing and spluttering on the tasteless burnt dough with horror I realized how terrible it was. It tasted like burnt pieces of coal- actually worse than that.  Yuck!

Holy chocolate cow! How in the world did Devlin eat this? I could barely bear the smoky taste. Unscrewing the cap of my bottle, I chugged down the entire bottle of water.

I turned over the brown spotted cookies to find they were burned black from the bottom. "These are disgusting," I huffed. "He ate them without a single word,"

"What are you talking about?" Sandy raised her eyebrow, folds of her freckled cheeks lifting upwards as well.

"Nothing," I muttered, shutting my lunch box.

He lied to me. He lied right to my face. He thought it would hurt my feelings if he told me the cookies were pathetic. Alice Brown is a lot stronger than that. He thinks I'm some sort of wimp. He doesn't know. He doesn't understand. I've could have handled the truth.

"Alice, you look like you're about to kill someone," Sandy spoke, her voice terrified.

Running a hand across my face, I heaved a deep sigh. "You bet I am,"

Devlin Hutchins, you better get ready.

Standing by my locker in the packed hall with teens racing to their classes, I dug my hands into my locker shelf and tried finding my art brushes. Maybe I should clean my locker. Literally, I can't take a book out  without having fifteen more falling on top of me.

After minutes jamming and digging my fingers into the empty side slots, I found my favorite thick red brush. Grinning to myself, I carefully tucked inside the pocket of my blue bag.

I felt a tap on my shoulder- I turned around to find Oliver standing behind me, his hands buried in the pockets of his orange swim team hoodie. He had a cap covering the mop of curly chlorine bleached hair. His stormy blue eyes flickered to the students passing us. It was like he didn't want anyone to see us together.

He looked scared or was it embarrassment?

Ignoring his odd behavior, I smiled at him. Then I remembered what Sandy told me. Should I be angry at him for lying and for blackmailing my friend?

"Oliver-"I started out, deciding to ask him why he blackmailed Sandy and if he really would have told my dad about Devlin but he beat me to it.

"Look Alice," He breathed out, blowing a ragged breath of air. "About the other day-"

"I was about to ask you the same thing,"

"No listen," His stormy eyes met mine for fraction of a second. "Don't tell anyone about it. I didn't mean what I said. It was stupid of me,"

I felt my heart fall to the pit of my stomach. My eyes widened slightly. What in the world is he saying? "Huh?"

He ran a frustrated hand across his mouth. "I do like you. Well I used to like you when you were actually... never mind. Now Alice, things are different. I have a reputation and the guys on the swim will laugh at me if they find I got rejected by someone like you,"

Heat rushed to my face. It felt as though he had dumped a cold bucket of ice on me. Don't cry, don't cry, Alice.

Tears stung bitterly in my eyes. I laughed when I wanted to cry and hide under my bed. "What do you mean by 'someone like you'?" My voice shook with each word.

Guilt struck a chord on his face. Oliver's cheeks turned into a light shade of red. "Sorry, I didn't mean that," A groan left his lips as he grabbed a fistful of hair. "Here's the thing. I really like Beatrice and I want to ask her out to prom. She won't go with me if she finds out about you. This has nothing to do with you. You're cool Alice. It's just that I-"

"Oliver you know me and you know that I don't spread gossip. Whatever happened between us will stay between us. I promise," I grabbed my bag from the floor and slammed my locker shut.

Breathe in, breathe out. You're strong. Don't cry.

"Thanks and I didn't mean-"Oliver folded his hands together in a desperate plea, his eyes looking like a harmed doe.

"Forget it," I nearly yelled, some eyes snapped in our direction. Red painted Oliver's cheeks as his eyes noted the attention we receiving. I lowered my voice, my fist clenched into a tight ball.

"We used to be friends and now you're embarrassed to be seen with me. There was a time Oliver when you were the nobody and I wasn't embarrassed to hang around you because you were my friend. Because I loved you for who you were,"

I turned my back towards him and ran out of there. He didn't even try to stop me. Of course he wouldn't. My mind rushed back to the times when my friends used to tell me to ditch Oliver. They told me he wasn't cool enough for me. I remember telling them to back off because he was my best-friend. I remember standing up for him when the boys at middle-school would be mean. I remember being the hand that picked him up whenever he fell.

I remember every tear we shed. I remember every laugh we shared. I remember every single moment we spent together.  I remember everything.

Sadly enough, he doesn't remember anything.

I sat in the back of the art room near the bottles of paints and brushes. My hands furiously striking the white poster, the paint was leaving the pencil borders. I couldn't care less. I dipped the brush into the black pellet of paint, smeared it into the red. The bull I was painting for the exhibition was looking absolutely angry. The bull's eyes were bloodshot red which were peppered inside the whites.

Out of the corner of my eye I saw Oliver walk past my table- his head hung low- he went over to the paint inventory, his hands absentmindedly grabbing the bottles of paint. I could feel his eyes burn a hole through me.

If he wanted to talk, I'd have him get over with it rather than have him stare at me with that stupid guilt-ridden face of his. Mrs. Clark skipped over to my table in a purple jumper, leaping like a fairy in a garden of roses and unicorns. I wonder from where she gets all this cheeriness.

"Oh my," Mrs. Clark exclaimed, her mouth forming an impeccable circle as she took in the painting. "Alice, dear- this is so different from what you usually paint. It's much more darker and so austere. Oliver," She motioned him to join us. I released a low sigh, of-course she'd ask her favorite student to examine my sudden change in style.

"Look at it," She pointed at the poster.

Oliver eyes flickered to my face for a brief second before intently staring at the painting. "It's beautiful Mrs. Clark," He gave me a small smile which I didn't return. "Just like her," He added the minute I looked away.

My head snapped in his direction. I glared at him. He couldn't say things like that. Oliver stared back, unashamed by what he had said.

Mrs. Clark didn't seem to have heard him. She grinned, widely. "This will look absolutely amazing in the exhibition,"

"Thank you," I muttered.

Mrs. Clark danced away to the next table. Oliver stayed but he didn't say anything for a while.

Finally he opened his mouth to say something I never expected him to say. "Alice, you ruined your own life. Okay? I know you're better than what you've become,"

My heart skipped a beat or two at his words-in a frantic and gut-wrenching way. He still believed in me. There was redeeming glint in his eyes. It made heat stab my chest.

Sparing my painting one last look, he walked away before I could reply. I clenched my brush tightly. The wooden splinters from the brush dug into my skin.

Honestly, have I changed so much that Oliver thinks I've ruined my life? Am I honestly better than what I've become?

I haven't become anything. I'm still the same old Alice except this Alice isn't living her life anymore.

Oliver just doesn't understand that.

The winds were wild today, insanely fast. Trees and their branches swayed in the wind's direction. The sky was immersed in dark grey clouds while the sun was nowhere to be seen, hidden behind a curtain of thick clouds the sun's bright light was infused with darkness.

All my emotions were tightly bottled up inside me as I made my way out of the school's parking lot heading towards the sidewalk that led to Devlin's apartment.

Everyone rushed to their shiny cars and few of the Winterville high-schoolers rushed to parking-lot where the buses were parked. My eyes found a tall figure with blonde hair mixed with fading greys standing on the other side of the road in front the high-school's boundaries. It vaguely reminded me of dad. What was he doing here?

My feet carried me away- towards the side where he stood. It was dad. He was walking with Liza, a red cheerleading dress with yellow strips clung to her perfect stubby figure. A red statin bow tied her blond hair into a tight ponytail.

Oh God! How could I forget? Today was Liza tryouts for the high-school cheer team.  She was going to be freshman next year. I wonder if she made it on the team. There's only one way to find out, I'll ask her. My excitement couldn't be contained- a goofy grin forced my cheeks to move apart.

I began sprinting towards them. Hastily, I dodged the people walking in the opposite direction- few of them gave me annoyed looks when I bumped into them.

I was few feet away from them, so close that if I reached out for them- my fingers would brush against their shoulders. Liza's laughter could be heard till where I stood. Dad smiled at her as he gave her a side hug.

Judging from their good mood, I guess Liza made it. My little sister is going to be on the high-schools cheer team. I couldn't be happier. My hands reached for Liza's. I was just about to pat her shoulder when someone shoved me off the sidewalk.

The burly man carrying a trash bag muttered a grunt of apology before trudging away.

I turned back to look for my dad and Liza to find they still were walking a few meters ahead of me, their face bright with joy. It's the happiest I've seen them in years since the accident.

In that moment I realized something. I couldn't dampen their mood. If they saw me here, they would be reminded of everything- of all the bad memories attached with me.

I couldn't ruin this small moment of happiness. I couldn't. The reason I left home was so they could be happy and now they were.

A deceitful tear slid down my cheek as I turned my back towards them. My chest felt heavy and numb. A lump in my throat was making it hard to breathe.

I walked away, too weary and numb to cry again.

Mom, I never thought there would come a day when I won't be able to hug my own sister. I won't be able to share her happiness and tell her how proud I was of her.

# Chapter 14

The cold evening wind pounded on my window's clear glass panes. Every second or two a clacking sound would resound from the outside, making me feel not so alone in the empty apartment. I sat on the small twin sized bed, my legs pulled under the checkered quilt and a book propped open in my lap.

My eyes vacantly stared the glossy pages of my communication application book while my mind refused to focus on a single word. All I could think of was their hurtful words. The scenes were in flames behind my eyelids. The words were leaving unbearable scars etched deep into my flesh, coursing along my blood.

I was tired, tired of everything. I wanted my life back. I wanted to live again. I wanted be the old me. The Alice who was always on the top of everything- perfect grades, good health, and a huddle of friends always surrounded her.

I was tired of myself.

Before I knew it, the warmth of the blankets and wind's chaotic hum wove their magic around me and I fell into a dreamless slumber.

A banging on the front door jolted me out of sleep. I glanced at the digital propped next to my unkempt bed. 3:30 p.m. it said.

Strange. Devlin usually doesn't return before five and plus he has the keys to the apartment.

I got up from the bed, slipping on my slippers and walked to the front-door. My hand reached for the door knob. When I opened the door, I'm greeted by a tall, shy-looking girl who looks around to be of Devlin's age. Her cheeks are flushed pink as long waves of black hair cascade down her slim back. In her hands, she held a large woven basket filled with flawless white roses. She's staring at her feet, blushing furiously. Who is she?

I clear my throat. "Hi,"

Her honey colored eyes snap in my directions as a frown covers her lips. "Who are you?" She speaks, biting her lips.

"Um..." She's the one who's standing at my doorstep. Shouldn't I be the one asking her that?

"Are you Devlin's girlfriend?" She asks, nearly scowling at me.

Now it's my turn to blush. Color rushes to my face. "Err, no I'm his roommate," Well, sort of -except for the fact that I haven't paid my share of the rent yet.

Relief floods her face and a smile covers it. "Is Devlin here?"

"No, he's not. Actually he doesn't return from college before five,"

The smile drops on her face. "Oh," I'm caught up feeling guilty and jealous. Right now I want to chuck a bat across her face and hit it till her features are dismantled. Alice, be nice. This isn't like you.

"I can give him your message when he comes back from college," I try smiling but I think it comes out as grimace.

She looks at me, wearily. "You'll seriously tell him, right?"

I nod my head.

She chews the inside of her mouth and hands me the basket of roses. "Tell him that Elizabeth Chu came to visit,"

"Okay," I smile for the last time before shutting the door.

I set the basket on the kitchen's granite counter.  There is a small vanilla colored envelope lying in the basket. My hands are itching to read it but I resist. It's wrong to invade into someone's privacy. God knows, it could be love letter. Urgh.

Stupid, stupid Alice, stop feeling so jealous.

I sigh. Seriously, this is not the time for all this. I need to focus on my books. For chocolate's sake, I don't need to flunk again.

I'm about to enter my room when another knock resounds. Gritting my teeth together, I walk back to the door. Who is it now?

I open the door and surprise, surprise another girl stands at the doorstep.  She wears a tight red dress that cling to her faultless curves and flat stomach. Both of her hands are wrapped around a massive brown colored teddy bear.  Guess what? I want to kill her.

Painting an overly sweet smile on my face, I speak -since she's busy staring at me with her eyes bulging out of their sockets. "How can I help you?"

"Omg!" She half groans and half screams. "Is Devlin dating you? Are you two a thing?"

This time I don't blush. "No," I mutter dryly. "I'm his roommate,"

"Great!" She exclaims, holding the stuffed toy closer to her body. "Can I speak to Devlin?" Someone give me a sledge hammer so I can rip her Barbie-doll like face off her neck.

"He's not here," I reply through my teeth. "Still at college,"

She doesn't believe me- obviously, because she shoves me aside and barges into the apartment. "Devlin, sweetheart, Are you here?"

She yells on top of her lungs standing in the center of the living room.

Sweetheart- If I could I would strangle her with my bare hands.

I smile when a disappointed frown covers her face. Since when have I begun to take pleasure in someone's sorrow? That's wrong.

I pull the smile off my face. "See, told you he isn't here,"

She glares at me. If looks could kill. "Whatever,"

She places the teddy bear on the orange floral loveseat and marches to the door.

"Hey you," She shouts, turning around to look at me. "Make sure Devlin gets the teddy bear. Don't you hog it," She's freaking talking to me like I'm her servant or something.

My nostrils flare in anger. "I don't want your dumb bear,"

She doesn't hear me or pretends that she didn't and walks out smoothly in her red pumps. I want to kill her. Who the hell does she think she is?

Muttering some curses under my breath, I slam the door shut. When I reach my room, I pick up my communication application textbook and try to study. Which I'm unable to do since yes, you guessed it right- there are shouting sounds outside the door.

I bring my book along me and set it on the orange sofa before walking to the front door. Two brunette girls stand in front of the door, screaming and torturing their vocal cords. All good things chocolate, I feel bad for their voice box. It is probably bawling its eyes out and saying 'why did I do to deserve the throats of these monsters'

"I'm going to give it to him first-"The first girl shouts as she tries grabbing the box of chocolates the other girl held.

I rolled my eyes. "Excuse me? Can you go fight somewhere else?"

Their eyes snap in my direction, halting all the plummeting they were doing.

The first girl shrieks -her hands pointing at me like I'm some ghost.

The second girl looks between the number plate on the door and me. "What are you doing in his apartment?"

I sigh. Here we go again.

After two hours of opening and slamming the door shut, the hordes of girls coming here had finally ceased.  The kitchen counters were filled with expensive boxes of chocolates, cakes and flowers. I don't think there was any room left in the kitchen. About twenty girls visited the apartment and few boys which actually crept me out since they all were blushing furiously and were staring at me like I was some sort of disgusting insect. The same questions were asked over and over again by the time the last girl left, I was already feeling like Devlin's girlfriend because I heard the word too many times and in too many ways- not that I minded. A stupid grin lit my face. But seriously, what is going on? Why are there so many people visiting Devlin's apartment today?

I sat in the seating room on the orange sofa- my legs bundled together while a pencil was stuck in my mouth as I tried finishing a sketch. I had given up on communication app.  My mind refused to concentrate. All I could think of was the tangled mess of thoughts inside me.

So I did what soothed my frantic nerves. I drew. I know I shouldn't be drawing. I should be studying but in moments like these drawing is a better option than sinking into a hole of depression. My sketch book was wide open, the blank white page with a roughly sketched face stared back at me.

I don't know whose face it was. My hands were moving on their own accord, striking the paper faster than my mind could respond. The outline of the eyes was complete- it roughly reminded of a certain pair of eyes. I moved to the nose and lips.

Scratching of my pencil and the ticking sound of the wooden clock was all that could be heard. Few minutes later when the sketch was on the verge of completion- my heart stopped. Devlin's eyes from the page stared back at me. The sketch looked almost alive. The way I drew his smile- that smile of his when a small dimple would appear on the left cheek and the side of his eyes would crinkle as a strange lively spark would fill his eyes and how he'd stare at me warmly.

I almost cried. I don't know why. The pencil fell from my hand- I lifted my hand to my chest. I could feel it. My heart sped away faster than any clock.

Alice, a lifeless object can't give us happiness. Happiness is inside us. A piece entitled from one to heart to another always strikes happiness because it hits right on our heart

My mother's word echoed through my mind. A salty tear slid down my cheek.

I picked up the pencil from the cold ground and wrote the words down next to the sketch. Happiness is inside us.

I get what she meant. I finally did. The small gesture from earlier where Devlin had eaten my cookies without a single cringe despite the fact how terrible they were came into my mind. I smile because that small gesture had touched my heart. It struck a chord inside, igniting a joyful flame within me. No gift could be bring me this much of joy.

The opening of the front door caused to snap out of the daze I had been in. I quickly I set the sketch on the sofa, making sure I had closed the cover. I didn't want Devlin to see the sketch. It would be weird and awkward at the same time especially since he had indirectly told me to leave in the morning.

I was still upset about it. I know I shouldn't expect him to be nice all the time but I can't help it. It's scary to admit this but I do like him and I don't know how much.

With a hasty hand, I gathered my things from the sitting room and began walking towards my room when Devlin's tired voice stopped me.

"Alice," He says. I hear a strange longing in his voice.

I turn around to face him, my books clenched tightly to my chest. The erratic beats of my heart fill my ears- the drumming sounds echoes with all the other sounds on the outside.

He stands there, his warm brown eyes dull with exhaustion. He wasn't wearing scrubs today. It felt strange to see him in a plain t-shirt and jeans.

I set my books on the sofa. Suddenly feeling worried, he didn't look well. He wasn't smiling. The curves besides his lips were pulled downwards. With a gentle thud, his bag fell onto the ground.

He averted his eyes which were looking at me a minute ago and stared at his empty hands.

"Devlin," I almost whisper. Afraid. "Are you okay?"

He nods. He's lying I know. His eyes find mine and holding them in their place and for a second or two I forget to breathe. "You're mad at me," It wasn't a question. "Is that why you were leaving?"

I shake my head, biting my lips. "I was going to put my books away,"

"You're lying," There's no humor in his voice or in his eyes.

"I'm not mad at you," I reply. "Just upset,"

He furrows his eyebrows together. "Why?"

"Nothing big," I smile at him. I don't why but I feel Devlin isn't alright. He's trying to distract himself by talking about me or is he trying to distract me.

"Devlin, are you okay?" I ask again. Because no-matter how hard I try the nagging feeling wouldn't leave me.

He sighs- the piece of air leaves him with a shudder and then he massages his temple. "I'm fine. It's been a long day,"

"What happened?"

He doesn't answer my question instead he asks one. "Can I hug you? Please," The dejected tone of his voice breaks me.

I don't respond and run to him. Burying my head into his shoulder, I hold him tightly. I wrap my hands around his neck while he wraps his around my waist.

We fit together like two pieces of one puzzle. It feels good to hug him. His arms are warm and nice. All the chaos from my day dissipates into thin air. I feel calm and blissful. Under my hands, I feel his shoulders relax. I know he feels the same way.

His breath falls over my neck in an even rhythm- I close my eyes and sink into him. The soft smell of detergent and some nice masculine cologne fills my senses.

"It's going to be okay," I speak into his shoulder.

He hugs me tighter than before. "As long as you're here,"

I don't understand what he means but I don't question him either.

We stand there- in each other arms for few minutes. Before he pulls away, his face looks more relaxed than before.

He smiles at me. It's a small smile where he lips barely curve upwards but it's there.

I smile back, staring into his honey spilling eyes. They're truly beautiful and they look more beautiful when he's happy.

Then I remember all the girls that had visited. "Some twenty girls came to give you things. I tried remembering their names but there were too many,"

Devlin eyes follow mine to the kitchen. He shakes his head, sighing. "Looks like I have a ton work to do,"

"Work?" I asked, confused.

"Secret admirer day in college and you're supposed to give presents to the one person you like," He states in a manner of explanation.

"Looks you have a ton of admirers," I laugh.

He laughs too. "And now to send thank you cards to a ton of people,"

"You don't have to," I bite my lips. "They're your admirers. Remember?" I don't want him to reply to anyone. I want him to spend all that time with me. Selfish, I know. But I don't want to share him even though he doesn't belong to me.

He smirks- his eyes have a playful glint in them. "I can't keep the ladies waiting. Now can I?"

I try very hard keep my mouth shut so I wouldn't scowl at him.

"And the guys," I add.

A cringe escapes him. "Guys? Are you kidding?" He says in between a grimace.

I shrug, a teasing smile on my lips. "Go see for yourself,"

"I'm good," He breathes out.

Before I can stop myself, I blurt the words lying on the tip of my tongue. "Did you give someone a carnation?"

Instantly my face is fled with heat, I press my palms against my face so he wouldn't see. He sees the color nevertheless.

I expect him to tease me or laugh but he doesn't.  He looks away. "I did," A cloud of gloom lingers down his lashes.

My stomach twist in a painful manner- I can feels my chest swell up with melancholy. The joy inside me from a minute ago is replaced by despair. I can't let myself to get down, again. I won't be able to come out if I do.

"What did she say?" I hear myself say.

He laughs. I know there are tears in his eyes because he doesn't look at me when he laughs. "She rejected me, of-course,"

"She doesn't realize what she lost,"

He looks at me, hard. His intense gaze sears through my eyes.

"Devlin there are so many other girls who like you," I point at the clutter on the kitchen counters.  A sudden burst of confidence makes me advance towards him. I place my hand on his chest. The warmth flows into my palm.

His hearts beats wildly under my hand. Was it for me? "Because they know about the beautiful heart inside,"

He cracks a smile. "Thank you," It's the second time he has said that.

"Thank you," I repeat, letting my hand fall from his chest. "For eating those horrid cookies,"

A sheepish look covers his face. "They weren't that bad,"

I raise a brow. "Really now? You know you could have told me that they were bad. Honestly I wouldn't have cared,"

"You would have," He insisted. "Except you wouldn't show it,"

"I'm stronger than you think,"

"Do you even know what I think?" His tone is sharp and it catches me by surprise. Something about what I had said offended him.

His hands grip my arms as he pulls me closer to himself. I feel breathless by the small touch. Scorching fire smears my arms where his fingers are wrapped.  My pulse throbs in my neck.

He places his fingers under my chin, lifting them so our eyes would meet. A small gap separates our faces. I don't dare to breathe.

"What do you think?" The words leave me in a gasp.

The edges of his cool fingers trail down the side of my heat filled face. I fight the urge to close my eyes.

"You're not even trying because you think you don't deserve to be happy. You lie straight to my face. You lie to yourself. You lie to everyone around you. When I came back from college, you weren't studying. You had you're sketch book with you. You aren't even trying to clear your exams,"

I don't honestly know what to think at the moment: to be ashamed of myself, to be angry at Devlin for making these assumptions but he isn't wrong.

"I was studying-"

His hands lay on top of my shoulder. "What made you stop?"

I try to turn my head to look away but he wouldn't allow it. He pressed his palms against my face, forcing me to look right into his eyes.

"I-I couldn't focus,"

"Why?"

I don't answer.

'You stink'

'Haven't you heard of a thing called deodorant?'

'Looks like the loser ain't going to prom,'

'Prom won't stink. Phew'

'Someone like you'

The voices inside my head were only growing louder. They wouldn't go away. No-matter how I tried

"Stop!" I cried. I pull myself away from Devlin. He stares at me, terrified. The black in his iris widen. "Stop!"

I clasp a hand over my ears. "Make these voices go away, please,"

"Make them go away!" My body collapses onto the carpeted floors, pulling my knees together. I rock back and forth.

'He watches me, a helpless look on his face. He doesn't know what to do. I feel the panic grow inside my chest. My hands reach out for my chest. I press a hand across my chest. The pain was killing me. It started inside my chest and spread into my toes. I couldn't bear it.

Suddenly, I felt a pair of arms hold me. Devlin takes my childish hands in his large ones. "I'm sorry," He whispers, his voice stuck inside his throat. "I'm so sorry,"

He wraps his arms around me. My numb arms go around his neck. Tears stain my face and seep into his t-shirt. My fingers skim down his back over his taunt muscles.

I feel the voices die down. Now I only hear his voice. "I didn't know it was this bad," He touches my back, pressing me closer while his other hand smoothes my hair.

I squeeze my eyes shut, resting my head on his shoulder. "I don't know what happened," I speak weakly. "The things they said, I was hearing them again,"

He holds my shoulders and leans away. There is a frown on his face. "Who said what?"

I shake my head. "I can't-"

He doesn't push me further. Stark terror clings to his eyes.

"I couldn't focus," I begin talking when he doesn't say anything. "So I started to draw. It usually helps me when I'm upset. I know I should have been studying. There are only two weeks left till the retest. But Devlin, I couldn't. What am I going to do? I'm sorry if I scared you right now. I'm sorry for always being caught in problems. I- I"

He firmly plants a hand over my mouth. "Alice, stop apologizing for things you can't control," He smiles reassuringly and removes his hand. "As for the retest, you're going to pass them. I'm going to tutor you, okay?"

I nod my head, feeling overwhelmed. "Do you believe in angels?" I ask him.

He shrugs, confused on where I'm headed with this. "I don't know, do you?"

"Never did until now. I believe you're my angel,"

He looks dazed, after a while a breathtaking smile appeared on his features. He holds my hand in his. "And I believe you're mine,"

# Chapter 15

-----------------------------------------------------------------

Devlin sat next to me- on the floor of his study room, his knee brushing against mine. The gentle flicker of the blue lamps would try to pull me into a deep slumber but I resisted. Piles of books and paper surrounded us on the floor.

I folded my legs together, taking everything in. I breathed in the old smell of books and moldy carpet. My eyes took in the small smile playing on Devlin's lips, the quirk of his eyebrow, and the sound of his laughter mixing with the melody of the silent air.

Through the thick rimmed glasses, he looked at me briefly. "You're doing it wrong,"

My eyes fell back to the pages scribbled with dark blue ink. I sigh. My chest rising and falling under the pale green hoodie I wore. The human health textbook stared back at me. With a steady hand, I erased the labelings on the human skull diagram and set the eraser next to my knee.

I begin writing again. "Is it okay now?"

He looks up from his own textbook which is filled so many words that it made my head hurt. Again, he shook his head. For the past three hours or so, we settled on an agreement to study side by side. I didn't want Devlin to fall behind on his study schedule because of me. In between every ten minute that would pass, he'd check on me. It was kind of him to help me but I couldn't ignore the pangs of embarrassment whenever I'd get something wrong.

He was a genius... well in my eyes. After I had told him I had flunked human health science, communication application and botany, he told me that he'd help me with human health and botany since they were his fortes but he didn't really know much about communication application so he'll just try to accompany me while I studied. It was more than enough for me.

"Remember the basics Alice," He holds out his palm for the pencil. I hand it over, the tips of our fingers brushing. I try not to blush. "See the occipital condyle is right beneath the occipital bone. It's easier to remember if you put the adjoining bones in pairs,"

I bit the corner of my lips, my eyes pulled together in concentration. "Like the Maxilla with the Mandible and then the hyoid,"

"Bingo,"

"I finally get it," I grin, feeling accomplished.

"You're not dumb," He ruffled my hair. I swatted his hand away, narrowing my eyes at him. Great, I feel like a kid now. Does Devlin see me that way? A kid. Or like a small sister he has to protect. I cringe at the thought. That would be strange.

"What do you mean?" I ask, trying to ignore the pinching sensation inside my stomach.

"You know what I mean,"

"I don't,"

He lets go of piece of air before turning to face me. "You're not what you act to be. I honestly don't get how you failed. These exams should have been a piece of cake for you,"

"Guess what? They weren't," I reply, almost angrily. "What do you even know about me?"

I shouldn't have said that. The expression on his face falls into something grim.

"I didn't mean that," My voice breaks.  "Sorry,"

He pulls his arms over my shoulder and gives it a gentle squeeze. "I know you didn't but-" I hold my breath, waiting for him to complete the sentence. There's a mischievous glint in his eyes which glaze over my face.

"But?" I urge him to continue. He still held my shoulder so I craned my neck to look at him. Wrong move.

All my breaths halt. The lingering smell of cinnamon cakes we had for dinner fill me. I find myself inches away from his face. One idiotic move and we'd be caught in something we don't want.

He doesn't notice the lack of distance or pretends not to. "You weren't wrong," The cold of frame of his glasses touches my cheek. Color drowns my skin. A flustering sensation ripples from my stomach to my throat. I don't even feel my heartbeats.  They're so fast.

"Huh?"

He inches closer, his eyebrow quirked to one side while a small dimple forms on his left cheek. I instantly know he's suppressing a smile.

"I know nothing about you," I get a whiff of detergent from his clothes. It's pleasant, really pleasant.

"You know me more than Sandy," It was true. The things Devlin has seen, not even my own father has seen that side of me. I've

never cried in-front of him but in front of Devlin my emotion reel
out freely like a cassette's tape which is always compact and hidden.
Devlin understands me better than anyone. He knows what I'm
going through. Delvin knows exactly what to do when I'm upset. He
knows how to cheer me up. He knows me. He understands me.

He knows what I'm feeling by just a glance at my face. I wonder if
he knows about my feeling for him. I push the thought back into a
dark corner. I don't have any feeling for him. I don't feel anything.

My heart refuses to obey me. It still strums inside my rib-cage
wildly.

"I know you," He agrees. His tone is light but his eyes are stirring
with a strange darkness. A lost look hides them and that magical
quality. "But I don't know anything about you,"

"Does that really matter?" I whisper. Suddenly I feel this paranoia
cling to the sides of my chest.  He wants to know my past.

"It does,"

"I-I  don't- tthink," I stammer, coherent words refusing to form on
my tongue. "tthere isn't much to know,"

He tilts his head slightly causing our noses to touch. My lungs feel
like they're about to burst into flames. His arm is still wound around
my shoulder, actually it's frozen there.

The surface beneath my skin prickles in a haunting way. He
doesn't move back, the black in his iris widen. He finally realizes
how close we were. I feel scared. I feel scared about what's to come.

Unconsciously my eyes linger to his lips instantly I force them
away. A queasy expression covers his face. He looks uncomfortable.
I know why he isn't moving away.  He doesn't want to hurt me again.
A small part of my heart drops to the pit. Of course he wouldn't feel
anything for a girl like me.

I brush aside from his reach, moving away in awkward manner- his arm drops from my shoulder. From the corner of my eye, I catch him releasing a sigh of relief.

Something breaks inside me. Why do I fall so easy?

"What do you want to know about me?" I state stiffly. My hands wrap themselves around the wooden length of the pencil.

He stares at me for a moment -in a way, I can't decipher. His warm brown eyes are pulled together; the sharp counters are in a rigid position. It's like he's trying to solve some sort of complicated equation.

"Anything," He finally answers. I steal glance of his face. There isn't a smile on it as he bends his neck over the bulky book. I wonder why.

"You start," I label the bones in the spine column.

"What? This is about you,"

I ignore his quizzical expression. "I don't know anything about you either,"

"Okay," He drags the word. A bubble of amusement forms inside me. He looked at a loss of words- that's something new. "Well I'll start with my family,"

"Sure," I grin. Excited by the prospect of knowing something about his personal life.

A warm and content smile encases his lips. Our eyes meet for a brief second in which I forget the definition of breathing. "My mother- she's a housewife. Everything I know about cooking comes from her. She's the most amazing cook you'll ever meet and she gives the best advice ever- literally she's like a spiritual guru to me,"

My mom always knew what to say when I need it. A pang of pain surges through me but I don't pay attention to it.

"If we ever get the chance, I'll defiantly take you to meet her," We- my heart melts into a pool of chocolate at the word.

I don't realize that I'm smiling when I say. "I can't wait to meet her. Your mum sounds awesome."

"She is," The lights reflects in his eyes wistfully. "She's the type of person that can talk their way to your heart. I can bet you you'll like her instant you meet her and she cracks the funniest jokes. I don't remember seeing anyone stand by her side and not burst into fits of laughter. She's a lot like you. She can't take a favor without doing something utterly kind for the other person. She hides her pain so the people around her forget theirs,"

"Wow," I breathe out. Moisture make my eyes prickle. My mind couldn't even take in the strings of compliment he had just bestowed upon me. "I don't know what to say,"

"You don't need to," He looks up from the book, giving me a half-crooked smile.

"I feel like I need to. You just compared me to your mother. Devlin I'm not anything like that. I'm not that kind,"

"Actually you're right," My smile faltered for a moment. His brown eyes hold my green ones in a secure prison. "You're more than that,"

The sentence steals every single ounce of air inside me. I gasp. "I-I-"Heat rushes to my face and I don't try to hide it.

"I have a sister," Devlin continued speaking as if he had said nothing. His eyes leave mine and fall back onto the pale, worn pages. "She's roughly six years older than me. Last around June last year she finished her degree in law and now she's happily married with her high-school boyfriend," Devlin makes a gagging noise. "They call each other high school sweethearts,"

"What's wrong with that?" I flick my pencil the side of the page so I can turn over to the next chapter.

"Trust me, if you ever meet them you'll be acting the same way," He scratches the back of his head as wisp of black hair scatter over his forehead- uncertainty crosses his face. "Or maybe you won't. You are a girl," It sounded like a question.

"Did you just realize that?" I feigned hurt. "And what does this have to do with my gender?"

He shrugs his shoulders.  "I dunno. Don't girls like intense PDA sessions. And no, I didn't 'just' realize that you're a girl. Trust me, I figured it a long time ago," He even throws in a suggestive wink.

I punch his shoulder, trying to hide the burning blush. "Girls like PDA as much as you boys do,"

"As long as my sister isn't involved, I think I'd enjoy them very much,"

"Yuck! You're so perverted,"

He holds up his hands. "Who isn't?  Don't claim to be innocent, Alice,"

"I haven't had my first kiss," I try to defend myself. Even I know that I'm not an innocent little girl. I used to be well that is until Liza forced to read the fifty shades of grey.

"Doesn't make a difference," He slides the comments easily past me. "For all I know-"A spark of amusement lights his face. He angles his body so his lips would skim the air above my ear.  My cheeks burn for all I knew they could have been set into flames by a candle. "You could have shared everything but your lips," He completes his sentence in an allusive whisper.

I push his chest, hard; he stumbles to one side, laughing like a maniac.  The vessels in my cheeks refuse to return to normal.

I glare at him, mustering all the bits of anger I can. "You," I slam my fingers into his rigid chest. "Jerk," He doesn't stop and keeps on laughing like we might never see the tomorrow's sun. He rolls on the floor, breathlessly lying on one side beside me. I hover above his laughing frame- annoyed as hell.

"I can't believe you'd say that," A menacing growl escapes my throat. "You," I curls hands into a fist and knock it straight into his chest. "Jerk, idiot,"

"Ah!"He groans when my hand hits him. "Easy there, love. I'm made of flesh not steel," He locks my wrist in his hands so I wouldn't hit him again.

Love, it's the second time he's said that. Not that I'm counting or anything. Of-course not.

I still couldn't ignore the firework show erupting my stomach. All I could see was a hazy red filling my vision. This isn't good. How hard am I falling this time?

I narrow my eyes. "You crossed the line,"

"Oh really?" There is a playful smile on his lips. He doesn't make a move to get up from the ground and lifts his head to stare at me. "I don't see any. Mind pointing it out,"

"You're ridiculous," I tried biting off the smile as I feel warmth envelope my wrist from his hands.

He clicks his tongue. "Too bad, you'll have to deal with me for the rest of your life,"

Rest of your life. Is he implying something?

My pulse jumped out my skin. I'm sure Devlin can feel it too under his hands. Instead of questioning him about it- I peel his hands off my wrist and scoot back to my spot next to the human health science book. I don't look up -Scared my eyes might betray the thoughts running wild in my head.

I feel him shuffle beside me in an awfully silent way. "You were telling me about your sister," I shift my weight from my legs and cross them.

"I was. What can I say about her?" Devlin easily falls back into the conversation though I don't miss the puzzled look on his face.  His eyes were screaming 'Did I say something? What's going on Alice?' It's scary to think I understood the implications under his every gesture and notion.

"She may seem a bit cold on the outside  but she's really soft-hearted. It takes her time to warm up to people. She usually isn't the type to socialize," After a moment of thinking Devlin spoke again. "And that pretty much sums up my family,"

"What about your dad?" I ask, curiosity getting the best of me.

The nerves in Devlin's hand protrude outwards as he grips the edge of his book, holding the pages in place. He doesn't meet my gaze and stares at the book as if his life depends on it.

"Devlin," I place my hand on his stiff shoulder when he doesn't anything. "I'm sorry if I said something wrong,"

His eyes capture mine before he looks away. They hold a blank expression. "My father- he runs a small software company by the name of Enlighten,"

Enlighten- that's the company in which my dad worked. He couldn't be the son of the CEO. Why would he live here in this small apartment when his parents were in the same town?

"My dad's the senior accountant there," I whisper.

Devlin lifts his head. The usual kind lines of his face are twisted into something I don't quite like. He looks angry. "That's nice," There is bitter resent in his voice. "I was hoping you hadn't heard of my father's company," I don't miss the taunting edge.

"Well," I reply unsure. "Enlighten corp. is pretty famous here in Winterville. It's the only multinational company in town,"

"I know. I'm the God damn heir!" He stood up from his spot abruptly and walked to his desk. "Maybe this isn't a good idea,"

"What isn't a good idea?" I ask, standing up as well. What's wrong with him? I'm sure this has something to do with his father. Is that why he's reacting so negatively?

"Getting to know each other," Devlin's shoulders were hunched as he gripped the edge of the chair. For someone who didn't know him it looked like he was perfectly fine but I knew better. He was everything but fine. Something was off. The simple word father had brought so much pain to him. My heart ached for him. Someone as good as him doesn't deserve an ounce of pain.

"You should focus on your exam," He spoke in labored huff

I walk towards him- my steps are hesitant. I'm few inches behind him when I call his name. "Devlin," I whisper. "Are you okay?"

He doesn't answer my question and turns to face me. The expression on his face is neutral. Not an ounce of emotion seeps through it. It's like he's wearing an invisible mask over his skin. "I'm gonna to grab some fresh air," Somberness soars inside me. He doesn't want to share his trouble with me.

He arm nudges mine as he marches past me. My eyes follow him- he walks in robotic manner.

"Devlin," I try to make him stop but he doesn't.

"Don't wait for me. Go straight to bed after you finish studying," Even his voice sounded robotic.

Before I can even respond, he rushes out the door, leaving me alone in his room filled with books and saddening silence. The hushed icy autumn air sneaked from underneath the window panes, surrounding me.

I drew a hand over my arms, feeling cold- no, not because of the weather but because of Devlin. His sudden change in demeanor had chilled me till the core.

I have to know what had caused him to react this way. I have to and I'm afraid Devlin won't be the one answering my questions.

For a few hours, I spend my time finishing the last few chapter of human health science in the hope of distracting myself from Devlin. I don't succeed. Sometimes when I let my mind wonder- I would see his face- there were tears falling out his mesmerizing brown and I'd feel my heart hurt for him.

Maybe he was crying right now. Maybe he didn't want me to see him cry. Is that why he left?

After hours of restless studying, I finally retired to my room. This is when I heard the door unbolt and someone stumble inside. I stole quick glance at the digital clock beside my bed 12:30 pm it read.

I edged towards of door of my room, peeking through the small slit in it. Devlin walked down the hall, his hair in a tousled mess and his glasses were missing. He tossed the navy blue jean jacket he wore on the kitchens counter. I heard the opening of the kitchen's tap. Water rushed into the sink and then there was a splashing sound.

Few seconds later, Devlin emerged from the kitchen. His face dripping with droplets of water- even in the sparse amount of light, I could see the red tint in his eyes.

He stopped in front of the pale blue door of his room, briefly his eyes lingered to my door. Chocolate Fudge- I quickly scuttled away from the door and into my bed. My heart pounded insanely fast in my chest while a bead of sweat trickled down my neck.

I heard the door of my room creak open and his shallow footsteps fall on the carpet. He sighed, standing by the door. I try keeping my breathing normal and my eyes shut.

"Maybe bringing you here wasn't a good idea," He spoke in a hushed tone. I feel his eyes on my face. "I'm not good for you, Alice," There is a strong longing in his voice when he says my name. My stomach churns in a painful way.

"You should leave before I-" He doesn't complete his sentence.

A hollow sensation encases the center of my chest. What is he talking about?

He leaves my room, closing the door behind him with a gentle thud. I am left tangled in a yarn of secrets and questions. Nothing was making sense. Devlin isn't making sense.

I let my tired mind pull me into sleep before I can entangle myself deeper into the yarn.

Sandy jogs beside me as we try to make it to the biology class before the tardy bell rings. She's blabbering about something related to maths in which dividing zero by some number equal to two.

I usually drone out of these conservations. I make a sharp turn right through the brightly painted halls, there are large red bulletin boards decorating the walls.

I haven't seen Devlin since last night. He left early in the morning, leaving a small note on the fridge saying that he'll be late today. He didn't leave a reason for his absence. Something tells me- he's trying to avoid me.

I hear Sandy say something prom, pulling me out of the brief reverie. "What about Prom?" I ask her.

We edge towards the pavilion. Today our lesson was being held into auditorium. Apparently our teacher, Mrs. Sandalwal was getting an assistant student teacher.  The term is about to end and I have no idea why Mrs. Sandalwal would need extra help.

"My mom found out that I used the prom dress money to buy me a math book,"

"Is she mad at you?" I ask, offhandedly, my hands pushing the cold handles of the pavilion's entrance.

"Nah, she actually laughed at me," Sandy followed me through the open door. "She said that I'll have to go to prom in my old dress,"

Suddenly someone rudely shoved my shoulder- nearly causing me to drop my heavy biology textbook, I turned around to find Beatrice and her dirty blonde ponytail swinging back and forth. She shot me menacing smile.

"Watch it skunk," She hollered as she ran ahead of me towards the auditorium.

I mutter some curses under my breath. Sandy helped regain my balance, placing her hand on my back. "You okay?" Her eyebrows are bundled in concern.

I nod my head.

We enter into the auditorium- the cold air conditioning hits me with a surprise. My eyes scan the packed auditorium.  Beatrice already sat at the front with some of her friends. The only seats left were in the back.

"Great," I breathe out. "Now we won't see a thing,"

"The back seats aren't that bad," Sandy argues.

"Yah, if you don't consider the gum stuck underneath them," I'm about to turn around and trudge to the back end of the auditorium when I hear a familiar voice echo off the walls. "Miss Brown there're seats available at the right wing over here," All eyes snap in my direction.

My heart begins to pump blood faster than before. My eyes widen as I take in the person standing on the stage. Devlin stands next to Mrs. Sandalwal's petty frame with a microphone in his hands.He shoots me a polite smile.

What in the world is he doing here?

I think I'm going to faint.

# Chapter 16

----------------------------------------------------------------

R aven black hair are strewn across Devlin's pale forehead. He isn't wearing the usual blue scrubs- a red loosely fit t-shirt clings to his broad shoulders paired with an edgy black Levi jeans and russet combat boots. The casual clothes suit him- making him look like a typical American teenager. His thick-framed glasses are missing. There is a teasing gleam in his brown eyes as he takes in my shocked state.

Sandy digs her elbow into my rib- jolting me out of the trance. "I'd so exchange SpongeBob for him," She squeals into my ear.

I notice all the other students are staring at me- with a bored, dull expression. Beatrice and her friends including Carmen mutter something to one another and then burst into fits of laughter.

It didn't take a genius to figure that they were talking about me.

I avert my eyes from them and look at the right side of the auditorium. The entire front row close to the foot of the stage was empty. No-one really prefers to sit right in the face of the teacher. But if Devlin here then I don't mind sitting in the front row seats.

"What is your boyfriend doing in our biology class?" Sandy whispers into my ear as we walk towards the front.

He's not my boyfriend. I wish he were though.

I shrug my shoulders, trying not to look at the stage where Devlin stood chatting with Mrs. Sandalwal. Mrs. Sandalwal sagging wrinkles lift upwards as she laughed heartily. I don't think I've ever seen the woman laugh.  She presses a hand on her red-lipstick ridden mouth- a stroke of rose colors her cheeks.

Comfortably, I take a seat, setting my books on the adjacent empty chairs. Sandy gives me a pleading expression; the freckles in her cheeks tighten.

"I don't know why he's here," I sigh. "He didn't tell me anything about this," I steal a quick glance at the stage; he's hooking up the microphone back onto the podium. Mrs. Sandalwal trails to his side like a leech. Isn't she a bit too old for him? What in the world are you thinking, Alice?

"He's obviously here for you,"

I roll my eyes. "Sandy, I'm pretty sure he has hundred better things to do than follow me to school,"

Her pigtails swing back and forth as she shakes her head. "Patrick says Devlin is madly in love with you,"

"Yah, like I'm the only girl left on the planet," I scoff.

The girls in Beatrice's group make weird noise. Out of curiosity, I turned to look at them. Maybe one of them had a heart failure or something. Wait, they don't have hearts.

Beatrice's black-brown eyes smile shyly as she watches Devlin. She curls a strand of blond hair around her finger, biting the corners of her red lips.  Instantly, I feel sick. She likes him, of-course. Who wouldn't?

"Look," Sandy giggles. "Beatrice is so in love with your boyfriend. God, she looks like a pink jellyfish," I wonder if that's what I look like when I watch Devlin.

I raise my eyebrow. "And you're not?"

"Well, I have SpongeBob," She sounded unsure about that one.

"Beatrice has Oliver,"

Sandy wiggles her eyebrow. "Someone sounds jelly,"

"I'm not,"

"Aw, you are and you look so cute," She pinches my cheek and I swat her hands away. "Have faith in your boyfriend. He ain't going anywhere,"

"He's not my boyfriend,"

The playful smile on Sandy's face dampens. "Then why jelly?" She asked, her eyes are drawled into a confused line.

I'm about to reply when I'm cut by another voice. "Who's jealous?" Devlin towers over my chair. All the other sounds in the room fade into a suffocating silence. The stares of Beatrice and her friends burn a hole through the back of my head. I feel my heart rate ride up into my throat as my stomach twists in a flustering way.

"No-one," I quickly shoot back. Sandy watches Devlin wide-eyed- her eyes filled with curiosity and admiration.

Devlin smirks, his warm brown eyes searching my face for hints. "Really?" The tone of his voice is allusive.

I narrow my eyes at him. "What are you doing in my high-school?"

He holds up his hand in defense. "Whoa, thanks for the lovely greeting,"

"You don't deserve one. Now tell me why are you here?"

"Do you own this place?" He crosses arms, a smile still lighting his features. The stress and pain from yesterday seemed to have vanished into thin air.

"No," I mutter.

"Then I don't see the problem," Devlin is about to turn around and walk away when I grab his hand. Heat rushes to my face once I notice everyone in the auditorium is watching us. Chocolate triple fudge.  Instantly my hand drops his.

"Never mind," I sink back into the chair, silently wishing the earth would part open and swallow me.

Devlin ignores the stares. I don't think he would care even if the whole world was watching us. That's the peculiar thing about him-he doesn't care what others think of him.

Placing a hand on the empty seat's cushion frame, he leans down to my level. The faint smell of the masculine cologne he wears surrounds me. He tilts his head, so ours eyes would meet. My lungs ache because I'm not breathing. "I needed extra-credit so I took the assistant teacher offer. Okay?"

"Why are you really here?" Sound escapes my throat in a choked huff.

"Believe me, that's the only reason," His eyes don't agree with his mouth.

I don't believe him but I don't say so either.

I nod my head. He smiles at me. In the end, we both know the truth. He wasn't here for extra-credit. There is some other reason.

I watch him walk away- his shoulders are in a stiff stance, I can see his shoulder blades jutting out - an anxious air fills my body. What's going on his mind?

Sandy gives me a knowing look. "What did he say?"

"Nothing important," I answer, dazed.

"Yah, well I hate to point it out but you're face looks like a tomato and that too a ripe one,"

I pull my face into my hands. Great.

Before I can ponder upon my flushed cheeks, Mrs. Sandalwal breathes into the microphone. "Good morning," A loud beep encases the dark hall. Devlin frowns as he takes the mic. from her hand and taps its ends. He hands it back once he's done.

"Thank you," Mrs. Sandalwal bowed her head slightly, acknowledging him. "Well kids, I'd like to introduce you to our new student teacher Mr. Hutchins. He will be giving all you seniors and juniors a real insight to college life. Together we've put a small presentation. I hope you kids like it and I'll let Mr. Hutchins take it from here," A small giggle escapes Mrs. Sandalwal's lips as she heads down the stage's stairs and takes a seat next to Sandy. She must be excited to have Devlin for assistance.

"Isn't the boy just charming?" She whispers to Sandy.

Sandy nods her head feverishly. I bit down on my lips so I wouldn't burst into laughter. I don't know why I was finding all of this funny.

Devlin grins at the crowd and my heart melts. "So who's excited for college?"

A series of cheers and hoot break out in the auditorium.

"Wow, you' all sound pumped up," He strides to the right side of the stage where me and Sandy sit. The wood of the podium glows as Devlin turns on the projector.

A stop clock appears on the screen behind him, light reflects off the sharp counters of his jaw. I suck in a deep breath when I notice him observing me. He smiles at me. "When I was your age I was everything but excited for college,"

He looks away from me and leans against the podium.  In his long fingers he holds a stylus and in his other hand he held a mic. With a click, the slide changes into an utterly beautiful painting. It portrayed a small boy- no older than ten, dressed in muddy rags-staring at the navy blue sky which held a gazette of airplanes and jets.

"I might add that I was petrified by the thought of college,"

"How come?" A studious looking girl shouts from the center row.

He gave her warm smile causing my stomach to pinch in a strange way. "Dreams, we all have them, don't we? I was scared of not finding my dream,"

He tilts his head to look at the painting. "See this boy...You can already see bits and pieces of dreams forming in his hopeful eyes. College is all about dreams. It's the first step in making you realize your dream,"

"Anyone wants to share their dreams?" His eyes scan the audience. I spot a series of hand rise in the air. Beatrice held her hand high above her hand-she flung it in the air impatiently.

Devlin steps down the stage and makes his way towards the center front row where Beatrice sat. He held out the mic. for her to take.  I couldn't help but notice how Beatrice swept her hand across his when she took the mic.

"I dream to be an airhostess for the British airlines,"

"Impressive," Devlin responds, taking the mic from her.

He walks to the back of the auditorium. Mike Newton, who is in my Statics class, stand from his seat. As long as I remember, he's the only real human crush Sandy has ever had. He's a bit lanky-a typical nerd boy. He beat Sandy in the Algebra Triathlon and she's been crushing on him ever since.

"I want to be a physicist," He says boldly.

"Sounds amazing," Devlin grins at him.

Few more people tell Devlin about their dreams. All of them dreamed of something large and imposing -from being a neurosurgeon to a big league lawyer. I felt lost.  I wanted to be an interior designer. It's not something I always wanted to do. I always wanted to be contemporary painter and showcase my art in high class auctions but it wasn't a realistic dream. So I gave it up and choose something close to it like interior designing.

Devlin was about to climb the stage when he stopped in his tracks and turned around to where I sat.

"Alice, what do you dream of?" He didn't speak the words into the mic and was I thankful for that.

Then I realize what he is asking me. I don't want to talk in front of this large crowd. But I don't think I can refuse with Mrs. Sandalwal sitting two feet away from me.

I hesitantly take the mic from his hand- my hands sweating profusely as my pulse hikes up. Bubbling and rising inside me are pools of fear and terror. What if they all laugh at me?

I gulp, words leaving me before I can order them to halt. "I dream to be happy,"

There is silence in the room- a wave cold drowns me as my eyes begin prickling.

Devlin eyes hold mine- a strange kind of undecipherable expression on his face.

"Don't we all,"

Biology passed by smoothly. No-one laughed at me for dreaming something silly as that. The rest of the class was spent in the presentation which was quite impressively put together. Devlin didn't

look at me once during remainder of the class and left quickly once
the class bell was rung. I wonder why he was in such a hurry.

I sat at my usual lunch table with my mind far too preoccupied to
eat. My lunch box vacantly lay on the table. There're some bread-
sticks and cheese in it which I had gotten from Devlin's pantry.

Devlin, the simple name brings my stomach to lurch forward in
a strange manner. 'I was hoping you hadn't heard of my father's
company'

What had happened between Devlin and his father?

Whatever it was, it was something bad-something so bad that it
had caused Devlin to leave me and bare his heart in desolation.

I couldn't wait any longer. I have to find the answers now.

I got up from the table and picked my bag from the ground.
"Where are you going?" Sandy asked, looking up from her math
textbook.

I slung the bag across my shoulder. "Out,"

"But you can't. It's against school rules,"

"I don't care,"

I trudged-dragging my heavy bag along my aching shoulder. The
sidewalk is filled with people dressed in professional attires. Women
with buttoned up shirts and pencil skirts walk by me clicking their
high six-inch heels. Men, their hands burdened by heavy suitcases
and laptop bags stride in a proud manner- a dull expression painted
on their faces.  Shiny, expensive cars whizz on the road, stirring the
dirt on the sidewalk.

I stick out like a sore thumb in the crowd of grown-ups.

Tall, towering corporation buildings shoot into the blue sky- surround the roads. The glass windows of the buildings reflect the
sunlight- blinding me instantly.

My heart pounds in my chest in a fast and terrified way. Maybe I shouldn't be doing this. I shake my head. No, I need to do this.

My feet come to a stop in front of a dome-shaped building. The dome is gold and dancing in the sky like a temple of illusion. It's truly magnificent. The way the light bends around the sides makes it look like some sort of magic trick.

A large red lettered sign reads the Enlighten. Enlighten corp- develops web designing softwares and it currently hosts over one thousand different servers which is quite impressive if you ask me.

My step falter as I head towards the double-doored glass entrance, I can see people in regal suits and dresses standing at the reception area. I hear a loud chatter when I step inside- A group of sophisticated people standing in crowd are debating about something.  As I near towards the half-moon like reception counter- I can hear them more clearly.

"This is absolutely unheard of," A middle-aged lady- her hair wound in a tight brown bun, stands in the center. There is an air of dignity and power surrounding her. "They cannot pull out the contract without prior notice,"

"Mr. Hutchins will handle it. You don't need to worry about it-"A young man standing beside her mutters. Even though it seems like he's trying to comfort her- there were stress lines on his forehead.

"Handle it? Handle it my foot. He hasn't been able to stop the last four terminations. What makes you think he'll stop this one?"

"Have faith Miranda," The young man replies.

Miranda pulls her mouth into a menacing scowl. "Faith? We're going to lose our jobs and you're talking about faith,"

"Mr. Hutchins won't fire us,"

"He can't afford to keep us either. Our department is all in losses,"

The aged man, who had a dark look on his face, finally spoke - his white hair conveying a sense of worth. "Only one person can save this sinking mess,"

Something sparked in the weary eyes of the people around him. Was it hope?

"He won't come back," Miranda sighed, solemnly. "Not after what Mr. Hutchins did to him,"

"He has to," The old man's voice was firm. "He has to come back for our sake,"

"Instead of fussing let's get back to work, why don't we?" Another voice entered the conservation, drawing everyone into a stiff silence.

It was a young woman, she stood tall and proud. Black waves of hair were scattered along her straight back. She carried herself with arrogance- her eyes were bright blue. She reminded me of someone but I couldn't put of a finger on it. She looked familiar- the sharp counters of her face reminded me of a face I had seen countless times.

Who was she?

The group scrambled away into opposite directions like they had been attacked by a horde of long-horned bulls.

The woman's eyes snapped in my direction. I instantly averted my eyes, feeling a string of panic attack me. Something about her made me uncomfortable.

I turned my attention to the receptionist, sitting behind a sea blue screen of glass. She smiled at me amiably. "How may I help you?"

"I was looking for Mr. Brown, the senior accountant," I tried keeping my voice neutral. Out of the corner of my eye, I saw the woman with the bright blue eyes moves towards the reception counter.

I tucked a strand of hair behind my ear, praying that she wouldn't come here. It's silly but she scares me.

"Do you have an appointment?"

The receptionist frowns when I shake my head.

"No, I don't think I need one. I'm his daughter,"

"You must be Alice Brown," The bright blue eyed woman folds her arms on the cold counter- a chilled out look on her striking face. I gulp.

How does she know me?

"Ye-yes," I stutter.

"Come on, I'll take you to Mr. Brown's cabin," She waves me over to the right hall, which has expensive glass panes lining the walls.

"Thank you," I try smiling as I follow her into the hall. She's a foot taller than me so I have to crane my neck to meet her gaze.

She smiles back. There's a small dimple on her left cheek as she pulls her rosy red lips into a curve. Instantly I make the connection. Her smile is exactly like Devlin's smile. My heart stops beating for a whole point two seconds.

Words leave me in a jumbled order, rushing out of my mouth before I can stop myself. "Are you Mr. Hutchin's daughter?"

She quirks her eyebrow- in a way that eerily resembles Devlin. "How did you figure it out?"

What am I supposed to say? I know your brother on whom I have a massive, heart-breaking crush.

"Lucky guess," I laugh nervously.

"Lucky guess indeed," She laughs along me, her laugh sounded like the tinkering of thousand church bells. "I'm Sarah by the way. I rather not have you address me as Mr. Hutchin's daughter. It's outright weird,"

"Nice to meet you Sarah," She leads me down a narrow hall with sparkly marbled floors. My eyes widen when I take in the golden chandelier hanging from the ceiling.

"Is there a special reason you're visiting your father today?" It sounded like she genuinely cared. She's the total opposite what Devlin told me. She doesn't strike me as cold just a bit daunting.

Yah, so I can pry out Devlin's secret past and the reason for the bad blood between him and his father.

"No, not really,"

"Apparently I heard you left your dad's place. Takes guts to do that -though at your age I think it's a stupid idea. There is no way you can make it on your own unless you have help,"

I try not to be offended by her bluntness. "I do have help," Your brother.  "My friend's nice enough to let me stay in his apartment for some time,"

"Can I know your friends name?" She glances down at me. Why does she want to know his name? Does she know I'm staying with her brother? There's no point in lying if she knows.

"Devlin," I want to take the word back but the harm is done, instantly Sarah's face is fled with different emotions- one minute she's looks sad then angry which is replaced by a mixture of disbelief and relief.

Chocolate Fudge, Alice you make the most stupidest assumptions. She didn't know.

"Last name?" She stops walking- a few of the office's staff twist their heads to look at us. We stand next to room labeled as the printing lab.

I don't say anything and simply glare back at her. She taps her foot impatiently. "Last name?" She repeats in an angry voice.

By saving grace, my dad emerges out of the printing room, his hands carrying a stack of freshly printed paper. The blonde in his hair is filled with more white than before. My dad's eyes are tired and worn- wrinkles streak the side of his face. He looks old.

"Dad," I call for him- ignoring the pangs of guilt and fear filling me. I pushed back all my repulsion and regret into a dark corner of my mind, sealing it there.  I have to do this.

He stops in his tracks.

"Alice," Disbelief is etched deeply into his feature. "What are you doing here? Shouldn't you be in school?"

Sarah still stands by my side, her face glows with a red tint but Dad doesn't notice her.

"I had to get some forms signed for the retest," My hands dig into the bag and pull out a sheet of crisp white paper which had consent form  sprawled across it.

"Let's go to my cabin. I'll sign them there," He motions me to follow him towards a small, sliding door at the left side of the corridor.

Perfect, I'll be able to ask dad about Devlin without having to worry about anyone hearing me.

I face Sarah. "It was nice meeting you and thank you once again,"

She narrows her eyes at me- a sudden dislike for me fills her blue eyes. "My brother won't like it if he finds out you're here," With that she stalks off into the opposite direction, her six-inch red heels clicking on the floor.

If he finds out that is.

I stand in-front of dad's cluttered desk filled with files and more files. He usually is a very organized person. There is no way he'd sit in a mess like this one. The computer screen would flicker every two seconds.

Nothing looked right. Tension lines were forged onto dad's forehead.

"You look worried. Everything okay?" I ask him, watching as he signed the forum with a shaky hand.

"Not really, Alice, there're some massive budgets cuts I have to deal with. The company is going into loss and the stock rates are falling so fast," Dad never opened up to me about his job. So it takes me a minute to comprehend all that he had just said.

He sets the pen down and hands me the form. I shove it back into my bag.

"How come? A company can't just go to down without a reason," I push back the green cushioned chair and take a seat in it.

The gray in dad's eyes dulled. He didn't realize that he was talking to me. Whenever he's tensed, he would start muttering things to random strangers. It's a strange habit my father has had for as long as I can remember. "It's nothing you need to worry about,"

"Dad, seriously can you please tell me about it. Does this have to do with Mr. Hutchin's son?"

Dad's eyes widen. "How do you know about him?" I don't miss the accusing tone in his voice.

"I overheard some of the staff talking about the bad blood between Mr. Hutchins and his son," I shrug my shoulders, trying to sound causal about the whole ordeal even though my lungs could burst open any moment.

Dad buys it, he looks relieved. "For a moment, I thought you know his son personally,"

I don't just know him.

"Why? What's wrong with his son?"

"Wrong?" Dad laughs- The hollow sound of my father's laugh makes my heart fall to the pit of my stomach. I feel queasy.  "You should ask what's right about him,"

I bite the inside of my cheeks to keep myself from yelling.  The metallic taste of blood seeps into my mouth.

"Dad, how can you judge someone like that? You don't even know him," I blurt the words, my heart hammering fast with rage.

"What make you think I don't know the boy? I know him alright," A skeptic look covers my father's age worn face. "Alice, why do care about this boy?"

I take a deep gist of air, in the hope of calming my agitated nerves. "I don't care about him. It's just I don't like it when you judge people,"

His eyes are overflowing with unshed tears. "Just like your mum,"

I avert my gaze. I'm nothing like her, dad. The only reason I'm defending Devlin because I like him way too much.

"Devlin, that's his name right?"

Dad doesn't notice my attempt to change the flow of the conversation and quickly follows along. "Yah, that's his name alright," I couldn't ignore the deep distain in my father's voice as he spoke about him. "He jeopardized the entire corporation for his worthless desires,"

Dad shakes his head as if to rid himself of a bad memory. "When I met him, I actually liked the boy. He was polite, respectable sort of chap with fine mannerism and steady, honest opinions. You don't find boys like him anymore. I thought to myself how nice it'd be if my daughters could find themselves a boy like that,"

It would be nice. I silently agreed with him.

Dad laughed at his own folly. "It was all an act. Of-course- the boy was too good to be true," An anchor of dread clung to my shoulder. I fear what's about to come. Devlin couldn't be too good to be true. Right?

"Mr. Hutchins boasted about his son. On and on he went how his son would take the world by a storm. We all believed him. His son was truly something. After four months working in the company, the boy already had brought two important clients into the Enlighten's ring,"

"He worked here?" I asked, shocked. All this time I thought Devlin was a simple medical student. He couldn't have worked at Enlighten- I just couldn't imagine it. Devlin in a buttoned up shirt with a tie and coat instead of blue scrubs- the idea seemed impossible.

"I wish he hadn't," Dad grunted, bitterly.

"Why?" I whisper.

"He lost Enlighten's biggest investor because of his carelessness. Apparently the boy never wanted to a part of the company. He wanted to be a writer not the CEO of a million dollar company,"

I couldn't digest the information. Devlin- a writer, how had it never occurred to me? The shelves of books lining his room- they weren't textbooks. All of them were fiction novels.

The reason why his desk was always cluttered and why he didn't let me study on it was because he had his writing journals scattered there.

"Neither was I,"  He never wanted to be a doctor but he still chose it anyways.

"I can't believe that. He wouldn't risk the jobs of the people around him. If he gained two important clients, how could he possibly loose an investor? Something isn't adding up,"

"At the time, I found it hard to believe as well but as we began losing investor after investor, we were forced to believe in it,"

"Devlin would never do something so carelessly. He isn't like that," I press a hand against my mouth when I realize what I've said. Dad stares at me with a blank expression- it takes him a moment to react.

When he does, there is pure rage and fury on face.

"I meant by the description you've given me. He doesn't sound like that sort of person,"

The anger on his face dissipates and I feel my breathing rate return to normal.

"Oh," Dad presses a hand to his chest. "You had me there for moment. I rather not have you deal with likes of him,"

"Of-course, dad. I should get going," Before I utter something else. "You probably have work to do,"

I scurry out of the chair and jog towards the door when dad's voice stops me. "Alice,"

I turn around, forcing a smile on my face. "Yes,"

The wrinkles on his face deepen as he smiles back. "Liza told me you're staying with a friend. You know you can always come back,"

He sounds so hopeful. It makes my chest ache- I quickly turn my head to the other side- not wanting him to see the tears flowing down my face.

"When the time comes, I will," With a heavy heart, I dash out of his cabin. Tears making a waterfall down my face.

Be strong Alice. I whisper to myself, inconspicuously wiping the tears from my cheeks.

My vision is blurred. I can barely make out the faces in the halls as I pass. The path ahead me twist and turn in different ways. I realize that I'm lost in the enormous building.

Hazy black spots are beginning form behind my lashes. The world around me slowly starts to spin. I realize that I'm having another chocolate emergency. Moving to the side, I lean against the wall. My breathing labored as black clouds the surrounding.

Hold on, hold on.

I open my bag, fumbling and drop the contents onto the floor- no-signs of my glucose tablets or chocolate.

The ground sinks under me; my legs give up, causing me to collapse onto the hard marbled floors.

The throbbing in my head increase- I don't have the strength to utter a word. People surround me in checkered shirts and heels, congesting the small pocket of air around me.

"What's wrong with the girl?" They mutter amongst themselves.

"Are you okay dear?" A kind lady asks. I want to tell her I'm not but I don't have the voice.

The crowd grows in size and I feel more suffocated.

"Move aside!" I hear a familiar voice. "Give her some room people!"

In the blurred state, I see a figure emerge through the crowd. A blue-black striped shirt clings to his broad shoulder as a tie loosely hangs off his neck.

He kneels down beside me and takes my hand in his, his skin is ghastly pale with fear. "Go bring something sweet!" He shouts at someone I don't recognize. "Why are you standing there? Damn it! She's having a low-sugar attack! For God's sake Hurry up!"

I want to laugh at Devlin's worried expression. I want to tell him that I won't die from a chocolate emergency.

But before I can do anything, the curtains of conscious fall and everything descends into unfathomable darkness.

# Chapter 17

----------------------------------------

The scariest part about being in love isn't the feeling itself. It's the moment when he reciprocates the feeling. When your heart collides with his, it's an impact that's meant to leave some scars. The moment when his eyes reflect the emotion deep inside your heart, the moment when you can't hold yourself and fall- are the most terrifying yet exhilarating fragments of love. You break away from everything; eyelids are closed as you fall, deeper and deeper into a bottomless ocean. You can only pray for the collision to be perfect- to tie your broken pieces and not to shatter everything apart.

Breaths leave me in a slow drag. There is light as the surrounding come to life. The first the thing I see is a portrait. Golden beading pulls the frame together, inside it there is a painting- not just any painting. It's Devlin. It's a Devlin I don't know.

Pale pastel pallets of colors weave through the canvas- brown eyes are painted hauntingly on the panel- he isn't smiling. He looks lost as he holds himself in a daunting manner. The softness of his contours reveals his younger self. A regal black coat holds his arms in place. His midnight hair are combed neatly to one side. The man in the painting doesn't resemble the Devlin I know.  There isn't a playful light in his eyes or the teasing smile on his lips. The pits of his eyes are hollow and dead. The man appears to be a dead corpse.

A cold shiver runs down the length of my spine. I avert my eyes from the painting and take in the surroundings.

My body is sprawled across a black leather sofa and there's a pillow neatly tucked beneath my head. The room is enormous and forebodingly dark. There is a spherical mahogany table opposite to me, long chairs with intricate craving of roses and thorns are placed by the table. The walls are painted black, pitch black. If it weren't for the coral shaped lamps, I would have never seen the walls.

I lift my sore body from the sofa, nearly falling back down in the process.  My breaths halt when I take in the figure leaning on the windowsill.

He stares at me, his eyes blank and dark. The placid expression on his face doesn't change as he watches me sit up on the sofa. A blue tie hangs off his neck while a grey coat covered his shoulders. His hands grip the ledge- the skin around his knuckles is white. The starless sky peeks in from the parted window.

He doesn't make a move to advance towards me.

"Devlin," I speak up, my voice resounds in the silent room. I feel scared. "Does my dad know?"

He shakes his head, his lips drawn in a tight line.

"Where are we?" I ask, standing up from the sofa. My legs give up and I fall back down. The room spins around me; I grip my head which was hurting like I've been hit by a cargo ship. The side of sofa sinks as Devlin takes a seat beside me. His cool fingers are pressed against my burning forehead. The beats of my heart increase drastically.

He doesn't say anything and massages my temple- the tips of fingers running in small circles. The pain subdues to some extent. A sigh of relief escapes my lips.

In a fraction of a second, his hands fall down and I instantly miss his touch. I pressed my spine against the sofa, trying to control the wild, flustering feelings inside me.

"Where are we?" I repeat, my voice sounded hoarse.

I turn my head to look at him. He holds my gaze, fiercely and protectively. I wait and wait for him to utter a word but not a sound leaves his chapped lips. My heart falls inside me. Why isn't he saying anything? Is he mad at me?

"Devlin," Fear makes my breathing harder. "Say something," I can't hide the longing in my voice. My voice betrays me- it betrays all the feelings I've been hiding.

He still doesn't say anything. There isn't an ounce of emotion on his features. The intensity of his gaze scares me. Goosebumps rise on my skin.

"Please," I whisper.

No reply. Dull, haunting eyes stare back at me.

I'm not going to give up.

"Are you mad at me?" I grab his shoulders, the fabric of his shirt slips between my fingers- heat from his skin seeps into my hands, scalding the skin beneath my palms. I search his eyes for something, anything- where are the warm brown lively eyes I love?

"It shouldn't matter to you," His voice is quite, so silent that the passing winds could have easily stolen it.

"It does," I say without a speck of hesitation. "It does matter to me and there is nothing you can do about it,"

He shrugs my hands off his shoulder- I let them fall to the side. A wave of pain tries to pull me under. I don't let it.

He looks away, out the window where the night sky is darker than it's ever been. I realize why. Because the sky is empty- no stars, no moon fill it tonight. Just like him. He's empty today- there isn't warmth nor happiness inside him.

"Your dad won't like it if he finds out you skipped school,"

"I don't care,"

"You shouldn't be here with me. Go back home Alice. It's the best thing for you," His voice is heavy.

"I am home,"

His head snaps in my direction. "What do you mean?" Panic crowds his face- he fumbles with his hands before taking my arms in his grasp.

"I can't go back to a place which doesn't feel like home anymore," Few tears leak out of the side of my eyes. "It's feels like home with you. After years, I've finally started living again. It's because of you. I can't leave you when you need me,"

He brushes away the tears with his thumb, a saddening smile danced on the corners of his lips. "You shouldn't worry about me. I'll be fine,"

"I'm not leaving you," My voice is firm. I stare right into his eyes when I say the words.

"This isn't about me," His hands still hold my face. "It's about you,"

"No, this is about us,"

The space between us seemed to be vanishing. I edge towards him. He doesn't move back. The brown in his eyes glows -with what?

I don't know. Maybe it was my drowsy mind that pulled tricks on me. Maybe it was night that peppered magic. Whatever it was, it was beautiful and strong.  A bundle of courage grew inside me. It soared from the center of my chest and encased the tips of my toes.

It caused me to press my lips against his. He froze against me. My heart hammered against my rib-cage- I'm afraid that it might break my bones, creating cracks which won't ever be healed.

The gentle warmth from his lips sinks into me.

I pull away after a second. My cheeks are stained red. Where did this courage come from?  I feel horrified, embarrassed, and terrified at what I've done.

I just pecked his lips.

With terror pulling its string along my center, I steal a glance at his face.  He looks shocked- the skin beneath his dark hair is colorless- ghastly white. He sucked in a sharp piece of air, his eyes briefly find mine- they were stunned to silence.

My hands curl around my chest. I tip away from Devlin.

He doesn't let me and grabs my wrist, his nails digging into my flesh.

"You deserve a better first kiss," He whispers.

He pulls me into him, his arms curl around me. Before I can even react, his lips meet mine. Cold shivers run down my spine. Devlin's hands cup my face, bringing me closer to him. The autumn air whirls around us.

My cheeks are buried in heat and red. The subtle taste coffee seeps from his mouth and drowns me. Our bodies are pressed against the others. He lowers me to the sofa, my head rests on the soft pillow as my heart beats drum inside me like a dangerous winter song. His fingers trail along the side of my face, caressing my cheeks gently. It sends my heart into overdrive.

His lips move against mine in a perfect, slow synch.

My lungs ache.  I'm on the verge on fainting from the lack of air.

I pull away, breathless and flustered. His eyes capture mine- they're glowing with a warm golden light.  He smiles at me; his arms pressed to the side of the sofa as he props himself above me.

The faint smell of his fresh winter cologne surrounds me.

I can't help but smile back.

"Let's get out of here," He breathes out, his voice husky. "You have school tomorrow,"

I nod my head, unable to find the voice to reply. It warmed my heart to see how much he cared for me.

"I'll take you somewhere for dinner," He lifts himself off me and sits on one end of the sofa. The tone of his voice is light and happy. The Devlin I know is back.  "There's this awesome place I know. They serve the best kind of Chinese. You do like Chinese food?" He asked, worried that I didn't.

I couldn't help but laugh. "I do,"

He helps me sit up, his large hands taking my small ones. "Perfect,"

I wrap my hands around my arms, a pert smile on my face.

"Come on, we have to try their stir fried noodles," He led me out of the room, his hand wrapped around mine. It's an amazing feeling.

"Devlin, where are we?"

The merry expression on his face falls and turns into something grim. "My cabin in Enlighten," He muttered under his breath. "I don't get why they haven't cleaned it out yet. I'm not coming back,"

I want to ask him about it but I'm afraid that it might dampen his mood. Something about my expression catches his attention. He sighs. "I promise I'll explain later, Okay?"

"Okay," I smile.

With his free hand, Devlin reaches for the golden door knob. The instant the door is flung open,  bright, blinding yellow lights flood the cabin.

On the other side of door, stood a chubby middle-aged man- he wore a regal designer suit and tie. The color of his hair is a shade too light to be considered black and a shade to dark to be brown. The front part of his head is bald and his sharp jaw has a small beard twisted into a single wisp of hair at the chin.  His brown eyes vaguely resemble with Devlin but their nothing like his. His eyes are sharp and calculating with a strong cunning undertone.

The way his eyes pierce through me make me feel very uncomfortable. As if sensing my discomfort, Devlin tightens his hold on my hand. From the corner of my eye, I see a bead of sweat trickle down Devlin's tensed forehead.

I gulp when I see my dad appear beside the man. Dad's gray eyes are burning with fury. His eyes narrow down to our entwined hands. The wrinkles on his face deepen as a menacing scowl forms on his face.

I want to bury my head into Devlin's shoulder and hide behind him but my legs are paralyzed. Devlin and I look at each other- we both realize the deep trouble we're in.

"Mr. Hutchins, I honestly did not know my daughter knew your son," My dad's voice is strained as he speaks to the stout man.

So he's Mr. Hutchins- Devlin's father. I glance at Devlin- his jaw is in a taut position and veins in his neck were jutting outwards.

I wove my fingers through his sweaty hand and gave it a reassuring squeeze. His eyes meet mine-panic clouded them. Don't worry- I try to tell him with my eyebrows drawn together and my lips curved into a small smile.

"The knowing part is not of my concern," A voice ringing with authority and power echoes through the glassed hall- outside the floor-lengthened windows I see the city lights flicker to life. Cars headlights and streetlight appear like glowing fireflies.

"Who doesn't know my son? Afterall he's the son of the most prominent businessman this town has seen in ages," Arrogance is thickly laced with Mr. Hutchin's voice. "Something else troubles me here," His eyes briefly glance at out tangled hands- I don't let go nor does Devlin.

I clearly understand what Mr. Hutchins is trying to imply. He doesn't like the idea of Devlin and me together.

Dad stares at me, accusingly. "Mr. Hutchins I can assure you my daughter won't be seen near your son,"

My eyes widen. "You can't decide that," I nearly yell, horrified. For a moment I feel my heart stop beating. Devlin holds my hand so tightly now that I'm sure my skin is bleeding from his nail marks.

"You're coming with me. I've had enough of this rebellious teen act," Dad states, his voice firm. Nothing I say is going to change his mind..

"I'm not going anywhere,"

Mr. Hutchins clicked his tongue- giving us a pitying smirk. "Alice," He directly addressed me. I don't like how he said my name- as though I'm some kind of filthy rag doll.  "I think it would be in your best interest to listen to your father,"

"Why are you doing this?" I cry- my eyes flicker to Devlin who looks shell-shocked by the turn of events.

"Well dear I have a reputation which my son cares nothing about," Even though his voice is coated with sugar, I don't miss the threating leer to it.

"What does your reputation have anything do with me?" I snap.

Dad shoots me a warning glare which says shut your mouth right now.

"Reputation?" Devlin laughs. His laugh sounded forced and ner vous."The owner of a sinking company is talking about his damned reputation,"

"If this troubles you," Devlin wrapped his arm around my waist, holding me protectively. My dad looks like he's about to blow with anger. "That's your problem not mine,"

He stroked his beard thoughtfully, curling his finger around the thread of hair hanging from his chin. "We'll see whose problem it is,"

Mr. Hutchins pulls out his phone and swings it to his ear. "Security, we're having some trouble on the third floor. Send in the guards,"

He cannot do this to his own blood in flesh.

"Mr. Hutchins you can't possibly force them apart!" Dad shouts, color drains his face. "They're kids if we reason with them I'm sure they'll listen,"

Mr. Hutchins shakes his head. "I'm done with reasoning,"

Devlin hand drops from my waist and he grabs my hand. He doesn't look surprised by his father's decision. He leaned down to my level and whispered. "Don't think. Just do as I say,"

I nod my head. Petrified by the thought of being separated.

The bulky men dressed navy blue and black uniforms approach from the left end of the hall. Their hands are burdened by hefty guns.  Fear churns my stomach painful.

"Run!" He hollers and drags me along him towards the right hall.

The surroundings pass in a blur. Blood soars inside my veins,  We run hand in hand. I hear Mr. Hutchins scream on top of his lungs. "Catch them! I'm going to fire each one of you if you don't catch them,"

Devlin laughs, breathlessly. "They won't get to us,"

We dodge the office's staff giving us peculiar glares. I nearly knock into a lady carrying a tray filled boiling coffee mugs but Devlin catches me in time.  The entire building is thrown into chaos and disorder.

People are shouting after us. I dare to look over my shoulder and see the guards approaching us- frantically their beefy bodies collide with the staff members. A lady with whom the one of the guards collided with slapped him straight across his face. The poor guy shook his head. I bet he's thinking this job isn't worth the pay. I stifle a laugh.

"This is crazy," I breathe out- my legs aching as we take the stairs. Devlin almost tumbled down the stairs. I grab his collar before he could fall.

"Crazy is not the word I'd use," He smirk, his face dripping with sweat. "I'd say mad,"

"The difference?" I raise my eyebrow, my hands leave his collar.

"I just wanted to contradict you," He shrugged his shoulders.  He took my hand and brought me to a pale colored door at the end of the stairs.

"You don't have a fear of heights, do you?"

"Why?" I ask him. He pushed the door to an open. The cold autumn wind blows the sweat off our skin. Strands of my brown hair move along the breeze.

He walked outside. In the dim light, I see that we're standing on a roof. Broken beer bottles and newspaper pages are scattered across the roof.

"We're about to climb down a ladder," He edged towards the metal railing of the roof. I see a long, bamboo ladder clinging to the side of the glassed wall. We're at least one story above the ground- around hundred meters from the crowded sidewalk filled with people dressed in expensive suits.

I gulp. "Devlin, how many times have you done this?"

He gave me a lopsided grin, the sharp counters of his face glow in the scant light.

"You don't want to know, trust me,"

Devlin tipped his feet onto the railing and then he jumped off it- I nearly scream.  I lean over the edge to see his hands firmly planted on the ladder's step.  He peels one of his hands and holds it out for me. "It's perfectly safe,"

"I doubt that,"

"I'll be here if anything goes wrong," He tries smiling reassuringly.

I hesitantly place my hand in his and pull my leg over the railing. Bile rises up my throat as I tightly grip the rungs of the ladder. The splinter from the wood dug into my hand.

Suddenly the door flies open, a guard steps out onto the roof. His eyes meet mine, instantly he starts yelling like a mad man. "They're on the roof,"

"Hurry," I yell to Devlin who's quickly climbing down the ladder. In the dark, I carefully make sure my feet are properly placed on the steps.

The guard begins to climb down the ladder.

I look over to Devlin. He's standing on the sidewalk, waiting for me. "Alice, jump! I'll catch you,"

The guard is nearing towards me. I feel my pulse rise as I throw myself off the ladder.

Devlin catches me like he said he would- his arm around my knees and the other under my neck. He quickly set me on the ground. "I parked my car just over there," He points to the other side of the crammed road with cars and people skidding down the sidewalk.

We run to the other side of the road. Horns blare in our direction. Devlin's red Toyota Camry  is parked by some café. Fumbling, he quickly jammed the keys into the door and throws it open.

He climbs into the car and throws the other door open for me. I hastily shuffle myself inside. In a second, Devlin has the car running. Pressing the accelerator, he zooms through the traffic.

From the rear view mirror, I see the guard with his mouth hanging open watching us leave.

"What the hell did just happen?" I exhale, my lungs burning inside me.  "You have a ton of explaining to do, Mister,"

"Where do we start?" Devlin stared hard at the road ahead of him.

"From the part why your father nearly got us killed,"

# Chapter 18

"From the part why your father nearly got us killed," I huffed.

Devlin cracked a smile- a small dimple made an appearance on his cheek. He shook his head ever so slightly, wisp of black hair danced across his pale forehead.

"So," I dragged the word. The streets were packed with cars and yellow-black taxis. Buildings- lighted brightly in the dim night whirled into a distant blur. We were headed to towards his apartment- I could tell. Old, age-worn apartments, parks filled with utter vibrancy, street-food stalls came into view.

"He wasn't gonna kill us, you know." Devlin slipped a finger under his collar and undid a few buttons; silver skin peeked through the shirt. He loosened the blue tie hanging off his neck- as though it had been choking him few minutes ago.

I rolled down the window, letting in the cool, autumn wind dry off the sweat sticking stubbornly to our skins.

"Nah," I folded my arms across the dashboard and rested my head on it. Nothing other than a good-night sleep (and maybe him) seemed tempting right now. "Of course, he wasn't going to kill us.

I mean we both know how much your father enjoys a good game of chase. Let's take a moment and ignore the fact that he had a freaking army of guard trying to haul us,"

Devlin chuckled, glancing in my direction before turning his attention to the road, swerving though the traffic smoothly as though he was running a knife down a chunk of butter.

"Don't mock so much, love," He said in between laughs. Love, my heart melted into a pool of chocolate and seeped into my toes and the tips of fingers.

"I haven't even started," I replied, lightly.

"Honestly, dad, well- he was just trying to scare us. He would never hurt you or me,"

"Really?" I quirked an eyebrow. "Because from what it looked like I'm sure he wouldn't mind having me dead,"

Devlin stiffened, his grip on the steering wheel became tighter- the veins in his hand skimmed above the papery skin. "Don't say that," He whispered, barely loud enough for me to hear.

"Say what?" I asked, confused- leaning away from the dashboard.

"Nothing, nothing at all," He breathed out. I don't know how to explain this but Devlin looked tensed, his brows were pulled together and his lips were drawn into a thin line.

"No, tell me,"

He shrugged his shoulders. "I dunno- I just don't like having you talk about your death... it's that..." He trailed off.

It took me a moment to understand what he was implying. My suicide attempt- he was scared that I was going to try to kill myself. The fear humming in his warm brown eyes was almost palpable. Suddenly, I felt embarrassed for all that I had done. No-matter how hard I tried I could never get over the subtle grit of guilt grinding my aching bones.

Imagine what would have happened if my father and my sister who loved me more than anything found out about it. I cringed. They would be crushed-no doubt- Dad would blame it all on himself and Liza- she would become so frightened by the news. I could imagine seeing tears roll down her cheeks and her face lose its sunny, joyful light. That made my heart twist achingly inside me.

I had acted out of cowardice-not wanting to face the bundle of worries life had served me. That's life for you- you have to stand up and face the storm head on. There is no place to hide from the harsh winds and cold reality. I will live my life. Not for my family for loves more than anything, not for my friends who listened to me when I was lost, not for Devlin who picked me up and helped me stand up again- I will live this life for myself because I matter as much as everyone else in my small world.

If I want to love and comfort the people around me, I have to learn to pick myself up first. A sinking ship can't possibly save another until it repairs its own torn sail.

"I won't do it again," I wanted to sound strong but the words slipped out in a hesitant murmur. "it was in the spur of the moment- things fell apart so fast- I didn't even know what I was doing-"

"You don't need to explain," His hand found mine. My stomach churned in flustering manner- the gentle billowing of my heart thrummed inside my ear drums.

With a hint of gentleness, his fingers wove in between mine- our hands fit like two lost reels of the same photographic film.

"It felt like I needed to,"

He stayed silent for a second- his eyes trained on the twisted path ahead of us. The once tight hold he had on my hand-lessened to an extent where I couldn't feel his fingers- they were merely there hanging from my pained flesh.

"Whatever you did," He spoke so detachably that it made my heart fall to the pit of my stomach. The caring warmth on his face dwindled into a chilling nihility.  "It was for your own sake. Who am I to question it?"

Ice glazed my eyes. That shouldn't have hurt but it did. He had kissed me a couple minutes ago and now here he was deny-ing everything between us. He was treating me like an absolute stranger. Taking a deep breath, I smiled- almost sourly as his words from the time he had saved me came haunting back- 'After all who am I to question what you did? It's your life. It's your choice to do whatever you want with it,'

"You're right. What-," My voice was cut by a loud shriek.  My heart literally jumped out of my chest. Chocolate Fudge! His hand slid through my grasp. Then there was sound of tires skidding on gravel. What's going on?

Devlin pressed the brakes, the car screeched to a stop. Horns were blown on the busy central park streets. A shiny, bright con-vertible with a girl in tight-black dressed holding a bottle of beer in hand shouted a bunch of curses and drove past us. If Devlin hadn't stopped the car on time- the girl would have definitely crashed into us.

"Girls these days- always in a rush," He muttered under his breath, shaking his head. In an instant he had the Camry speeding away. I liked how drove- not too fast, not too slow- just a notch above the speed limit.

"And Boys these days don't mean a thing they say," I sighed.

"What did I say now?" I wanted to laugh at his comical worried expression. His mouth was slightly ajar and his eyebrows were puckered. Under normal circumstance, I would have but right I couldn't do anything other than fret over things I could never control (his past and my heart). Why do we human beings always want to be the puppeteers and control our fates? Was it because we're afraid of the unknown? You know the kid was never afraid of the dark- he was afraid of what hid inside it aka the unknown.

"It's about what you didn't say," It's about the things you didn't ask me (if I liked you or not) It's about to the four letter you won't ever say. It's about why you haven't given our friendship or whatever it is a name. What are we Devlin? You haven't tried to ask me once.

I watched him meet my gaze. For a moment, I felt breathless staring into those golden hued eyes which were peppered with this intangible magic.

He causally shrugged his shoulders. "I don't say a-lot of things I want to say,"

"Like?"

His eyes left mine and he stared straight ahead. There was lesser traffic on this side of Winterville. The crowd scattered away behind in the main central park area. A couple jogged on the road- neon earphones plugged into their yoga pants. An elderly woman walked with her granddaughter, laughing as they went. There was a mother speed walking with a stroller in which lay two adorable children. I loved the community in which Devlin lived. The people here were really friendly. They're the type who would invite you for dinner without a reason and send you oatmeal cookies whenever they made some at their place.

We were growing closer to his apartment. I could see the tall, rugged brick buildings of Oak Apartment Complex peak out in the distance.

"Like," He repeated as he shifted the gear. "Like how the sweater you're wearing,"

I looked down at my knitted sweater- it was orange and had a big pumpkin in the middle. I remember getting it from the thanksgiving clearance sale.

"It's three sizes too big for you," He bluntly stated.

My mouth fell open. I couldn't believe he would say something like that. I should have known. With him, you can never tell what he's going to say. He's like a dice- you can never predict the side you'll receive. It could be a one (when he's distant and cold) or a jackpot of six (in which he says something utterly loving and warm).

I crossed my arms over my chest and narrowed my eyes at him. Stupid chocolate eyed jerk.

"I like wearing loose clothes. They're comfortable," I wish I didn't sound so defensive.

"Comfort is one thing and you're over doing it. It's like you're hiding underneath that sweater instead of wearing it,"

He knew nothing.

He didn't know that I wore oversized clothes because I hated the way my body looked. He didn't know how it killed me. He didn't know about the insecurities that were corroding my insides the same way rust does to iron.

Whenever I went shopping with Liza, she'd force to wear those beautiful, white-lace covered dresses.

Then in the dressing rooms, somehow I managed to squeeze into the dress and when I would to stare into the mirror. I hated everything I saw.

A girl with her mother's bright peacock, green eyes and slightly long, brown hair curling around her shoulders- wearing no smile would greet the empty walls. A dress would be clinging off her curves and showed the flab she managed to hide behind the loose clothes she usually wore. She wasn't skinny nor was she obese. Just ten pounds overweight. According to the society norms, she wasn't considered to be beautiful. Compliments were never bestowed upon her. She didn't want them either. In the end, she hated herself- she hated what she had become and the way others saw here. Never the girlfriend, always the friend.

I would turn my back towards the mirror. Liza would call my name and tell me to show her how the dressed looked. I'd quickly slip out of the dress and change into my clothes. I would lie to her and tell her that the dressed didn't fit.

Dishearted, I always ended up buying baggy clothes. Liza would click her tongue and say 'why do you buy these? They're so dull'

"I don't care," I muttered under my breath, turned my head to look out the window. This is the last thing I wanted to share with him.

"You'd look amazing if you wore clothes your size," Amazing, yellow red Butterflies, blue jays, and humming birds- fluttered uncontrollably inside my stomach.

Don't pay attention to them- they'll fool you again.

"This is my size,"

Why were we even having this conversation? He was supposed to explain everything that happened in Enlighten  today. It's like he's purposely avoiding the topic.

"It's not," He argued, fiercely. Why does he care? From the corner of my eye, I could see him getting all worked up. "All you ever wear are these baggy hoodies and sweaters,"

I snapped- I knew I wouldn't last long- my temper was as brittle as a thin icicle placed under the pounding summer sun.

"Why do you care what I wear and what I don't? It's not like we're dating. You kissed me and you haven't even tried to ask me about my feelings! I know we barely escaped Enlighten. I know I shouldn't be yelling at you for something as stupid as this but I am! Okay?"

There goes keeping your mouth shut part. Air filled my lungs as rapidly as it left.

Devlin didn't look shocked or hurt or angry or confused. He looked amused and that made me feel like a little kid.

He opened mouth and said the dumbest thing I've heard. "Are you hungry?"

"Seriously?"

"Well you wanted me to ask you something so there you go,"

Can someone give me sledge hammer? Because I want to kill him at this freaking moment. Yet at the same time I wanted to hug him tightly and never let go.

I began laughing and soon he joined me. We laughed and laughed. Honestly because it was all we could control at the moment. We couldn't control our feelings, our twisted reality, and our impending doom.

# Chapter 19

The car's engine was cut, its loud and energetic roar stopped beneath my feet. Laughter had abandoned us a long time ago, leaving a suffocating silence in its place. Devlin turned the keys and pulled them out, smoothly tucking them into the pocket of his grey pants.

The night was dark, swirling around us like a hidden blanket of gloom and deception. Welcome to Oak Apartments Complex – said a wooden board with green painted borders hanging off a small rusted pole. Residents of the apartment were shuffling in and out the tall, brick building containing numerous black framed windows and straight staircases. Some of the small, metal paned windows led out to the wooden planked patios.

Devlin had parked his Toyota Camry in the parking lot near the entrance of the apartment's shabby enquiry office. Besides us, cars were leaving their spots and some were being parked. It was a busy environment. Everything was bustling with life and activity unlike us. He wasn't talking neither was I. Time seemed to have come to a strange standstill. Both of us didn't know how to make it tick forward.

Maybe only I felt that way. Maybe I was the only one who didn't want things to move on.

Why?

Because I was scared of what's about to come, I'm scared of reality, I'm scared of his rejection which I know is bound to happen.

He was about to exit the car, the door was opened as he shifted to move out but I stopped him.

I had to. I didn't have a choice. There were questions that needed answers.

My hands trembled as I held his shirt's cuff, the fabric felt nice under my cold skin. His brows were creased as his eyes watched me wearily- it was like they could read each and every thought creating a ruckus inside me.

I bit down on my lips to stop them from quivering.

He moved back and closed the door with a gentle thud.

"What?" He spoke, dryly.

I gulped. My hand still held his wrist. I didn't want to let go. I wanted to hold his hand because I needed to. There aren't words to explain that necessity.

I let go nevertheless, a lump forming inside my throat when I did.

"I went against my father today," My voice was hesitant, flickering like an open flame placed outside in the stormy winds. "I need to know why,"

"Because Mr. Brown didn't want us to be together," The expression on his face was blank as he said the words.

"Are we even together?" The tone of my voice was sharper than I had intended it to be.

"Are we?" He held my gaze, indifferently. My pulse quickened as I stared into those spellbinding eyes.

When I realized that he had turned the question back on me, my heart fell to the pit of my stomach.

I didn't know what to say.

"How old are you, Alice?" I had no idea where he was headed with this.

"Eighteen,"

He averted his eyes to stare at the cold night. "Do you know my age?"

"No," I whispered. I had a brief idea on how old he might be. He had already completed grad school so he's probably older than twenty-two. How much older? I really didn't have clue.

He looks really young, which he is. I mean if I didn't know him I'd probably say he's still in high-school but he isn't.

"In a few months, I'll be turning twenty-four,"

He's six years older than me. Liza would freak out if she found that I had a crush on a guy who's older than me. She will totally pull out the 'I told so' card on me.

'I knew it, I knew it. There is a boy in your life. No-wonder you've changed so much' I could already hear her voice inside my head.

"So?..." I trailed off, my eyebrows furrowed together in confusion. Why is he suddenly bringing up our age?

"You don't get it. Do you?"

I shook my head.

He sighed. "Never mind,"

I let it drop because honestly Devlin can be really weird some-times and doesn't' make any sense so I'm pretty much used to it. I wasn't wrong when I had said he'd make a pretty girl, chocolate syrup, he acts like one too.

"Will you explain everything that happened today? Because I'm pretty sure my dad won't want to see my face again," well I don't think he'll mind that.

I only reminded him of the bad things in life anyways.

"When the time comes," His tone was evasive.

"Yah, you mean never," I retorted, crossing my arms over my chest.

His eyes snapped in my direction. I didn't realize he was angry. As much as  a lion ready to shred his prey into pieces. His jaw was tightly clenched while his eyes burned with uncontainable amount of fury.

Chocolate Fudge, what bit into his butt?

"Like I said I will explain when the time comes," He spoke through gritted teeth. If I said I felt scared, it would be an understatement. I felt petrified. What's wrong with him?

I know I should have dropped the topic right then and there but I couldn't. For obvious reasons, I had the right to know. I needed to know what we are running away from.

"Basically you ruined my idea of going back to my family once I clear the retests. Because hell, I'm sure my dad won't let step me in the ten meter radius around his house. And now you don't have the decency to give me an explanation. I'm pretty sure I deserve one,"

"Don't worry I'll fix everything," He breathed out, running an agitated hand through hair.

I felt angry. I've had enough. What is his freaking problem? He cannot possibly expect me take the shit he throws at me.

"Oh, okay! Is that how you Hutchins work? First you wreak everything then you fix it. Like how Mr. Hutchins hasn't been able to stop the last four terminations-"I quickly stopped myself when I realized what I was saying.

All good things chocolate, I shouldn't have said that. Ice glazed his eyes. I had offended him. There is one thing I've learned over the measly eighteen years I've managed to live, man and his pride don't mix no matter what. One blow on the pride is equal hundred blows on his heart.   It was my father's pride and my stubbornness that killed our family. I should have known better.

"What terminations are you talking about?" He was watching me wide eyed and cautiously.

He didn't know about them.

"I don't know," I replied honestly, sensing a sudden urgency taking control of him. "I overheard some of the staff talk about some contract being pulled out without prior notice,"

"Damn," He slammed his fist against the steering wheel. "No-one told me about this,"

"If you don't mind me asking, what were you doing in the office today? I thought you had left it after you-"I stopped not wanting to complete my sentence.

"After I lost our biggest investor," He finished it for me- his shoulders were in a stiff stance.

I didn't reply. If I did, I would have said something totally inappropriate -like how I wanted to hug him tightly because he looked so vulnerable right now, like how I wanted to bury head into his shoulder and tell him everything will alright, like how I wanted to kiss the misery off his face.

"Sarah called me up today- she needed my help with something. I think you've met her," He gave me a sideway glance. There was a slight teasing spark in his eyes.

I tried really hard to control the cringe at her name. "She doesn't like me," A grimace was about to encase my mouth.

I forced it into a smile.

He caught my repulsion nevertheless. "I told you before it takes her time to warm up to people,"

I wanted to argue about it but decided against it. There was a child like admiration on his face when he spoke of his sister.

"What were you doing in Enlighten?" He asked, even though he secretly knew the answer.

"I had to get some forms signed,"

He rolled his eyes, a small smile tracing his lips. "You expect me to believe that,"

"As much as you expect to believe that you were in my school for extra credit," I muttered.

He gave me a full blown grin. "Mhm, what forms are we exactly talking about?" He spoke in a playful tone.

I reached for my bag which wasn't there. Frantically, I looked around the cream-leather seats of Devlin's car. I even checked the glove compartment which was filled blue CD cases.

"Chocolate Fudge! Where's my bag?" That bag had my retest forms, books, and most importantly my favorite paint brush.

"Oh God," I pressed a hand across my mouth. Literally, I couldn't breathe.

"Relax," Devlin placed his hand on my shoulder. A shiver ran down my spine as heat drowned my face.

This is when I remembered a minor detail. "My bag- I think when I had fainted, I left it there,"

"Calm down, I promise to bring it back tomorrow. You think you can make it without your bag for one day?" He asked, looking into my eyes.

No I wanted to yell. My most precious brush was stuck in there.

I nodded my head instead.

"Okay good, after I make amends with your father, I'll look for your bag," He removed his hand from my shoulder, instantly I missed his soft, caring touch.

"Wait, you're going back? But you can't. Mr. Hutchins will definitely try to get his hands on you and how in the world are you planning to fix things with my dad? He hates your guts,"

Here I was fretting for his wellbeing and here he was laughing his heart out. I narrowed my eyes at him.

Chuckling, he leaned down and pressed his lips against my cheeks. "You're so cute,"

I didn't blush because my cheeks were already the brightest shade of red they could manage.

Chocolate-eyed jerk, I hate him.

"I'm glad you find my concern amusing," I replied, dryly.

"Do you seriously think this was my first time getting into trouble with my dad?"

I should have known. The way he had expertly led us down the ladder and through the building- it didn't seem like his first attempt at it.

"How many times have you done this before?" I didn't think he would answer the question.

He grinned, showcasing his perfect rows of teeth.  "Counting this one, I think it's my thirtieth,"

I stared at him, baffled- my mouth agape. I certainly did not expect this. "Wha-what?" Coherent refused to be formed on my tongue. "Are you kidding?"

"No,"

"Was that some kind of joke because it seriously looked like your dad wanted to kill you?"

"Yes and no. I guess that's his way showing resent,"

"It's a very weird way if you ask me," I muttered.  "Can I ask you something?"

"Depends," He smirked, a small dimple made an appearance on his left cheek. For a whole two point three seconds I forgot to breathe.

I had to pressurize my brain to remember the question I had been meaning to ask.

So I ended up blurting the first thing that came to my mind. "Are all of the Hutchins this crazy? Or are you and your dad an exception?"

Devlin laughed, the sound flowed freely in the small, compact area we sat in. His laugh echoed inside my rib-cage making my heart pump blood faster than before. I loved the simple, enchanting sensation.

"Maybe," Was his reply.

Honestly, All I wanted right now was to sleep in my bed and hide under my brown checkered blanket but when I heard the commotion coming from Devlin's apartment as we approached it, I instantly figured that no such thing was happening any time soon.

My first instinct was to tell Devlin to call the police and report that had buglers broken into our place. I was about to say so when I saw Devlin, looking perfectly calm, he had a  grey coat neatly folded on his arm as he strode beside me.

We stopped in front of his apartment. A silver number plate read 303. The maroon door was slightly parted, small amount of light fell through it.

Devlin briefly glanced at me, an apologetic look on his face. "Sorry, I forgot to tell you-"

He was interrupted by two guys tackling him to the floor.

"Holy shit! He looks like a business man," The African- American guy hollered. He had a clean shaven head and a short, muscular body. A loose pair of trousers and sleeveless red shirt which had the number the three in white printed on it covered his bulky physique. I couldn't see his face because he pinning Devlin to the floor. The other guy had olive colored skin- he looked Indian- he was wearing a bright yellow t-shirt and low slung jeans. He was laughing hard as he held Devlin to the floor by his waist. The Indian guy had a sharp nose and thin, angular jaw. He could easily pass for some high-profile actor, he was that good looking.

"Brandon, Get that darned thing off him," The Indian guy said, chuckling. I suppose Brandon was the name of the African guy who had his hands wrapped around Devlin's collar "Code one of the medical student manual- no coats, shirts, and ties,"

"For once, I agree with Yuv," Brandon replied. Yuv- nice name for a handsome guy.

"Argh! Dude get off me. You'll scare her," Devlin screamed, breathlessly.

I watched them half horrified and half amused. Devlin squirmed under them, kicking his legs wildly. Should I help him? Nah, I was actually enjoying myself. They had ripped his shirt - the buttons popped open revealing the silver skin underneath. Devlin didn't have a bad body- he may be lean but he sure kept himself fit.

Almost all the buttons in his blue-black stripped shirt were un-done and torn and now it only hung off his shoulder like a jacket. Brandon jerked the shirt off Devlin's shoulders and tossed to Yuv.

They let go of Devlin and stood up. Devlin got up as well, the tips of his ears a dark shade of pink. They threw his shirt around like they were playing ball. I noted with awe Brandon was just as handsome as his friend Yuv. He had the most piercing pair of honey colored eyes I've ever seen.

Devlin cleared his throat, obviously catching me checking them out. He stood in the hall, awkwardly- only his grey pants hanging low on his waist.

I coughed to stifle a laugh.

His eyes snapped in my direction. "You find this funny?" He nearly growled.

I simply shrugged my shoulders.

Yuv caught the sight of me- he gave me a friendly smile. "Wow! Who is this pretty lady?" He spoke, curiosity piping thick in his voice.

Brandon with Devlin's torn shirt in his hand, ran over to me. I was scared that he might knock me down, judging by the excited look on his face.

He gave me a hug, almost choking the life out of me. "Finally!" He cheered once he had let me go. "Our boy is growing up,"

I glanced at Devlin- in the hope he might help me because I felt clueless. To my not so pleasant surprise, Devlin looked like he was going to blow up from anger. I'm pretty sure there was steam escaping his ears.

"Amen, master, your teachings have been put to use," Yuv placed a hand on his chest and closed his eyes. "Your disciple has finally got himself a girlfriend.

If someone had called me Devlin's girlfriend few days ago, I would have died from blushing like a drunk monkey  but now all did that title bring was a handful of bitterness and gloom. It reminded me of things that I could never have.

"I'm not his girlfriend," I breathed out. Out of the corner of my eye, I saw Devlin's entire body stiffen. "He's letting me stay at his place for few days. Basically I'm his roommate,"

Yuv was quick to notice the tension hanging in the air. "So you're not dating anyone?" He walked over to me and wrapped his arm around my shoulder. Devlin's eyes were narrowed at his arm. Why does he care? It shouldn't matter to him. He averted his eyes, almost like it was hurting him.

"No-one," I replied, staring hard at Devlin. His hands were held in a tight fist- the veins protruded outwards. Black strands of hair shadowed his eyes, masking the emotion in them.

Brandon smacked Yuv's head.  "Don't try anything on her. She's too young for you,"

"Hey," Yuv yelled a cheeky grin on his face. "She doesn't care. Right? Afterall age is a number,"

"Right," I laughed, nervously.

"Deva!  Darling, look at you," Yuv's arm left my shoulder. I almost breathed out a sigh of relief.  He strode to Devlin and pulled his cheek. "All worked up,"

"What's Deva?" I whispered to Brandon, watching him fiddle with Devlin's shirt as though it were something filthy.

"Huh? Deva?" Brandon scratched his bald head. "Apparently Yuv's nickname for Devlin my pal- it means loved one in his language, Bengali," He whispered just for me to hear. "Don't tell him but I find it absolutely ridiculous,"

Yuv was pulling Devlin's cheek with both of his hands. Devlin swatted his hand away. It amazed me to see that Devlin wasn't strangling Yuv with his bare hands, considering how annoyed he looked.

"Sorry we didn't really introduce ourselves, did we?" Brandon spoke, tossing Devlin's shirt on the hall's carpeted floors.

"Guys! stop the romance!" Brandon went over to Yuv and jerked him off of Devlin. "For some damn reason, I feel like your mother Yuv,"

Yuv fluttered his lashes. "Mommy," He threw his hands around Brandon and hugged him tightly. "I love you too," Brandon face turned into a bright shade of green like he was going to throw up any moment. Devlin made a gagging noise.

I couldn't help but laugh. Laughter escaped my lips before it could be stopped. I bet I looked like a mad buffoon. Air filled my lungs as quickly as it left. I laughed till tears left my eyes. I don't think I've ever laughed so much.

When I did stop making fool of myself, everyone was staring at me with awe scribbled on their face. I wanted to die. They probably think I'm sort of freak.

Yuv bent down on his knee and held out his hand, his long fingers waiting for mine. Everything blurred into different shades of red.

He placed a hand on his heart, closing his striking black eyes briefly. "Oh, your laugh- my' lady- are those angels I hear?"

I blushed- the color crept to my cheeks like a sneaky song

"Will you do the honor and marry me?" He stared at me expectantly and in all seriousness.

I dared to look at Devlin. He shook his head, muttering something to himself.

"Cut it out," Another voice entered the hall, all head turned in the direction of the voice. A tall, skinny girl dressed in edgy, black jeans and a red, net t-shirt which revealed her smooth skin underneath, stood in the entrance of Devlin's apartment. She had short black hair that barely went past her ear and hauntingly beautiful grey eyes. Her entire arm was covered with tattoos of roses and sinking ships. A small, ruby nose ring was clasped to the side of her cheek.

"Get your ass inside Yuv or else I'll slice your vocal cords," I winced at her choice of words.

Yuv, like a scared puppy, scrambled to his feet and rushed inside the apartment. I almost felt bad for him.

"Do I need to send an invitation for you guys? Get in. We don't need to create a ruckus in the halls. Our reputation is bad enough,"

No-one questioned twice her twice. Brandon and Devlin rushed inside wordlessly. Before Devlin went in, he kissed the girl's cheek. My stomach churned in a way that made me feel sick. "Take it easy, Bre"

The girl cracked a smile; her lips tainted with black lipstick were drawn upwards. Her smile was absolutely breathtaking. "You too,"

She was about to close the door when I walked to it.

I placed my foot in the door to stop her.

"Excuse me?" She furrowed her eyebrows together. I bet she wanted to lock me out of here on purpose.

I slipped through the small opening in the door. She didn't try to stop me.

"You're excused to go to hell,"

# Chapter 20

"**Y**ou're excused to go to hell,"

I know I shouldn't have said that. It wasn't meant to be heard by anyone anyways but everyone in the cluttered living room with pizza boxes and gaming console flung into an awkward corner was staring at me. Disbelief was deeply etched into Devlin's features. He couldn't believe I would say such a thing.

God, what's wrong with me? This isn't me. I've never spoken to anyone this rudely.

Bre dragged her sneakers and skidded to stop beside Devlin, her lips pressed together tightly.

"What did you just say to my cousin?" Devlin spoke, his arms crossed over his bare chest. I didn't like the tone in which he spoke. He never talked to me this shrewdly.

Cousin? My eyes widened when I realized Bre was Devlin's cousin. Color rushed to my face.

Fumbling, I wiped the pool of sweat gathering in the center of my palm against the rough fabric of my jean, a strange lump forming inside my throat.

I ignored Devlin's piercing stare and faced Bre. "I'm sorry I didn't mean it. It's just I'm really tired and all. I hope you understand," I averted my eyes and stared at the blue carpet, ketchup stains adorning it. "If you'll excuse me,"

Before any of them could reply, I rushed out of the living room and into my room. I slammed the door behind me, the ground sinking beneath me as I pressed my back against the wood.

"What's happening to me?" I whispered to the silent night air entering through the parted blinds. "He should not affect me this much,"

'But he does,' A voice inside my head said. 'What are you going to do about it?'

"Nothing, absolutely nothing,"

I lay in bed, wide awake and bleary eyed. Running my hands through my tangled, brown tresses, I turned over and pulled out my earphones. The wires of the earphones were knotted in ugly ways. I didn't have the strength to straighten them. I tossed them to the floor- a pained sigh escaping my lips.

The loud echo of hearty laughter, shouts, and rock music seeped through the small crack in the door and into my room. A strange longing entered my heart. I missed the times when I used to part of such gatherings.

I sat up in bed, the blanket falling to my feet and resting there. I stared out the window, it was dark outside. Collecting my strength I trudged to the window, the gentle wind blowing my hair haphazardly. I watched the city come to life. Darkness faded into golden, red hues of light.

It was like the ground was trying to imitate the night sky, hoping that someday it would look as beautiful those stars shining high above.

I smiled. My fingers curled themselves around my arms.

Aren't we all the same? Like the ground. We see stars shining in the sky. We see the joy and radiance surrounding them. We want to be them. Abandoning the sparse time we have, we chase, we run after the illusion of light. If all of us could just appreciate our own pockets of happiness, wouldn't this world be a better place?

I rested my head against the cold glass, my breaths fogging the vision, distorting the reality laid ahead of me.

Once I had been the same, never really valuing the things I had, not knowing that could I even loose them. I had taken everything for granted. I always thought no-matter what I did my mother would be there to help me, to lift me off the ground when I fell, to love me.

On this day, it will exactly be fours years since her death.

A sharp ringing sound pierced the silent air around me. Who would call me at this hour when the clock was striking close to midnight? I went over to my bed and tossed the pillow aside. My phone lay underneath, untouched and abandoned.

The caller ID read Liza. My heart contorted inside me, so agonizingly that it caused tears to stain the glowing screen.

I pressed the phone against my ear, breaths leaving me in a vapid drag.

My legs could no longer hold me- I collapsed onto the bed, my back pressed painfully against the hard wall. "Liza?" The name sounded foreign on my lips. It had only been days but if felt like time had passed by in years and centuries.

"Sis," Liza croaked. Her voice wavered with emotion. I shut my eyes tightly. I could see the tears falling from her usual bright green eyes. "Today is mom's..." Death anniversary-She didn't complete her sentence. She never did. "I called up to see if you're okay. You usually aren't,"

Since the past four years on this particular day, I'd lock myself in my room and cry. I would cry until I couldn't feel my eyes. Liza would sit outside my door the entire time, waiting for me to come out and when I did she would hug me tightly. She always stayed strong, for my sake, for dad's sake. I never realized how much it might have been hurting her to be strong.

"I'm fine. Actually I'm more than fine. I've never been better," Deceitful tears burned a trail down my cheeks.

"You're lying," She whispered. It was no surprise that she could see through my lies. She always did. Just like mom, she understood me better than anyone.

I took a deep breath. I can't make her worry for me.

"How are you? Is dad okay?"

"I'm okay and dad" She trailed off into silence. "He hasn't come back yet," She added few seconds later.

Dad never comes back home today- maybe because we reminded him of mom or maybe because our house was filled with her memories. Whatever it was, he never talked about it and we never asked.

"You're alone?" I didn't like the idea of having Liza staying at home without anyone by her side. She may be a grown up girl but she was my little sister.

"No, dad arranged me to stay at Mrs. Jackson's house," Mrs. Jackson was a pleasant old lady, living couple blocks away from our house. Mr. and Mrs. Jackson didn't have children of their own so they never minded when Liza and I visited. They actually enjoyed our company as much we enjoyed theirs. Mr. Jackson was a veteran from the army. He served in the American army during the cold war. Now he earned a living by teaching as substitute in the elementary school.

"Did Mr. Jackson pull out his service awards?" I asked Liza, remembering that every time we visited Mr. Jackson he would show us the various badges and medals he had gotten during the time he served the army. He was in the superior ranks- one of the highest ranked officers. It's a shame that he quit the army after the wars.

"He did, I never get over the fact that he has so many of them," Liza's voice was filled awe and wonder.

I smiled. Now she won't ponder too much on mom's death.

"My favorite one is the Legion of Merit. It's so cool,"

"I like the Soldier's Medal, actually no, not that one," I could picture Liza waving her hands frantically and biting the inside of her cheeks as she tried remembering the one she liked the most. "I like the Silver Star. Do remember that one?"

I laughed. "I do,"

We spent the next hour or so chatting aimlessly. We talked about the beautiful shell jewelry Mrs. Jackson made and the new pair of conch earrings she had just completed for Liza and I. Then we joked about Raulf, our neighbors pet bulldog, who had gotten a bad case of ticks and how the poor dog won't be able to get catch the eye of the poodle in the park.  Never did we bring up mom. I felt proud that we hadn't because only God knows how much we needed that.

Liza ended the call, saying Mrs. Jackson was getting worried that she was talking to a boy and was planning a wild rendezvous with him.

"I love you sis. No-matter what you do," Liza said before the phone's line went dead.

Her words echoed inside my head. No-matter what you do.

I held the phone close to my chest, my hollow heartbeats reminding I was alive even if I didn't feel so.

My eyelids fell to a close.

There was fire everywhere. Yellow, red flames rose high in the air, soaring like a phoenix's wings, encasing the crumbling building in its expanse. Inside the firestorm stood my mother, smiling at me, she held out her hand for me to take. I stepped back in denial.

Orange clouded my vision. There was smoke, black soot, and ashes. From the ashes rose another hand. I blinked, once, twice. It couldn't be. The ashes whirled around me; the ashes were taking a form, a man's body. There was a scream. It was my scream

I opened my eyes, gasping and pressed a hand against my mouth. Devlin sat beside me on the bed, his hands stroking my face.

"Alice, what's wrong? You were screaming," He asked, a crease separating his brows. He looked worried.

"What are you doing here?" I rasped. My hands still held the phone close to my chest. Something trickled down my cheek, a moist liquid. I didn't realize that I was crying.

His warm palms were pressed against the side of my face- the tears flowed through the spaces between his fingers. "I was about to call you for dinner. You haven't eaten anything for God knows how long,"

I don't know what caused me to wrap my arms around his neck and fall into an embrace. He wound his arms, holding me tightly, his body flush against mine. I didn't mind the lack of distance. If I could, I wanted to bring him closer to me. The scent of detergent from his shirt filled me, drowning me in a pleasant sensation as I rested my head on his shoulder.

His uneven breath fell on my neck. "Al-Alice, we need to-"

"Just stay here with me," I buried my head in the crook of his neck. "Please,"

"Is that what you want?" He asked after a moment of hesitation.

"It's what I need,"

He didn't say anything after that. With a gentle hand, he pulled me to the bed, his legs straddling mine. We lay, intertwined in each other arms. I rested my head on his chest, the rapid beats of his heart soared beneath me.

He pressed his lips against my forehead. "I'm sorry for every-thing,"

I nodded my head, not having the voice to speak.

# Chapter 21

-----------------------------------------------------------------

I was sat on the orange couch, wedged between Devlin and Yuv while they talked about something totally out of my understanding capacity. A steaming hot bowl of strawberry oatmeal was propped in my lap. I stuffed another spoonful of the gooey pink liquid. It scorched my tongue, leaving it numb for two seconds before becoming normal again.

Bre and Brandon sat on the Prussian their legs pulled together with video game controllers in their hands as they played some sort of fighting videogame on the television screen. I could barely look at the television without wanting to throw up the entire bowl of oatmeal I had eaten.

Lord of all things chocolate, how is killing and punching the guts out of 3D character considered entertaining? There were pools of blood and disarranged faces with massive scars surrounding Bre's character in the game who was wearing a tight red dresses and suicidal heels. Brandon's character was currently chocking a cop to death. The cop's nose was broken. Dark blood poured out of it. I averted my eyed and poked the glob of pink oatmeal.

After Devlin had hugged me for exactly eight minutes and thirty
–six seconds, he forced me to come outside into the living and join
his friends from medical school. Brandon was in third year of med
school with Devlin. Yuv was in his fifth year. It was his last semester
in medical school after which he's going to be joining the interns.
Bre was in her second year at Johns Hopkins.

By just watching the group of friends, I figured the lines of friendship that ran along them were very deep. It was like they could
understand each other by a simple look.

When I stepped out of my room, I expected to receive a cold
shoulder from Bre and everyone else but I got the opposite.  They
were all really warm and nice to me. I felt really guilty for snapping at
Bre earlier. If you ignore the consistent stream of profanities leaving
her mouth, she is a really pleasant person (better than Devlin's
sister actually).She asked me about what my hobbies were and
trivial questions as such. I could tell she was trying really hard to
be friends with me. I don't why though when I had been nothing but
mean to her.

"Isn't it cool?" Yuv nudged his shoulder against mine. I looked up
at him, furrowing my eyebrows together.

"What is?"

"That Scientist have been able to create an artificial strain of DNA
using six nucleotides instead of four,"

I thought about it for a moment and then nodded my head.

"But there's no point of creating something that won't last in
nature. The E.coli strain will just revert back to the four nucleotides
sequence to survive. So the experiment is pretty much a waste," I
replied.

What? Don't look at me like that as if I'm an alien species sent from mars. I know I'm Alice Brown the girl who is on the verge of flunking American high-school but that doesn't mean I don't have any brains. I have plenty. The thing is I just don't use them in proper place and time.

All of us have brilliant minds. The only thing that separates the good students from the bad ones is the amount of effort they put in. I've been on both sides of the door. I know what it is like to sweat buckets and lose yourself in books. I know what it is like to avoid books for the sake of sanity.

"Exactly," Devlin snaked his arm around my shoulders, pulling me closer to himself. His skin flush against mine. It took all my power to prevent myself from placing my head on his shoulder. "The experiment is of no use unless they find a way to express the DNA sequence as new strains of proteins,"

Devlin gave me a crooked grin. I bit the side of my lip, smiling.

"Whatever," Yuv rolled his eyes and ran a hand through his oak brown hair-the muscles in his arms flexed as reached up for his hair. "You guys can pair up against me. It won't make a difference,"

Devlin's arm left my shoulder. I missed the warmth and comfort it had brought.  "Just admit it-you're dead wrong about this one,"

Yuv scoffed, crossing his legs on the sofa. He edged towards me. "I'm never wrong. I wasn't wrong when I said Diana would reject you,"

"Diana?" I asked, looking in between Devlin and Yuv's heated stare.

"Hey," Devlin spoke to me. "You've finished that. Let me get you some more," He grabbed the bowl from hands and walked to the kitchen.  He was clearly avoiding the topic

"I'm full," I yelled frantically, waving my hands. God, the oatmeal was really good and all but if I have another spoon full of it then I'm going to throw up. "No more oatmeal for me!"

Yuv laughed beside, clenching his stomach.  "Dude, you look like he's about to chuck you behind the bars,"

I made a face. "I can't help it. One more spoon of that and I'm going to jump off a cliff,"

"Alice," I heard Devlin's reprimanding voice from the kitchen. The sound of opening of the sink's tap followed. "I rather not have you talk about jumping off a cliff,"

Color fled my face. I buried my head into the orange pillow. "Urgh!"

Yuv jerked the pillow out of my grasp. "Don't hide that pretty face of yours," I could tell he was teasing me again- the way his sharp nose was wrinkled upwards to stifle a laugh.

I punched his shoulder. "Shut up,"

Nevertheless, there was a plum red blush adorning my cheeks.

"Ignore him, Alice," Bre spoke up, placing the controller by her knee and turned around to face me. I couldn't help but stare at her arms filled with tattoos. There was a long brown rose steam winding along her arm. The thorns were sticking out in odd angles.  "He's having trouble landing himself a girl. Though I doubt his pathetic moves are getting him anywhere,"

"Burn," Brandon snickered, his eyes still glued to the T.V. screen.

I found it hard to believe that someone as good looking as Yuv would have trouble finding a girl. I guess his loud mouth shooed the girls away.

"At-least I'm better than Deva," Yuv muttered, begrudgingly. "I didn't try to snag a senior doctor,"

"What?" I asked, confused.

"Let me explain," Bre jumped up to her feet and plopped herself on the sofa beside me.

"No one needs explain anything to Alice," Devlin shouted from the kitchen. I laughed at his panicked tone.

Bre didn't pay an ounce of attention to his words. "Your roommate here gave Diana Evans- our mentor and a senior pediatrician- a carnation on secret admirer's day. Dumb ass move if ya ask me. She's engaged. Hell, he asked her out her in-front of the entire class,"

"Seriously?" I couldn't believe Devlin would do such a thing. He doesn't seem the type to make a public confirmation of his love.

Bre bobbed her head, slowly. Her short, edgy black hair brushed the side of her ear.

"Diana was so embarrassed. It was funny as fuc-"Bre burst into fits of laughter. "She was this close to suspending Devlin from her class,"

I laughed with her, halfheartedly.

"See I'm tens times better than Deva," Yuv butted in.

"We all know how much better you are," Brandon scoffed, chucking the control to the side. He sipped on soda from a red cup.

"Hundred times better!" Yuv made a superman pose and stood up on the sofa.

"Hate to say it, but it was a stupid move on Devlin's part," Brandon shrugged, resting his elbows on his knees. "Really stupid,"

Bre's grey eyes met mine. It was like she was searching for something. "Love is blind. Fu_king blind,"

Yuv smiled, sadly. He was staring at Bre, a strange longing in his black eyes. "You can't control who you fall for,"

Brandon groaned. "This isn't a chick flick guys. Bre come on- you don't talk like that. Yuv, we can't expect better from him but you Bre-"

Yuv dragged his long legs and sat down beside Brandon. He gave him a sloppy kiss on the cheek. "Awh! Someone doesn't feel loved,"

"Dude," Brandon shoved him aside. "Keep the love. I don't want it,"

Bre placed a hand on my shoulder. There was an urgent look in her eyes. She cupped my ear and was about to whisper something when a voice interrupted her.

"Are you guys done gossiping about me?" Devlin leaned against the wall, watching me with a fond smile lighting his features.

In a flash, Bre moved away from me. She gave out a nervous laugh. "We weren't gossiping,"

"Right," I muttered under my breath.

Bre was about to tell me something. Why did she back away the instant Devlin came? It doesn't feel right. I don't know why it felt like whatever she was about to tell me was important, real important -something that was connected to Devlin.

Or maybe I'm imagining it all.

It was around two in the morning when Devlin's friends decided that it was time to leave. After laughing at Yuv's quirky antics and Bre's irritated reactions, I felt tired. A sense of relief washed over me as I watched them exit the apartment. I had school today and needed at-least six hours of sleep for me to be fully functional in class.

Devlin and I stood in open the door. Yuv was carrying Brandon, who was screaming crazy, in his arms bridal style. Bre was the last one to walk through the door. Before leaving she came over to me and gave me a tight hug. She smelled strongly of cigarette smoke and some cheap store bought perfume.

She stretched her black lipstick stained mouth into a wide smile. The ruby nose ring flopped against her cheek. "You're cool," She said, before briefly glancing at Devlin who busy yelling at Yuv to put Brandon down.

"You too," I smiled at her. "I'm sorry for earlier-"

"Look," She interrupted me. Panic was clear as crystal in her grey eyes. Her fingers were in a death grip with my arms. I winced as her long nails dug deep into my flesh.

"You should watch out," She turned her head towards Devlin to make sure he wasn't listening. "Your a great girl and all. I don't want you to get hurt,"

"Hurt? What are you talking about?" My eyebrows were bundled up in confusion.

She met my gaze. "There are things you can't control. No matter how much you love him. You can't change him,"

"I don't love him," I argued, hotly. Red fled my cheeks. If I hadn't known better, I would have believed that someone has set them on flames.

"Whatever. Be careful. That's all I'm saying,"

Before I could say anything else, she quickly rushed to Devlin's side. "See you at college," She spoke to him but her eyes were fixed on me. There was a warning inside them that I couldn't ignore. With that she marched out of the apartment, the soles of her black boots clacking against the hardwood floors.

The door closed was closed with a gentle thud. Devlin smiled at me, his brown eyes shining brightly. Inside my head Bre's words were echoing like a thundering storm. What did she mean by I couldn't change him?

He said something I didn't quite hear

"Yah?" I muttered absentmindedly.

He walked over to me, taking long strides. Hesitantly, the tips of his fingers lifted my chin. There was a slight frown on his face. "Are you okay?"

I looked up into his warm, inviting brown eyes. The faint smell of the cologne he usually wore surrounded me.

I smiled at him. How could he possibly hurt me when he did everything to make sure I was alright?

"My study schedule is messed up," I pouted.

A small dimple formed on his left cheek as he chuckled silently. "You can make it up. Can't you?"

I thought for a moment. "I can if my amazing tutor joins me,"

He gave me a loop-sided grin. "You tutor shall be at your service in the evening,"

"Evening?"

"Yah," He sighed, his shoulders slumping. "I have some work to do so I'll be late,"

Then I remembered the art exhibition was today. "Never mind. I won't home either. I have to set up my painting at the exhibition,"

"See," He folded our hands together, his thumbs making small circles on the back of my hand. "Things always turn out in our favor,"

"I hope it stays that way," I whispered.

# Chapter 22

------------------------------------------------------------

The art hall was bustling with activity and never seen before excitement, students laughed together in unions. The usual shunned out artists, wondering in their own nonexistent worlds were now fidgeting with their batches and making last minute amendments to the stands on which their masterpieces lay.

I stood in the back corner of the hall, the glorious afternoon sun bathing me and my painting in a warm glow. The painting I had picked for the exhibition, against Mrs. Clark's suggestion, was Devlin's eyes. The canvas bare white, only two pair of eyes stared out it.

Oliver was standing few rows ahead of mine with his painting of a girl sobbing into her hands. I noted, enviously, he was in his best clothes today, unlike me in my usual pair of jeans and hoodie; he was dressed in perfectly ironed white shirt and cream colored trousers. He secretly looked my way. For a brief second, I saw his lips curl into the faintest of smiles.

I gave him a menacing glare. If he thinks, he's going to be forgiven for all he said then he has got the wrong idea. I will never forgive him, never. He was my friends, the closest to my heart. There used to be a time when even words weren't needed to convey what the other felt. Now it was like we were on two different planets, where even words can't makes us understand each other.

A heavy weight dropped to the pit of my stomach. Why? Oliver, why did you do this?

I looked away and surveyed all the other paintings in hall. Everyone had put up their best sleeve today, hoping to catch the eye of potential buyers. It's been the same every year; all students put their painting and sell them for a fair share of money. I was selling Devlin's painting because I couldn't keep it. It keeps making me love him with a more devastating intensity.

Sodden sneakers squeaked, breaking my reverie. It was Oliver; there was an abashed expression on his face. The tousled mess of dirty blond hair was combed to one side of his head.

"Alice," He said in a low voice. His stormy eyes watched me, warmheartedly, the same he used look at me when we used to be friends. Warmed surged through my chest, all of the sudden I felt giddy.

No, please, don't trust him again. He could hurt you again, Alice.

I gulped, swallowing the lump of happiness that had just formed in my throat. "What is it?" I snapped.

He winced. "I'm sorry,"

"You're not," I barked back, curling my hands around my arms. "You think it's my fault. You think I choose to be this miserable brat. My mother died right in front of my eyes, Oliver. Do you seriously think it's my fault I turned out this way?"

"You're reacting the way I thought you would. That's why I don't talk to you anymore."

Bitterness entered my mouth. He was expecting this: for me to react negatively.

"Save yourself the trouble and don't,"

"I want my friend back and you're not stopping me,"

"You don't want her back. She embarrasses you,"

"Like I said, I'm sorry for that. I was being a jerk. But for one moment, can you just stop expecting the world to pity you? You have to stand up for yourself, Alice" My name almost sounded like acid on his tongue.

"Pity?" I felt my eyes widen. "Because I don't laugh as often I used to, doesn't mean I want the world to pity me. People change, Oliver. Sometimes they can't go back to who they were in the past"

Oliver heaved an ached sigh. Apparently, he didn't agree with me. The blue in his eyes became slightly lighter. He blinked, once and twice, searching for the right words to say but they seemed to have failed him tremendously.

Giving up on all attempts, he grabbed hand, firmly and took me towards his painting. Students stared, some whispered amongst themselves, their chins jutting in our direction. I could see Beatrice's fellow 'friends' as their lips thinned to show disapproval. This news will probably be ringing in Beatrice's ears by tomorrow.

"Oooh! Olivar, better watch out! You don't want to be caught with me," He stopped in front his painting, briefly glancing over his shoulder to look at Beatrice's friends.

"Found someone else," He replied, testily. "Don't care about her anymore,"

Wonder who the new girl was? I suppressed my curiosity with an overly sugary grin. "Already?" I quirked an eyebrow, heavily amused. He scowled, obviously not amused. "What? Did she dump you into that trash outside school grounds," I pointed a finger towards the window.

"No, I came to my senses,"

"Nice to see you still have some left,"

"Snarky, huh?" He smiled, solemnly- almost nostalgically. "My best-friend is still in there, isn't she?"

I averted my gaze to hide my smile. It felt good, even though for the smallest amount of time, to be on friendlier terms with Oliver. My happiness dampened when I realized it won't be for long.

"This is what you became when Mrs. Brown died," Oliver breathed out, staring hard at the painting. A girl, her brown hair mangled in all different directions, had her face buried into her hands. The scarlet dress she wore was slipping over her shoulders. She sat in a field of grass, her lap stained with teardrops. There were red marks on her arms; she had been hurting herself, wanting to kill that guilt pulling her under.

The painting brought too many memories. It was dark yet bright at the same time. It made my stomach lurch forward. My chest felt heavier than before.

"She just stopped living. The girl who taught an idiot like me to laugh freely had stopped living. I was scared. Okay? My best friend was a mess and I couldn't do anything. I was scared that I would collapse with her."

"But you didn't," I added, my fist clenched together. "Because you abandoned her,"

"Alice, it was scary. I didn't want to go down with you. I was popular then and the newly selected member for the school swim team. I was in the honor roll society and in the national junior league for artists. I had everything except one thing,"

My breathing was rapid and uneven from anger. In a way, I understood Oliver yet I didn't want to. How could he do this to me? Friends are supposed to be with you even in your worst times.

"You," He finally whispered. "I didn't have anyone to share this with. Yes, I had other people around me but I wanted to share my achievements with you. I wanted to see you cheer me from the sidelines when I went for the interstate swim competition. I wanted you to be the first one to hold my trophy. I wanted you to be the first one I could call late at night. I wanted to you to sit with me when we worked on homework. I wanted you to be one with whom I could talk about the new anime series. But I no longer could..." At this moment, his eyes were glistening under the bright lights.

"You were so far from me. Whenever I tried to talk to you, you'd act like I was a total stranger. I realized that I lost you until recently... you started changing again. You were behaving more like yourself. Hope sparked inside me and... I'm sorry, Alice. I know sorry can't lessen what I've done. I want you back. Please, can we be friends like we used? I miss you,"

"It took you four years to say this," I croaked, rubbing my eyes with the back of my hand.

"Boys, argh!" I laughed in between tears. "You guys take so long to figure things out,"

I punched his shoulder. "I swear if you do that to me again. I will kill you and I mean it. Oliver Stale, I will rip each and every bone out of your body,"

"Does that mean I'm forgiven?" He asked tentatively, a smile threatening to break loose.

I nodded my head vigorously, sending strands of hair flying out of my bun.

The biggest and most happiest grin broke out on Oliver's face. He leapt into the air. "Whoo-hoo!" He yelled on top of his lungs.

Everyone, by everyone I mean every single living being in the hall, was staring at us. The peculiar looks on their faces didn't faze Oliver for a second. He grabbed my shoulder and pulled me into the most bone-crushing and heart melting hug any human being could manage.

Our hug was broken by the booming voice of Mrs. Clark. "Students take your places! Our sponsors and guest are about to arrive,"

"Thank you so much, Alice, thank you!" Oliver spoke, breathlessly, his grin growing wider.

I simply smiled before scuttling away to my spot. Mrs. Clark was pacing about the entrance of the hall, her usual playful demeanor fading away. She was sporting a patched up, black coat and khaki pants. A paint brush was stuck behind her ear.

There was a ceremonious toll of the ancient, wall clock. At once, guest began filling the hall. My heart began picking up its pace. I never felt so anxious. It's a scary feeling to have your work to for others to judge and stare at.

Some of the guests were dressed in casual attires while others were dressed in tight fitted suits, who possibly could be talent scouts for art universities. A familiar face entered along the wave of others, the figure stood out in its own segregated space, as though she thought she was superior to the rest. It didn't take me a second to recognize the woman in the huddle of strangers, something about her made her hard to forget. I suppressed a fearful shiver that was about to escape my spine.

Sarah Hutchins, Devlin's elder sister, had just stepped inside the hall. She was a wearing a regal, navy blue blazer and tight, black jeans. Even though, she was dressed for a causal occasion, the foreboding aura of prominence still swept around her like a magnificent ocean wave.

She had something to Mrs. Clark which had caused Mrs. Clark's plump cheek turn the brightest shade of red. I couldn't tell if it were from anger or embarrassment. Whatever it was, Mrs. Clark didn't look pleased but she didn't say so and gave her a polite smile instead.

Sarah strode through the place like she owned it. Carelessly, she walked between the rows of displays, not bothering to reply to the eager smiles the students were giving her.

I angled my face away from where she was standing; desperately praying that she wouldn't see me here.

Few visitors came up to my painting and asked me brief questions about it like: did this pair of eyes belong to anyone, what kind of paints I had used, was there a story behind the painting and many more as such.

A question of my own began irritating me. What was Sarah doing here? She doesn't strike me as the type who would be wondering at a high-school art exhibition. Ignoring the pangs of annoyance that sprung inside me, I focused on my current visitor.

A middle-aged man tapped his chin, thoughtfully. He was wearing red suspenders and a large bomber jacket. After a moment, he scrunched up his mustache which quivered over his upper lip.

"It'zz a vary ze simple painting," He spoke in a thick French accent. I had to strain my ears to understand him. "All ze otherz have vary complex and beautiful paintingz,"

"Well, isn't simplicity beauty? Sometime white can be more beautiful than all the other colors combined because it lets them shine and bathe in glory while it vanishes into nothingness. The white canvas here lets the eyes shine through. The colors become clearer against white..." When I saw the man give me a frazzled look, I trailed into an awkward jumble of words. "That's ....err... what I believe,"

"Awe-striking thinking," An elderly man with greying hair, stood beside the French man. He was dressed in gym clothes and had a rather relaxed smile on his face. He looked like the type of person who spends their Sundays on the coach, eating fries. 'Quite rare to see a young woman with such high ideas,"

The French man shook his head, muttering under his breath. "Zis is insane. Ze have uh horror-e-ble taste in zis art," He walked away, stiffly.

"Beauregard" The man in joggers whose relaxed smile had vanished into a frown, glared after the French man. "Someone needs to knock manners into his fat brain." He smiled at me. "Oh, you don't listen to a thing likes of him say. I tell you, you've got some serious talent. Keep up that good skill shinning,"

"I will, thank you sir,"

"Ah." The man waved his hand. "Don't call me sir, makes feel old prat and not to mention plain and boring." He stifled a cringe. "So call me Abelard, will you? And that was my lovely, younger brother, Beauregard who seriously needs to think out of the box," He laughed merrily. I laughed with him.

"See you around," His eyes, surrounded with wrinkles, squinted down at my name tag pinned to my hoodie. "Alice. Lovely name," He winked at me before heading to the other tables.

As soon as he left, the moment I had been dreading arrived. Sarah was smirking at me, her arms neatly folded across her chest. "So, so we meet once again. What a pleasant coincidence?"

"Coincidence," I scoffed.

She gave me a scathing glare, her eyebrows perched higher than usual. "So you think I'm here for you. That's quite narcissistic if you ask me, darling." She dragged the last word.

"I never said such a thing," It was my turn to smirk.

"Very well, doesn't do me any harm to tell you why I'm here. I must admit you're a part of the reason," She shifted her blue piercing eyes to stare at my painting. "You're better than I expected,"

I couldn't tell if she was talking about my painting or something else.

"I've heard you've met Bre," She smiled, sweetly whilst running her nail along the canvas's edge. To onlookers, it would have looked like we were having a friendly chat. "Warned you about my brother, didn't she?"

I couldn't find the voice to speak in. In the end, I resorted to stare at her with my eyes narrowed and to see where she was headed with this.

She continued talking as though I had replied. "It was the right thing to do. I guess my cousin took a liking to you. What surprises me is that you didn't run away? Not that you have a place to go but still you should have left him,"

"Why?" My voice icily stiff. "Why should I leave him?"

She clicked her tongue, as though I were five year old child who was misbehaving. "I only have your best interest at heart and so does my brother. If he found out, you're harboring feelings for him. I can't imagine what he might to do,"

I furrowed my eyebrows together. "He already knows that. He stood up for us against Mr. Hutchins. He ki-" I didn't completed my sentence, feeling heat rush to my face and drown my cheeks in a dark shade of pink. He had kissed me. Of course, I wasn't going to tell Sarah that.

"Kissed you? Do you even how many girls my brother has kissed before you?" She laughed, mockingly then shook her head at my immaturity. My heart slowly began falling to the pit of my stomach.

"He went against Mr. Hutchins-"I stood firm on my ground. I wasn't going to let Sarah put me down so easily.

"He told me that he stood up for your friendship. He doesn't think of you more than a friend,"

I felt at loss of words. I opened and closed my mouth repeatedly. It felt like someone had slapped me straight across the face. My cheeks burned with embarrassment at my own foolishness. Friend? Friends don't kiss each other, do they?

"It isn't like he and dad are particularly on the same boat either. Picking a fight with dad probably wasn't a big deal for Devlin. He's done it countless times before-"

"Why are you telling me of all this? Why do you care what I think of Devlin?" I cut her out. None of this was making any sense. "As of a matter of fact, what happens between Devlin and me isn't your business,"

Sarah coolly shrugged her shoulders and retracted her hand from the canvas. "Looking out for my brother, that's all. He's too soft-hearted for his own good. Probably blame himself if you had your heart broken because you mistook his kindness for love," The cruelty of her words hit home. I found myself laboring to keep my breathing under control.

"Point noted. You can leave me alone now,"

Her eyes flashed like ice under broad daylight.

"Wonderful," She smiled. With that she left me struggling to hold up and keep strong. I felt more confused and agitated than I ever had. What in the world is going on?

I groaned into my hands. Oliver shot me a puzzled look. "Everything al 'right?" he mouthed.

Nodding, I smiled the widest smile I could manage. He didn't look convinced but didn't bug me about it either.

I was greeted by an empty apartment when I arrived home. Messaging my forehead, I collapsed onto the orange, floral sofa. The cushions sunk underneath me while my bag landed on the floor with a soft thud. Devlin was still out. That gave me plenty of time to think about all that happened today.

I was having a hard coping with all that Sarah had said. This makes her fourth person to warm me against Devlin: first Oliver, then Dad, Bre and the latest addition, Sarah. For once, I want to make my decisions without having people remind what is right and what is wrong. It's not that I completely (and stupidly) trust Devlin. I would be an idiot if I did after so many people telling me he's not the 'right' type of guy.

My heart, on the other hand, doesn't agree with me. It's just hard to believe that Devlin would actually try to hurt me when he's done so many things for me. He risked his career for my sake by giving me unprescribed glucose injections. Why would he do that if he didn't have any feeling for me?

It's official. I'm going insane.

My phone began ringing uncontrollably. I pried it out of my back pocket and pressed it against my ear.

"Ello?" I breathed out.

A frantic voice greeted me from the other. "Alice, I want to see you right now!" It was Liza and she sounded like her hair had caught on fire.

I sat up a bit straighter. "What is it? Everything okay at home? Is dad okay?"

"Yah, everything is okay. I'm coming over to your place. Give me your address." She spoke in a hurried rush.

There is no way Liza is coming here. She'll probably ask questions that I won't be able to answer. I quickly made a hasty cover up. "Let's meet at our favorite dinner-"

"No, tell me your address or I'll ask Devlin."

I froze in my spot. My grip on the phone loosened slightly. I could feel my eyes bulge out of their sockets. "Dev-Devlin? How to do you know about him?" Has Dad already told her about him?

"I'll explain when I get there," Her voice sounded strict, almost like mom when she got angry at me. "Address?"

"I'll message it to you," I mumbled in a daze. This can't be good.

Fifteen minutes later, there was a loud knock on the door. I didn't need to open the door to guess who stood on the other side. I walked towards it, trying to delay it as much as I could but the knocking grew more frantic and urgent.

I sighed in defeat and yanked the door open. Liza was still in her cheer uniform. Her hair blonde hair had been tied into a tight pony-tail. I didn't dare to meet her furious green-eyes.

I stepped aside and let her come inside, silently closing the door behind her.

"I can't believe you would do this," She screeched like a strangled cat caught between two stray dogs.

"I was going to tell you," I spoke, earnestly. Liza gave me a disbelieving look. "I was trying to find the right time,"

"You weren't going to tell me. Admit it."

"Please Liza, don't act like this..." I gripped her shoulders... "I'm sorry dad had to be the one to tell you about –"

"Dad? He didn't tell me anything. Devlin came home today. He was there for several hours, talking to dad." Liza watched with me carefully, weighing my stumped expression. "Didn't he tell you that he was coming to our place?"

He did say that he would fix everything between me and my dad. I guess he was just fulfilling the promise he made but I didn't think he would go talk to my dad about everything. Why am I so surprised?

"Yah, he promised me would talk to dad," I tried to conceal my astonishment. It was of no use though; Liza could read me like an open book. She frowned.

"I kind of eavesdropped on them. I mean I didn't know who he was. He just randomly arrived at our doorsteps, wearing scrubs. I got worried that he was here to check up on dad or something but he wasn't. They were talking about some business deals. Then he mentioned your name. He looked really worried and apologetic. When he was about to leave, dad introduced me to him and told me you were staying at his place,"

"Really? Was dad angry at him?"

"Was he supposed to be?" She asked, confused.

"I guess not,"

"Are you dating him?" Liza suddenly blurt out, looking really flustered.

"No," I muttered and looked away. The air between us had become thick with tension.

"He's really old... I mean...not old, old... you get what I mean. Don't you?"

"Yes," I stated firmly. "He's older than me but that shouldn't make a difference. We're just friends,"

Liza began twiddling with the hem of her dress before meeting my gaze. "I dunno, sis. I just find it strange. Why is he helping you? You barely know each other. It doesn't make sense unless he wants something from you,"

"What can he want from me?"

She raised her eyebrows slightly, her lips puckered together. "You're really innocent. You don't what men want..." She trailed off into silence.

It felt as though the roles had been reversed. She was the older sister and I was the younger one. Wasn't it always like this? I was always the idiot and she was always the know-it-all.

I laughed a manic laugh which didn't sound like me at all. "You ...(gasp)...think " I spoke in between breaths. "You... think (gasp)... he wants...(gasp) ....sex."

She didn't seem amused. She looked rather sad. Was it pity I saw lurking beneath her eyes?  "Yes. If you had any self-respect, Alice, you'd get the hell out of here,"

"Liza. You've got the wrong idea" I reached out to hold her shoulders. She backed away, disgusted.

"I'VE HAD ENOUGH! Seriously, I'm tired of playing mom. For once, can you step up to the plate? It's always me who has to fix your mistakes. WHY DON'T YOU GET IT? WHATEVER HAPPENED IN THE PAST WASN'T YOUR FAULT. IT WAS A MISTAKE. WHY CAN'T YOU LET IT GO!"

My mouth fell open, stunned.

"DAD CALLED YOU A SLUT AFTER DEVLIN LEFT. HE BLAMED MOM FOR MAKING US THIS WAY. HE THINKS I'M GOING TO END UP LIKE YOU. WHY DO I HAVE TO SUFFER BECAUSE YOU DON'T LIVE UP TO HIS EXPECATIONS?"

Liza was breathing hard. Sweat trickled down her forehead and traveled along the side of her face.  Out of the corner of my eye, I saw Devlin standing there, a stethoscope dangling from his hand. He wore a grim expression, his lips pressed together.

"Good-bye," Liza briskly stated, unfazed by Devlin's presence. She walked past him, her eyes narrowed menacingly at him then she turned away and slammed the door shut.

Different emotions collided fiercely against me, leaving me feeling all too weary. I didn't have the strength to face Devlin. I didn't have the strength face myself either.

"Sorry you had to see that," I whispered, heading for the door.

I was about to reach for the door knob when he grabbed my hand. "Where are you going?"

"Not now...please Devlin" The lump in my throat made it hard to talk.

He let go of my hand, allowing me to rush out of his apartment. The thoughts in my mind were ringing so loudly that I couldn't hear anything else. All I could hear was Liza voice calling me a slut.

# Chapter 23

Whenever turmoil rages high above my head, I always get that feeling of being insignificantly small like a bird whose wings have been clipped while the big wide world watches it desperately flapping its wings. I wrapped my hands around my arms, tugging the sleeves of the sweatshirt forward. It covered my fingers which were numb and cold as I briskly strode past the apartment building on the sidewalk.

That feeling of being so small wouldn't go away. As people watched, some glared, I wanted to do nothing more than shrink away. How could she? I tried blinking fast so tears wouldn't form. How could dad call me that?

In a wet puddle, I caught my own reflection- my feet pulled me to a sudden halt. Liza's words came crawling back to me. They moved uncomfortably under my skin, prickling and making it hard to breathe. I loathed myself. I despised my body. My own father had called me a slut. I wasn't a slut- the only boy I've kissed was Devlin. And I loved him.

I still loved my father though and I still loved Liza. Even if death came knocking on my door, it wouldn't be able to rip that love out of my heart. No matter what they say, I will always love them.

Suddenly long, bony fingers wrapped themselves around my wrist, holding it with a hint hesitation, the grip on my wrist felt warm and to some extent soothed my heart.

Devlin stood behind me, panting like there was no oxygen in the air. "Could-couldn't let you go?" He sounded winded.

"You messed everything up," I groaned but then smiled warmly at him. I couldn't put my troubles on him. Never. "But it's okay. At-least you tried. It's the thought that matters,"

"I-I" Devlin looked dumbstruck. "Are you alright?"

I shrugged. "I guess. I know Liza didn't mean what she said. They're family and you know I've been really careless and she was meant to burst eventually,"

There was an incredulous expression on his face. "You were expecting this?"

"For a while now," I breathed out. It was a little easier to breathe when he was around. Strange, isn't it?  How one person can steal your breath and be the one to grant it to you.

But then I remember everything everyone had been telling me about Devlin, instantly my smile dropped.  I couldn't force myself look into his eyes, knowing that it was wrong. I shouldn't be in love with him.

I noted with an unbearable ache that he was still holding my wrist.

"I want to take you somewhere," He whispered, softly.

"Right now?" I asked, surprised. "But why?"

He smiled to himself like he knew something that I didn't. "I have feeling that this might the last chance we have,"

When I asked him what he meant by that, all I got in response was an airy laugh.

Devlin had brought my schoolbag from Enlighten and it was lying on the backseat of the car so were my other bags. I turned to face him. We were currently sitting in his car, driving off to a place of which I had no clue. Wind rustled through my hair as I watched him. His lips were pressed tightly together while his warm brown eyes were now staring at the road in a pained and sad manner.

"Why did you tell me to pack my bags?" I spoke in a tone higher than usual, dread settling itself deep in my chest. "Where are you taking me? Are we moving to a new place? I don't see your bags anywhere,"

"That's because I'm not moving," He answered in a tone that told me he didn't want to talk.

I realized that he had said I not we that meant I was the only one who was moving.

"Is this some kind of surprise? Because let me tell you, I don't like it." I muttered, testily.

"I'm sorry," He briefly glanced my way. I could see he sincerely meant it. "But please bear with me for a little while,"

I didn't reply, feeling more scared than I've ever had. I wasn't scared for myself rather I was scared for him. It looked as though one slight blow might break him apart.

We were on some highway which was winding in odd angles like loops on a roll coaster. Lush greenery surrounded the six lane road. Cars passed in a blur, unaware that of the beauty they were missing. Slowly, I felt my eyelids become heavy and I slipped into a dreamless slumber.

I felt someone pat my shoulder. Peeking one eyelid open, I saw the evening sunlight cast an ominous shadow over Devlin who was standing in the open passenger door. It was a magical moment. Snow fell from the sky haphazardly, carried away with wind.  Someone had pulled a curtain of grey clouds over the purple sky.

"We're here," He said in an icy voice, staring everywhere but me.

I got out of the car, almost in a daze. It never snowed this early into the year. Snow barely covered the cemented parking lot and melted away the instant it came contact with ground, leaving behind wet spots.

"Where are we?"

I glanced around the small parking lot. There were barely any cars here: an old model of Mercedes was parked few feet away from Devlin's car. A little further, there was a towering building with sparkling glass panes. The building was surrounding by several smaller counterparts. It looked like they belonged to the same institution. What caught my breath was the zigzag outline of snowy peaked mountains in a distance. A strange golden halo surrounded the mountains as the sun began to disappear behind them.

"Mount Pleasant Mental Health Institute," He stated, his hands stuffed inside the pockets of his scrubs. The sharp counters of his face were twisted with worry, anxiousness.

"Why are we here?"

"Remember I made you a promise," Devlin tried smiling but it quickly turned into a grimace.

I racked my brain trying to remember any promise he made which involved me coming with him to a hospital.

"I promised I'd take you to meet my mother,"

A heavy weight dropped to the pit of stomach. Now I was the one who felt nervous enough to cry.

I was standing beside Devlin in the spotless hospital hall which separated from this small room by a floor length glass pane. We stood outside the glass window, staring into the room where a woman was cackling loudly as the nurse chased after her around the room.  Silvery hair fell down the woman's back, curling around her waist. She ran swiftly, squinting her eyes when the sun from the room's window got into her eyes, and clapped her hands animatedly. I couldn't hear what she was saying and why she was running around in a child-like manner.

I noticed the nurse held a cup filled with some colored liquid. Finally the woman gave up on running and collapsed onto the bed. The nurse handed her the cup. The woman drank it one go then made a gagging face once it was done.

The nurse exited the room and gave Devlin a nod of acknowledgement before heading off in the other direction.

"Alice meet my mother, Dorothy Hutchins" Devlin spoke misty eyed, pointing at his mother who was now sitting on the bed, knitting a sweater.

I didn't know what to say. I wanted to ask him what's wrong with her but thought it would be too rude to say such a thing.

Almost as if he had read mind, he answered my unspoken question. "She suffers from Alzheimer's. It's in the fifth stage,"

"Does she still know you?" I said the first thing that came in mind. It never occurred to me how bad I was at this sort of thing. It also never occurred to me that man who was standing beside had his own scars to hide. I was always worried about my own scars that I never saw the wounds bleeding under his skin.

Devlin smiled, a mirthless smile. "Why don't we find out for our-selves? You'll be surprised by how much she still remembers. The last time I came she remembered my name and almost everything about me,"

"When was last time?"

"That day you asked about my father," He whispered.

"Oh," That's where he had gone.

"Shall we?" He motioned towards the door then a sudden appre-hensive look crossed his features. "If you want to, of course, you don't have to come with me,"

"Don't be silly," I smiled, wholeheartedly. "I really want to meet your mum,"

"Really?" An kind of innocent glee overtook his face.

"Why wouldn't I?"

"Because she's..." He looked away but didn't finish his sentence.

I pressed my hand against his. There was a slight tremble in his hand as he wrapped it around mine. Heat from his hand seared into mine. My heart began leaping inside my rib-cage while my stomach twisted and turned in ways I never thought possible. He led me into the room; the incandescent lights caused the tiled floors to gleam.

Mrs. Hutchins was devotedly knitting a coral pink sweater, only when Devlin cleared his throat did she raise her head to stare at us. She gave me the most sincere smile I've seen. Her pale brown eyes sparkled with joy as she set aside the sweater and got up from the bed.

She stood in front of me, her hands clasped by her chest. Mrs. Hutchins was few inches shorter than me and had the most beauti-ful set of features: almond shaped eyes and perfect, austere cheek-bones. Age had done little harm to her beauty.

"She's beautiful," I gasped.

Devlin smiled fondly at his mother. "Mum, this is Alice,"

Mrs. Hutchins pointed to him then me and folded her hands together. Devlin flushed into different shades of red. This was the first time I've seen him like that. I tried really hard to bite away that laugh about escape my throat. I failed nevertheless. It earned me annoyed yet embarrassed glare from Devlin.

"What did she mean by that?"

"Nothing," He muttered grumpily.

"I di-did not mean no-nothing by that" Mrs. Hutchins wagged her finger angrily at her son. Her speech was slightly pressured. It seemed like she was having a hard time talking. "Yo-you scoundrel," With that, she lightly cuffed Devlin's ear who now was turning into the color of a ripe red tomato.

"Wh-why didn't you tell me about Alice? These teenage boys, I tell you. "

I pretended to not have heard Mrs. Hutchins call Devlin a teenager.

"I did," Devlin sighed exasperatedly "When I came here the last time. You know what? never-mind." I don't think it was possible for Devlin to blush harder than he already was.

"Anyways how's your dad? Is he taking the cold medicine I left it f-for him on the table? And how's your first year in college going? Are you happy with the English major? Y-you -always w-wanted be a writer for as long I can remember. My, my since you were five,"

Again, this piece of information stuck out oddly. Devlin, a writer. He had English as his major in college.

Devlin shook his head. "Dad doesn't have a cold anymore. That was last September," He completely ignored his mother's question about college.

She seemed shocked by the news. "September? What is th-the date today?"

Not wanting to distress her any further, Devlin effortlessly changed the topic. "Mum, I told Alice that you're the funniest person I know. Tell her one my favorite jokes,"

Mrs. Hutchins features lit up. "Ah! That one about.." She rubbed her palm against her head. "It was the one about the student and the teacher. The teacher was..."

"What the teacher doing? I knew that joke. Darling, I know that one. This stupid disease..." Mrs. Hutchins rapped her knuckles against her forehead. "Argh!"

She grabbed a fistful of hair and tried to yank it out of her head.

Delvin wrapped his arms around his mother, trying to comfort her. "It's alright mum, it's alright. Everything is fine," He chanted over and over again. "Shh...it's alright,"

The nurse walked into the room with a tray of medicine. "Sir, Mrs. Hutchins needs to rest now. Please, could you please exit the room?"

"Take good care of her, Mrs. Smith" Unwilling Devlin let go of his mother.

Mrs. Hutchins suddenly looked fear stricken. "Don't go," She wailed. "I don't like it here. Son, look! Look! I'm perfectly fine. Ta-take me with you,"

"I will mom. I promise. Soon I'll be ready to take care of you. Mom, until then please stay here,"

That seemed to have calmed her down. She settled herself quietly onto the bed and started knitting again.

Devlin took my hand. "Come on," His other hand wiped the tears from my eyes. "Don't cry love,"

A serene silence stretched on between us. My forehead was pressed against the car's window, watching the dark shadow of the foreboding mountains in a distance. Even at the speed we were travelling at, the mountains remained clear as a freshly taken Polaroid picture.

Devlin had his window open and air rushed inside. The air brought along the smell of wet grass and sodden soil.

"You're strangely quiet," Devlin said, risking a brief glance at me.

"Is that why you became a doctor? Because of your mother." I suddenly blurt out.

He didn't speak for some time.

When he did, it was in a cold and robotic voice. "Yes." He held his jaw in a tight position. "I had just started college when my mother was diagnosed with Alzheimer's. She refused to accept that she had the disease. You see, my mother was an independent and strong willed woman and meaning that she had Alzheimer, she had to give up her independence. Small tasks like driving a car, going shopping became dangerous tasks for her. The doctors had strictly advised her to stop driving but she refused. So one day she took off without telling any of us,"

"She landed herself in a terrible accident, thankfully no one was hurt. Strange things started happening after the accident. Mum couldn't remember what day it was and became increasingly grouchy. What the doctors had feared come true. Her Alzheimer was progressing at an alarming rate because the car crash had somehow made a powerful impact on her brain. She was unable to recover from the trauma of the accident. Finally, my family decided to send mother to this hospital. We could no longer take care of her even with a full time nurse at service...it was too much for us to handle. Things really got out of control then,"

"How did you end up for working for Mr. Hutchins if you were going to be a doctor?" I didn't think he would answer me but I was surprised again.

"Well," Devlin drawled slowly. "I was mess back then. Friends with the wrong kind of people and did all the kind of stuff you're not supposed to,"

"Like what?"

"I'm not giving you any ideas," He replied sternly.

I let out an annoyed groan. "I'm not a kid,"

"Fine," An amused smirk curled his lips upwards. "Tattoos,"

I scoffed. "Everyone gets those these days,"

"Well that's all I'm telling you. "

"By the way, where did you get the tattoo? Can I see it?" I edged in my seat to see if there was any black ink visible on his skin.

"It's somewhere I'm sure you don't want to see,"

I blushed and ducked my head to the other side. "So you were a bad boy what next,"

"As I was saying," He easily pulled himself back into the story of his past. "I was a rebellious teenager but that soon changed. When my mother nearly died, it hit me in this way that literally tore me apart limb by limb. I loved her more than anything and I just did not want to do anything that would upset her, knowing that it could worsen her condition. Of course, my father realized this too. He didn't want to upset mum so tried to tame me-"

"Tame you? Like you were some kind of wild horse?"

Devlin laughed. "Something like that. After my graduation, he forced me to join Enlighten and I obviously didn't want to work there. So I did everything I could to escape which always ended me making it through the door at the last second before the security could catch me. Eventually, I gave on the stupid chase game and circumstances were bad enough for our family. I worked hard, eventually my hard work paid off and we gained many clients and investors. At the time, mum condition began to worsen. She began to throw fits of rage at the hospital, demanding them to let her go. It was ho-horrible-"Devlin sounded like there was a boulder stuck in his throat. I placed my hand on his shoulder while he continued press his hands hard into the steering wheel. The skin skimming above his knuckles was pale white.

"I finally broke. It was the final straw. I flung everything down the drain when I lost an important investor. All the burden came on Sarah and dad's shoulder. Dad despised me for what I had done. I had wrecked Enlighten. That day he insulted me in front the entire company. I can never forget that day,"

"Yet you still go there and help them. Why?" I whispered.

"The same reason why didn't get offended by Liza's words. They're family, Alice. I can't watch Sarah struggle by herself. They need me,"

"I can understand," He gave up his dream, his pride for his family. Could someone really love thier family as much as this?

"Well that was really heavy, wasn't it?" He smiled at me, a kind of secretive smile.

I don't why I felt scared. Why was this strange fear trying to clap my heart shut?

"Why are you suddenly telling me all this?" I ran a hand through my tangled tresses, confused. "I mean you never told me anything before. Why now?"

"Because I trust you now,"

And I don't think my heart has ever sped this fast.

# Chapter 24

----

"Do you want to stop for a drink?" Devlin titled his head to meet my gaze.

"A drink?" I whispered apprehensively. Was he talking about alcohol? Looking outside the window, I realized the sky had fallen into vicious darkness as a half-moon had risen to the solemn occasion.

He smirked, in manner that reminded of a charismatic wizard, weaving enchantments through the cold air, unaware of the hearts speeding away faster than ever.

"Let me rephrase myself if you will," He cleared his throat. "Would you like to have some tea? It's a perfect night. The sky's clear, there's absolutely no chance of rain."

I smiled. It was hard not to smile when he was around. "But where?" I gestured towards the winding roads, stark snowy-peaked mountains, and forests of pines and aspen trees.

"There's a place few miles from here,"

"There is?" I quirked an eyebrow.

He turned his attention back to the road. "You'll love it, trust me," Somehow it felt as though there was hidden meaning beneath his words.

"I'd trust you with my life,"

Devlin had pulled over to a empty patch of forest, devoid of trees. Several other cars were parked here, some along the sides of the road, some on the bare grass fields. It was loud outside. The chatter and noise could be heard within the car. There was light outside, a strange halo of golden and red.

Devlin departed from the car and came over to my side. 'come outside' his mouthed knocking on the window. I motioned him to move back a little so I could open the door. He did move back and I tumbled out the car.

"It's just right past that bend of aspen," He pointed in a distance, where the light grew stronger. There was a little opening between the towering, white barked trees.

We walked side by side. Devlin didn't seem to be in a rush, he walked slow, in small and steady strides.

"I would give you my jacket," He whispered, his breath washing over my cheek. "But I don't have one,"

"It's really not that cold,"

He shrugged, a boyish kind of grin forming on his lips. "I always wanted to do that. You know?Give a girl my jacket,"

I laughed without meaning to. "Do you even realize how cheesy you sound?"

"Cheesy!" He exclaimed. "Alice, you're killing me here,"

"Well," I drawled. "I already killed your manliness,"

"If someone heard us talking, I swear they'd get all the wrong ideas."

"Do you care?" The opening between the trees grew nearer as the light grew brighter.

I realized that the light was coming from golden, umbrella-shaped lanterns hanging from strings of wire all which connected to the roof of a small wooden shack like stall. There were people standing in a line in-front of the stall. Few oak tables and benches were scattered throughout the small square of trimmed wild grasses.

Couples, families were sitting on the worn tables, laughing, talking with one another. Eyes lighted with joy, faces adored with soft, indulgent smiles greeted me. There was a small campfire at one end, bodies were huddled close to the fire. Their skins glowed with a orange hue. The smell of cinnamon and pumpkin pie drifted through the air. A sudden kind of homely, nostalgic feeling tightened its reigns around me.

"No," Devlin finally answered. It was a strange moment, his warm, honey spilling eyes gazed into mine. He was staring at me yet he wasn't looking at me. Despair glazed his eyes, hopelessness was all I could see.

"I'll get us some tea," He began making his way towards the stall, leaving me standing near a empty bench frazzled.

"Okay," I whispered to myself. He was already gone.

I sat down, my eyes still following Devlin as he walked, causally, his head hung low, his hand tucked away in the pockets of his scrubs.

What's wrong with him?

I plucked a dandelion from the ground, twirling it in between my fingers. Eventually its stalk grew limp and the dandelion began dropping into my palm, its soft hairs brushing against my skin caused red spots to form wherever it touched my hand.

"You shouldn't do that," Devlin spoke, setting two small paper cups of tea on the table. Steam rose from the cups and danced in the air for few seconds before disappearing. He was balancing two plates of pumpkin pie on his arms in a quite comical manner: his tongue stuck between his teeth, his right eye squinted a bit, and a dimple on his left cheek.

If I could capture this moment and I'd replay it over and over again.

"Do what?"

"Play with wild grass, you'll get an allergy."

"Are you always like this? Or am I an exception?"

He settled himself comfortably across me and propped his chin in his hand. "Like what?"

"This worried big brother,".... I. Did. Not. Just. Say. That. Devlin, my brother, hell no. Seriously, Alice, mum wasn't kidding when she said that I should consider becoming a clown. Let me ask you, how many of you have referred to your crush, your first love as your big brother? Anyone? No-one. I knew it. It's only me.

The words had already left my mouth and I could not take them back.

My words hadn't fazed Devlin for a second. It was like he got asked this sort of thing everyday.

"Is it bothering you?" He asked, earnestly.

"No," I smiled, warmth seeping into my fringed cheeks.

He took my hand into his. Fireworks soared through my stomach, flashing lights and warm sunsets filled my heart which thumped swiftly, faster than the strumming of a viola's strings.

His cool fingers were pressed against my heated hands. "I'll have to give you an antihistamine tablet when we get home-" He stopped mid way through his sentence. A uneasy realization settling itself across his features.

"You're not taking me home, aren't you?" I had conjured up this much. There was reason why my bags were sitting packed in the trunk of his car. I already knew what the reason was going to be. My father had said something that had upset Devlin.

He let out a resigned sigh, not daring to meet my eyes. "You're right. I'm not." His hands trembled slightly as he raised the cup to his lips, drinking its entire content in one gulp. He set down the cup, the papery pale skin around his knuckles reddening. Raven black hair covered his forehead and his eyes. Strand of hair were curved around the nape of his neck. I sat there, taking in his beauty. A breeze picked dust off the ground and spread it in the air like a winter morning mist.

The way he held himself, in a dignified manner, prideful yet enough to know he was not arrogant. The way he my hand, lightly yet tight enough for me to know he was still here with me.

"I'm taking you to Bre's place,"

"Why?"

He did not reply.

"What did my dad say?"

Again, I was greeted by silence. I hated it when he was quite. I abhorred it with each and every bone in my body. By now, I knew what his silence meant. I knew he was blocking me out, I knew he was blocking everything out. Is that how he is? Is that why his sister and Bre warned me? Is it because he never lets anyone break through the walls guarding him. He told me everything about himself because I am leaving him today. He wanted me know, not because he trusted me, because it was his last chance to explain why I went against my father for him.

It hurt me more than I thought it would.

"This isn't about what he said and what he didn't. This about is you,"

"Devlin, look at me," I had an urge to slap him straight across him jface, to knock some sense into his, now, lifeless self.

He begrudgingly raised his head.

"I am perfectly fine, as a matter of fact, I'm feeling better than I have ever had for these past years,"

"That's not what I mean. Do you even know what people are talking about? Your dad thinks you've slept with me!" Devlin nearly screamed, disgusted, the whites in his eyes were a wine red color. For a moment, it did not matter what dad thought or what people said. All cared about was Devlin. It was an insane thought and it scared the daylights out of me.

"As far as I know Devlin Hutchins does not care what others think of him"

"I don't," He breathed out. "But I can't hear anyone shit talk about you. I just can't. Do you even know how close I was to shouting a bunch of curses at your dad?"

I began laughing. I couldn't help it. I clenched my stomach and laughed to my heart's content. Why was I laughing? Even I don't know. Somehow it felt right.

"This isn't funny," Devlin glared at me.

"I dunno. Your face, it's worth laughing at,"

"Alice, you're impossible,"

"Okay, okay," I held up my hands in defeat. "I'm serious now,"

"You're going to stay with Bre until your exams then you can return to your family, once you get the results back. I don't think you're dad will have problem with that."

"I'm staying with you," I crossed my arms over my chest, defiantly.

"No, you're not,"

"What's the point?"

"What's the point?" Devlin shook his head, disbelievingly, laughing a mirthless laugh. "What's the point? Are you seriously asking me that?"

I gathered my courage. My heart picked up its pace. My surrounding, the people, everything was beginning to blur into different shades of red. The flustering sensations inside my stomach told me that I had made the decision. It was now or never. The thought of saying these words felt like dying yet at the same time they remind me of the peaceful moments. The moments where we watched the stars through our entwined fingers, where he held me close to his heart when the tears wouldn't stop, where he brought me back to life when I was drowning in an ocean of darkness, where he chased me around the sofa, where we laughed till the sun disappeared behind horizon, where he held me in an embrace, where our breaths met and became one.

Words were beginning to form on my tongue as my eyes widened when I realized what I was about to do. "Because I already love-"

A hand was tightly pressed against my mouth. It was not my hand but his. "You will not complete that sentence," He grabbed my hand, tightly, almost painfully. "Come on, we're leaving," It wasn't a request.

Moisture prickled my eyes but I did not cry because I felt too confused to do so. He dragged me towards his car through the clearing in the forest. Owls hooted loudly, yellow eyes stared from within the forest.

"Why?" I jerked my hand out of his hold. "You are not taking me anywhere! Do you get that?"

"No, please, Alice. Don't do this to me," He was literally begging me.

"What the hell is going on?"

"Not right now. Not here," He whispered.

This was going nowhere and I gave up even before I fought with him because I could honestly not fight with him, not when he looked so vulnerable.

"Where does Bre live?"

"East Winterville,"

I closed my eyes and tried keeping my breathing even. "Let's go,"

Bre lived in a huge mansion with her parents. Considering what a bad-ass Bre was, it came to me as a shock that she lived with her parents. If I weren't in such a terrible mood, I'd probably be freaking out by how big her mansion was. There were four stories, all joined by Victorian styled staircases. The furniture was old, probably antique and more expensive than all my belongings combined. The ceilings were dome-shaped and painted with vivid scenes of bright blue skies and soaring birds.

I lay on the bed in one of the guest rooms. The pillow was too soft for my liking and my body felt like it was sinking into the mattress as it were made of quicksand. I missed the teddy bear quilt at Devlin's place. I missed the faint smell of detergent from the pillow covers. I missed listening to him come into the apartment and sometimes into my room.

He hadn't said a word since our not so much of an argument, not a single word. No goodbyes, no I'll see you later, no I'll call you, no I'll miss you.

Maybe I should have fought with him. Maybe I should have punched him till he finally gave in. Maybe I should have smashed his walls. Maybe then I would still be in his apartment, listening to him talk.

There was hesitant knock on the door. "Come in," I got up in bed and sat cross-legged.

Bre peeked into the room, smiling kindly, the ruby nose ring flopping against her cheek. She had been really nice about this whole ordeal and had welcomed me into her house like I was family, not a stranger her cousin had met few days ago.

"Keeping your head outta water, huh?" She leaned against the door frame, crossing her long, black net covered legs. Her hauntingly beautiful gray eyes inspected my face with a slight frown.

"Barely,"

She sighed, closing her eyes for a fraction of a second. "Warned you earlier, didn't I?"

"It was already too late by then,"

"I figured," She smiled.

"Then why?"

"I thought it might lessen the blow. You know what, babe," Bre watched me with a certain fierceness. "Let him do what he wants. He's an idiot,"

I laughed. "Seriously,"

There was a strange look on Bre's face. It was like she had suddenly remembered something. " I'll talk you tomorrow,"

With that she left me to find a cure for my aching heart.

I got up from the bed, threw the blanket on the floor and laid down on it.  Somehow the cold floor felt more comfortable than the warm bed. Before I even knew it, I had drifted into sleep where once again I was surrounded by flames but this time there was no-one to rescue me when I cried.

# Chapter 25

------------------------------------------------------------

It was a bleak, starless night when the twenty-three year man stumbled upon his apartment, fumbling with keys, he opened the door and was encased by the darkness of the interiors. He didn't bother turning on the lights. He never did.

"Why am I not good enough for you?" He was talking to himself, yet again. He muttering about lies he couldn't possible hold in his heart.

The tie around his neck seemed to be choking him like a serpent coiled around its prey. He gripped it with both hands and yanked it off.

The lanky, bleary outline of his body was illuminated by the gentle, affectionate glow of the moon, who was again alone.

It was a cycle, the same old bloody cycle life played on him. The same old chain events he had never emerged out of.

He walked to balcony which was always hidden by the blinds. The man stood close to the railing, the rusty railing wouldn't hold up for much longer. Their inside were corroding away, the iron was unscathed, on the outside it was strong but on the inside, only a fool would assume the red rust was sign of strength.

"I did it again," He stared at the open view, tires hit the gravel, the wind whirled about, and the hearts cried.

"Congratulations," A woman had entered the apartment to whose presence the man was unaware. She had been watching him for a while, pained to see him like this.

"Why did you follow me?" The man snapped bitterly.

"I had to see if my little brother was okay,"

"I think you've seen how I am, now get lost,"

"Devli-"

"Kindly leave me alone. You've done enough for me,"

"Fine. I know I haven't done anything for you," The woman was half in tears. She wouldn't be able to hold herself much longer. Her usual posed and poignant facade was cracking like a glass vase under pressure. "I know. If it weren't for you taking the blame for my mistakes, dad would have probably kicked me and my husband out of Enlighten,"

"For Christ's sake, Sarah don't start on that again," The man was gripping the railing as if it were the last raft of wood in the turmoil stricken ocean.

"It wasn't my intention to use you for your talent. I wanted dad to be proud of me for once. Everything was about you. He never gave a damn about me. That fucking sexist pig,"

"Don't" He couldn't tolerate her talking about their father like that. Even though, he knew she was right. He hated it whenever she brought him close to his father's reality. "Look, I'm giving you credit for all my work. What more do you want?" He stood there like a man who had admitted his defeat and was greatly ashamed of it. He had the face of defeated warrior who had a sword pierce through his chest.

"You are well aware that I'm not here to talk about this,"

"The answer is still no,"He would repeat himself a million times but the answer would remain the same.

"Do you like her?"

"No," He replied without missing a beat.

"Yes, you do,"

"No, I don't," These words came from the bottom of his soul. He did not just like her. There was so much more to it than just that.

"Just because dad disapproves of her, you shouldn't give up on her. Okay?" The woman stood taller than before. "It isn't my fault that she didn't go running in the opposite direction. I did as you said. I warned her against you. But she did not so much as wince at my cruel words,"

"That's because you weren't being cruel enough,"

"Brothers," She placed a hand on her head, looking a lot younger than she really was. It was as though she had regressed into her teenage self where her brother used to annoy her to death.

"She doesn't deserve someone like me,"

"She's not going to find someone perfect either. Human's aren't meant to be perfect. Jesus! Bless that girl's soul for dealing with you. I don't know how she did it,"

He completed ignored her statement, his eyes were lost in a world of their own. "She'll find someone better than me. Someone that isn't a mess,"

"You are not a mess! You're just confused about your life. That's all,"

"Mom had fought with me that day. The day she was in that car crash. Do you know what we fought about?"

The woman did not reply. She merely watched her distant brother.

"She was telling me to stop hanging out with Zachery and his group. She had her doubts about them luring me into doing drugs," He slammed his hand on railing. The impact's sound reverberated in the silent air. "Damn it! Damn it!"

"You're not going to lose her,"

"I will."

She gripped his shoulder and forced him to face her. "I am only going to say this once, so you better listen up. Just because life screws you up this one time doesn't mean it's going to screw you over and over again. I know sometimes things aren't in our control. I know nothing will last forever," She opened his clenched fist. "Time is all we have and you're letting it slip away. Don't let her go, just don't. Only few us are lucky enough to find love . I can't even tell how lucky you are to have someone who loves you as much as you love them,"

She was out of breath. "Do you understand me?"

The problem was the man harboring a empty steel heart did not want to be wielded.

"Of-course,"

Behind the locked doors of apartment 303 lay Devlin on Alice's bed. His eyes were wide open while his head rested on her pillow. The smell of her perfume still lingered on the bedsheets. He closed his eyes. It had only been twenty-three hours and he was already beginning to lose his mind. He wondered how she was doing, was she missing him the way he was?

He would never know, of-course.

# Chapter 26

I heard someone once say the only thing that remains the same is change itself. That phrase has stayed with me ever since, always lingering behind my hazy thoughts. It's true, isn't it? Everything changes, even love does. A passionate young love gives way for affection when youth withers away.

Change is what I was feeling right now. As the weekend passed, I spent my time in the guest room, studying-my eyes fixed upon the blinding white pages of the book, a part of my heart was slowly becoming a stone. Yes, that's the aftereffect of rejection. Once, a long time ago, I often wondered what made people to become so distant, cold, and cruel. It was my young self who was wondering about the stone heartedness of adults. Why are adults cruel? Why do they place worldly goods above friendship and love?

I found my answer. When a wave of hardship collided fiercely against me, I began losing wisps of my identity; I began losing kindness, sympathy towards the problem of others. I'm not the only one. Hardship and struggle does that to people. I vowed that I would resist these changing tides with all I had; I won't let the hardships of life kill my soul.

I lost that war.

And yet again, I was facing the same yet different tides of change. I wouldn't let them change me this time though. If there is one thing I had learned during the short time I stayed with Devlin is to never let life pull you down no matter what. His kindness and goodwill gave me hope. It made me hopeful that even in the war against reality, one can always fight the war together; you don't have to be alone in this war. Join other people; be kind, this isn't a race. This is Life. And Life was never a competition.

"Alice," Oliver's hand found my back, he steered me towards the lunch table at the end of the hall. His friends from the swim team were gathered around the table, few of the lower class girls were also sitting at the table, and I recognized some of the faces from middle school.

"Where are you talking me? I'm not sitting with your group,"

"Oh yes, you are," A pair of stormy eyes held mine. Small, red spots were peppered across Oliver's forehead. There was a small teasing smile on his lips; his eyes were almost challenging me to contradict him.

"I'll beat the shit out of you if you force me into sitting with them,"

For a moment, he seemed scared. I could see his mind going back to the time when we used to ride the same bus in middle school. Every time we would into a fight, which incidentally happened a-lot, I used hit Oliver so hard that there were purple bruises on his shoulders the following day.

Then Oliver smirked, his pale lips curled into a victorious smile, he straightened his back, his full height came into my view. I didn't miss the way he tighten his arms to reveal the muscles draping around its length.  "I'd like to see you try,"

I curled a strand of hair around my finger. "You wouldn't hit a girl,"

"You're the only exception," He finished with grin that reminded me of Lord Voldemort.

"What about Sandy?"

"She has her minute math competition today,"

"Right," I sighed as we began nearing towards the table. My old friends came into view, Zack, the boy with an electric smile and a personality to charm, Tanya, a girl who always puts up her brave front even when circumstances are opposing, Solida, who had a brain of a genius but a heart of an musician, Trever, a guy who is always willing to fight for his friends but didn't fight for me.

"Oliver, I don't want to talk to them,"

"You have to. Forgive them and move on. I'm not telling you to befriend them again. Just let go of the grudges,"

I didn't argue any further. Oliver was right in a way but I also could tell he was trying to redeem himself for all he had done.

The minute I placed my bag on the table, all eyes shifted towards me. Tanya and Solida readjusted their surprised expressions into kind smiles.

"Hey guys," Oliver spoke, taking a seat next to me, away from his friends. He rested his elbows on the table.

"Alice, isn't it?" The lean guy with a nose resembling the witch of the west, asked me.  He spoke in a slight French accent.

I nodded my head, wondering how he knew my name.

He grinned at me. "My uncle is a big fan of yours. You met him at the exhibition, Remember?"

My mind went back to the man in gym clothes and his brother with a strong French accent. "Abelard?"

"Yah, that's him. He said he never met a girl with such an imaginative mind." I felt heat rise to my cheeks. Suddenly, warmth and fuzzy sensations encased my toes and cold fingers.

"Well," Oliver beamed at him, placing his arm around my shoulder and pulling me towards him. I inhaled the strong smell of chlorine. "She's the most artistic person I know. No-one can beat her when it comes to colors," The sides of our heads were pressed against the other. I didn't mind though.

Tanya gave me a sideways hug; it was somewhat awkward with Oliver still holding my shoulder. "It's great to have you back," She whispered. There wasn't the slightest trace of malice in her voice.

"You just stopped hanging out with us," Solida spoke up, who sat on the opposite side.  She reached over the table, held my hand in her small one. "We really missed you,"

Trever was now standing behind me, ruffled my hair. "Garfield is back, guys," I laughed at his old nickname. What surprised me the most was that he still remembered it.

I turned my head to stare at him. He was smiling at me. Suddenly, I remembered what I used to call him whenever he smiled. "I see your smile still looks like the Grinch,"

On usual occasions, he would have gotten annoyed but this wasn't an ordinary occasion. He began laughing.

Zack with his short frame jumped to his feet and came rushing to my side. "You know what this calls for!" He announced with his hands hidden behind his back. "A Group hug!"

All six of us got to our feet and huddled around Zack, just like the golden days.  My shoulders were lighter than before.  The world was suddenly not weighing me down.

Having friends is the most blissful feeling in the world. If only I had gotten to them earlier, none of this would have happened. Sometimes you have to be the first one to take a step forward. I'm glad Oliver had given me the push to move on. I would have lived the rest of my life with stupid grudges.

After lunch, Oliver and I were walking through the crowded halls, heading towards our art class.  Few teachers strode past us, some gave Oliver affectionate smiles. The school swim team had recently won the state level swim competition. It was natural for them to be the favorites for some time.

He held my arm, as if I were planning to ditch him and run in the other direction. I didn't have the heart to tell him to let go, looking at the merry grin on his face.

"We should hang out sometime. Guess what?" Oliver started out.

"What?"  I tried sounding enthusiastic but I couldn't keep the tired tone out of my voice. Maybe I shouldn't have spent the night thinking about Devlin. Can you ever feel nostalgic because of a certain person? I don't think I will ever find home again without him around. He was my home, my solace, my safe haven.

And in that moment, as if answering my unheard prayer, Devlin was leaning against the pale cream wall beside the nurse's office with Mrs. Sandalwal looking up at him.

We were approaching them.  I wasn't even listening to what Oliver was saying. My minded seemed to have gone blank, the swirling stars, galaxies, the sound of our laughter, the nights we spent together talking aimlessly were now crowding it.

For a the shortest second, his eyes glazed over mine and being the emotional being I am, I couldn't help but feel my heart give out a painful squeeze. His eyes held no interest, no emotion, briefly they flickered to Oliver's hand wrapped around my arm. I was glad Oliver's arm was there for I was no condition to move forward in that point. He smiled, how dare he, here I was on the verge of tears, there he was, his lips curving ever so slightly, humored by some wicked inside joke.

I caught words of Mrs. Sandalwal and Devlin's conversation as we passed.

"So soon, dear, it's only been two lessons and you're leaving,"

Devlin replied in a polite, sincere tone. "I would love to carry on but my current conditions don't allow such luxuries.

"Oh my, is your schedule really that full?"

"I'm afraid to say that it is,"

Oliver drew my attention back towards him by muttering a bunch of curses under his breath. When he caught me staring, he flushed into the darkest shade of red.

"You have a mouth of a sailor," I commented, my eyes drawn together. "Seriously, Oliver."

"I just hate that guy,"

"Well, you shouldn't" I freed my arm from him. "He doesn't de-serve it,"

"Of-course you'll say that. You're staying at his freaking house,"

"No, I'm not," I whispered, my shoes looked more interesting than they ever had. "Not anymore,"

There was clear relief scribbled on his face. "Thank God,"

"You should talk to your sister before you go blaming someone else's mistakes on him,"

I should have been more careful. I had just found my friend and I was already beginning to lay out the trap to lose him again.

His mouth was pulled together in a scowl. "That's not even the reason why I hate him,"

I didn't even bother asking what was the other reason was. My gut told me that it wouldn't be a good idea to ask.

My legs were sore from sitting for long. I was sulking through the Pavilion corridors when a strange sight greeted me. A group of boys, seemed to be freshmen judging by the way they were giggling and bursting into fits, were ogling and snickering at some girl. This wasn't some girl. It was Beatrice, the girl who had been bullying me for the past year. Her dirty blonde hair were let loose in waves and cascaded down her hourglass like back. This is when noticed the entire back side of her jeans was stained red.

I glared at the boys, giving them my most menacing stare. They didn't even notice me.  "Assholes," I half-ran, half jogged towards Beatrice.

She was staring at her phone, the light reflected off her sharp features.

"Beatrice," I tried calling for her attention. Her eyes snapped towards me, she readjusted the neutral expression into one of disgust.

"What is it?" She barked. Deep breath in, deep breath out. Alice, stay calm. No girl deserves this kind of humiliation, not even Beatrice.

"There's blood on your pants,"

She watched me for a second; the words hadn't yet registered in her mind.

"No, are you kidding?" Her hands went to her back. She gaped horrified at her red stained hands. I don't think I've ever seen anyone look so embarrassed. There were tears glistening in her eyes.

I quickly shrugged off my green hoodie. It was my favorite one but this was more important. "Here," I held it out for her to take. "Tie it around your waist then let's head to the nurse's office,"

She did exactly as I said to do, her hands visibly shaking.

The group of boys was about to move past us.  "Have some decency from the next time. If she was your sister or if this was your mother, you wouldn't be laughing at them like that,"

They didn't have the guts to reply. I pushed past them and a numb Beatrice followed after.

The nurse took Beatrice in for a change. Before I left Beatrice, she gave me the weakest of smiles. The smile was just beginning to form on her lips like that of a bird who was about to take flight for the first time.  I just nodded my head and left.

One question was echoing inside my mind. Why can't all guys be like Devlin?

# Chapter 27

-----------------------------------------------------------------

One Week Later

The week passed by, the same way sand drifts through your fingers. Time is a slippery creature. My reigns upon it had been tightened. I studied past the clock. The afternoons melted into evenings before I even realized it.

Today was my last exam of human health science, the exam Devlin had promised he would help me with but never did. In the back of mind like a silent prayer, his name echoed, burning the little amount of peace I had. My days were surrounded by his memories and my nights were consumed by my mother's.

Love has a strange way of rewarding individuals, a way I will never understand.

"Alice, Alice!" Sandy approached me, her face flush with bright patches of red. She was walking alongside Oliver through the swarm of students trying to head for lunch.

Oliver has a sort of fear-stricken expression on his face which very much reminded me of Liza when she hid something from me. Liza-my throat suddenly tightened.

Sandy seized my shoulders with both her hands. "Alice, we've been looking all over for you," She wasn't wearing her hair in the usual pigtails instead they were cascading down her back, adorning her perfect heart shaped face.

Students rushed past our small huddle. There was so much noise in the hall, I almost felt suffocated.

"I just came out of the exam hall," I replied, wanting nothing more than to run away from here into a much more peaceful area.

Sandy lightly slapped her forehead. "Oh! I almost forgot. How was your exam?"

I shrugged. "It was alright. I'll pass."

"Hopefully these retest will help your GPA," Oliver who inconspicuously tried to loop his fingers around Sandy's wrist. Of-course, I didn't miss the small gesture.

"Anyways," I smirked at Sandy whose face was growing redder by the second. "Is there anything you wanted to tell me?"

She vigorously shook her head not before giving Oliver a pointed glare. He instantly let go of her hand. Oliver's bleach blonde hair contrasted heavily with his beetroot face. His stormy eyes didn't dare to meet mine.

"We should tell her..." He trailed off under his breath.

"Nah-uh, I can't do this," Sandy buried her face into her hands. "You do it if you can,"

"Is that a challenge?" He quirked an eyebrow.

Sandy peaked through her fingers. "No, stupid. it's an algorithm."

"I wish it were...."

"Just spit it out!" I cut Oliver off in mid-sentence.

"We're dating!" Both of them blurted out simultaneously.

I doubt that I have ever grinned this widely. Sandy was the girl Oliver had talked about at the art fair. She was the reason why he hated Devlin with a passion. Why? Of-course. Devlin was Sandy's replacement for SpongeBob.

"Now that wasn't too hard, was it?"

They shook their head in perfect harmony.

Tentatively, Sandy whispered. "You approve?"

"Only if that means you're letting go of SpongeBob,"

"He'll find someone eventually,"

"Then it's a yes! Hundred times yes!"

I pulled both of them in a group hug, my head rested on Sandy's shoulder and my arms was around Oliver's back. "I'm so happy for both of you,"

Despite feeling weary from all the exams and studying, I agreed to go shopping with Bre. It was the least I could do for her. She had been nothing but sweet as sugar in the past week. Even Yuv had been super sweet. He would occasionally drop by my room and help me with questions.

I collapsed onto the pink leather couch nearby. Bre's black painted finger nail skimmed past a hangers, holding up a pearly white sequined top.

"Bre, what in the world are you looking for?"

We had been going jumping from store to store. My arms were aching from carrying about twenty bags of shoes, dresses, and jeans. Currently, we were in Macy's. Apparently, they were having an enormous blowout summer sale. In the past hour or so, Bre had scanned half of their women section.

"Did you bring some money?" She pulled out a maroon satin top and held it against her chest. "How does it look?"

"Amazing. Yes, I did. Why?"

"Of-course, you're going to be buying something as well,"

"I don't want to,"

"Devlin, for the first time, was right," My heart skipped a beat or two, maybe more but who was counting.

She put the hanger back on the rack and continued looking.

"About what?" I sat up a bit straighter.

"You're attitude being a turn-off." I watched her finger enviously as she carefully judged the quality of stitching on the checkered blouse.

"Huh?" I furrowed my eyebrows together. "He said what?"

Bre sighed, placing a hand on her hip, she turned to face me. For a moment, I admired the way the she held herself in that confident aura of assurance and self-worth. Even in her worn leather jacket and black net leggings, she still held some class.

"If life gives you lemons, you make lemonade," Something in my frazzled expression made her say the next lines. "We're in a mall. You have money. Why not shop?"

"Whatever, I'll buy something,"

"I'll choose for you," She stated firmly. I didn't even bother arguing.

Bre and I walked through the almost deserted parking lot. Few cars were parked here and there. The cold wind nipped my bare arms. I clamped my jaw together to prevent my teeth from chattering.

A ominously dark sky loomed over heads. Bre had really outdone herself this time. She shopped till the minute before closing time. I wonder if she shopped this sporadically every time Even so, she managed to persuade me to buy a pale pink colored dress. It was the kind of dress I would have never bought. The hem was two inches above what I was comfortable with, the neckline plunged a bit too low, and there was barely any cloth on the back, just a little patch below the waist. But Bre being Bre and with her unhuman persuasion skills convinced me that the dress simply flaunted my figure not showcase it for prying eyes.

We were nearing towards Bre's motorbike which I'm absolutely terrified of ridding on when Bre broke the silence between us. "They won't ever like me,"    I nearly tripped on pebble because of her sudden outbreak. "Who are talking about?"

"Yuv's parent. Who else?" She let out an exasperated groan. "They won't like me. I mean no parent would want a girl like me for their son. I have tattoos. I roam around on a bike. I literally can't keep my hands off a cigarette for more than a day. I can't cook to save my life. Why would they want me?"

So that's why she had dragged me to the mall, to buy some decent clothes for meeting his parents. I couldn't believe that Bre and Yuv had started dating. It was great to hear that they were so ahead in their relationship. But this wasn't the time to express my happiness when Bre was in middle of a panic attack.

"You really do love him, don't you?"

She rolled her eyes. "No, duh" underneath her sarcastic tone, I could hear the worry.

"Well, then there's no reason to stress," I causally shrugged my shoulders. "You love him. He loves you. His parent can't really have a problem with that,"

"I can't believe he chose me," She ran a hand across her face, the creases of tension between in her eyebrows deepening.

"Hey, hey" I took hold of her shivering, cold fingers. "Don't be so hard on yourself. You're amazing just the way you are. He really, really loves you. I've seen it when he looks at you. It's like you're the only living entity in the entire universe."

Bre exhaled slowly, closing her eyes for a moment. Steadily, she was letting go, the worries, the stress, and the tensions wedeled away.

I continued speaking. "At least for him, don't doubt yourself. Bre, I don't know his parents but whoever they may they'll be lucky to have you. Plus you can always quit smoking and learn to cook,"

Bre smiled, her black lipstick stained lips twisted ever so slightly. "I'll try quitting but cooking..." She cringed, as though remembering an unpleasant memory. "I dunno about that....I'm really shitty with a spatula and knife,"

"Join the club." I grinned. "We should start our own terrible cooking skills union,"

With a very grave nod, Bre replied. "Definitely. We need get some rights for people like us. Let's go on a hunger strike,"

"Nah, I love food too much for that," I laughed.

Bre laughed with me. "Same-"she stopped speaking and suddenly exclaimed "Dr. Evans!"  Waving towards a couple in the block right next to ours, she approached a woman with long, brown curly locks and a man wearing a Eagles' jersey with the friendliest kind of smiles on his face.

The woman was a refreshing beauty. She had a short stature and warm, almond colored skin. Her features reminded me of the gorgeous Latina women in the commercial for dole bananas. The man juxtaposed the woman in that manner: while she was an exotic beauty and he was your typical southern Texas homie.

"Brianna," The woman spoke, apparently she was Dr. Evans. Why did her name sound so familiar though? "What a surprise! You and at mall. Wow, Yudishter has lot to be grateful for,"

Bre turned scarlet. "It's no big deal."

"Anyways," Mrs. Evans smirked on some inside secret. "Meet my boyfriend, Taylor."

Taylor shook Bre's hand politely. "It's always a pleasure to meet Diana's students,"

Suddenly, my surroundings were whirled away, I was standing in room full darkness and someone had rudely turned on the lights. The knowledge fled my heart almost like a destructive winter storm.

Diana Evans. She. Was. Diana. Evans.

Bre's words were drumming against my skull. "Your roommate here gave Diana Evans- our mentor and a senior pediatrician- a carnation on secret admirer's day. Dumb ass move if ya ask me. She's engaged. Hell, he asked her out her in-front of the entire class,"

I wasn't listening to the words they were speaking of. My eyes were fixed upon her. I saw something in her as I inspected her more closely. Something I wished I hadn't seen. Lips were moving but no sound was heard. My thoughts were barracking loudly in no ordered fashion. It was the rapid pulse in my rib-cage and the coldness of night that kept me steady.

"...I'll catch up with you tomorrow," Dr. Evans gave the final word before heading in the other direction with Taylor.

Bre was grinning from ear to ear. "She's my favorite teacher. I love her to bits,"

Her grin dimmed when I did not reply. "Are you okay?"

I closed my eyes, desiring with all my heart to forget what I had just seen. All I could taste was bitter regret stirring inside my mouth. I wanted to laugh and scream at my own folly.

I asked the next question even though I knew the answer. Then why did I even ask? Because reality doesn't feel damned with assumptions. It wants you to know the facts.

"Wasn't she engaged?" I opened my eyes. Discomfort meddled with her taken aback expression. She knew where I was headed with this.

"Yes but she broke away from her fiancé because..." I wanted Bre to stop talking but couldn't find the voice to tell her to do so. "He abused her,"

There was a storm inside me. Lighting slashed my thoughts apart ruthlessly. On Diana Evans arms, I had seen blue-black bruises and deep wounds jarring against her delicate, almond colored skin. How could anyone have the heart to hurt her so badly?

"Why did Devlin ask her out?"

The last stem of hope was on the verge of breaking.

Bre stared directly into my eyes. For a split second, I saw panic crowding her hauntingly striking eyes. "He wanted her to know that she deserved better, that she still could be loved."

"Funny isn't? How he takes pride in showing others love when he doesn't know to do so himself. He pities people, that's why he fools them in believing in love. Why is he like this? Why does he want to play the hero? Why?"

"I swear, Alice, listen to me for a second, will ya?" Bre tried stopping me when I began walking away. "You're a-lot more than that to him. He doesn't pity you. Just try to understand him. It's his nature to help people but you're different for him. I know you are,"

I shook my head, my back towards her side. A tear burned down a trail down my cheek. Even under the open sky, I felt suffocated, suffocated by these emotions. I loved him till the extent that it hurt physically.

"How do you know, Bre?" My fingers wrapped themselves around my arms. "How do you know?"

"Give me some time. I promise you'll see how much he loves you. I'm pretty sure even hell doesn't love heaven as much as he loves you,"

"I don't care about hell and heaven. I just care about right now and right here on the ground. He has shown me enough stars. I don't need you do the same, Bre."

"Just wait & watch, Alice. Just wait and watch. You'll soon be seeing stars in broad daylight,"

<h1 style="text-align:center">Chapter 28</h1>

Four and half years ago

Mr. Brown had always been Devlin's pillar whenever he slipped and fell during his time at Enlighten.  It was Mr. Brown's support system that had made Devlin who he was today. On his every step, Devlin knew that there would someone to stand by his side. Devlin knew he would always be there for him.

He was like the father he never had. The coldness in his own father's demeanor never let him open up to him. He never told anyone but he was terrified of his father. His insides screamed with fright whenever they talked. No-one knew this, no-one but his mother who would soon forget his small fear. He was losing his mother so fast. It felt as though if he dared to blink, she would be gone...forever.

Mr. Brown understood this. Devlin would share his burden with him and he would listen. He would never interrupt him like his father would. His father would laugh at him if he told him how much he was scared of the future. His father would tell him "You're my son, Charles Hutchin's son. What do you have to fear? You have all the money you'll ever need,"

Mr. Brown didn't laugh even though he was a senior accountant. He never laughed. There, he would sit by his organized desk, behind his files with a deep kind of understanding in his eyes.

Mr. Brown, in slight deep, age worn voice would reply "There isn't a man who doesn't fear something. A man who loves is the man who fears. You and I are the pawns of fate. But that doesn't mean we give destiny the power over our emotions. It is in your hand to make everything of the moment,"

In times like those, Devlin wished to have him as his father.

One late afternoon, Devlin wandered into Mr. Brown's office. He wasn't there yet. So Devlin took a seat on the cushion chair by his desk and looped his hand around the small rose-tinted glass paperweight, waiting for him to return.

There was a silver frame next to the paper weight. Devlin hesitated for a moment before picking it up.  A photograph was carefully slipped inside the frame. It was Mr. Brown's family. He stood proudly with the three beautiful ladies of his life. Both of his daughters were resting on his sides. The older one had her mother's eyes just like Devlin had his mother's eyes. She had the chirpiest of smiles. The way she clung to her father's neck, Devlin could tell that they were really close.

This made him feel angry. Maybe he it was more of jealously than anger. How he wished to share that kind of bond with his father.

Mr. Brown's office phone began ringing loudly. It kept ringing and ringing. Devlin contemplated whether he should answer it or not.

He ended up answering it after carefully placing the frame back on the table.

Even before he had the chance to speak, the person on the other side let out a loud, excited shriek. "Dad! Finally you picked up. I've been calling you non-stop on your cellphone,"

Devlin wanted to say something. He wanted to tell the girl that he was not who she thought he was but her excitement dimmed his courage for he had never heard anyone speak with so much happiness. Maybe he thought the world was a lot more brighter when you're a kid.

"Guess what? I won the junior art competition and Mom said we can go out for dinner. Come home soon, okay?"

The phone's line went dead even before he could breathe out the words stuck on his tongue.

He smiled at the silent phone. "Lucky girl,"

Years later, Devlin met the girl with the bright smile. There she was arguing animatedly with the cashier over ten cents for a chocolate bar.

Devlin instantly recognized her. How could he forget the face that had everything he ever wanted? Jealously was rising up his throat, bubbling like a poison inside his mouth. He felt annoyed at once.

Setting down his basket, he went over to the chubby cashier and thrust ten cents in his hand. Devlin took the receipt and the chocolate bar and placed them on her hand.

Scornfully, he spoke. "That's the thing about you, girls; they can't get one thing right,"

"Excuse me?" She bundled her eyebrows together, a strange weariness in her eyes. Upon closer inspection, Devlin realized that there were sleep deprived hollows under her eyes.

"Whatever," He snapped, quickly turning his back towards her, his blood running faster through his veins. She wasn't Mr. Brown's daughter. She couldn't be. Where was the light he had once seen in her?

When she fainted later from low-sugar, Devlin had never felt so bad in his life. Maybe he should have been nice to her. After all it was just ten cents. It's not like he had risked his life for her.

She wasn't breathing. Panic struck a chord, lighting a chaotic parade inside his heart. Alice wasn't breathing. Shivering from the cold river's water, he without thinking twice pressed his lips against hers.

Her chest rose while his fell.

After several minutes, she opened her eyes. Life had returned.

And suddenly he realised that there were greater things she was hiding. Because even though her breaths had returned, there was still that vacancy in her eyes, an emotional vacancy.

He wanted to help her, the way Mr. Brown had helped him through his tough years. Maybe there was another reason why he wanted to help her. Maybe he just wanted to see that face smile once more.

He had been following her since morning. He didn't trust her to not hurt herself again. A nagging feeling inside his chest didn't let him rest in peace.

Devlin began talking to himself, feeling creeped out by the fact that he following a girl to the library. "I want to make sure she's okay...for Mr. Brown's sake. It'll break him if he loses his daughter after he's lost his wife,"

"Yah, I'll just sit here and wait for her to come out. She'll go home eventually." He sat down on the bench beneath the lamppost. "Once she gets home safely, I'll feel better,"

He had gone to the hospital for his afternoon shift. It was emergency case and there was no way he could get out of it. During his time at the hospital, he kept fretting about the girl with the lost smile.  The minute his shift ended he rushed to the library.

"Maybe she left," He sighed, walking from the parking lot up to the library.

But she hadn't, there she was walking along the pavement, swaying ever so slightly on her feet. It was an almost instinctive reaction. He rushed to her side, catching her before she could hit the ground.

And so it began.

She wasn't the only who had fallen that day.

His heart had fallen as well.

# Chapter 29

I sat on the windowsill, watching the orange honey sun peak from the horizon, past the yellow haloed clouds. It was exactly two weeks ago when I had been sitting in my room back home, watching the sunrise with despair lurking inside my heart.

Now here I sat again, in Bre's guest room, watching the same sun, watching the same sky but everything felt different.

It would be unfair to say that Devlin changed me. He did not. He never tried to change me. Somehow it felt like he knew the old me. He knew that I was not who I pretended to be.

He has simply set me free, unbinding me from the shackles that had kept me down.

But still doesn't mean that he's the one who brought the real me out.

I myself brought this change. No human being can ever change you. You always have to be the one to take the initiative.

Everything had failed though. I wasn't supposed to fall for him, not this madly. Maybe he wasn't a blessing, maybe he was a disease, a disease that won't ever kill me.

"Alice!" I nearly fell off the bed, the novel I had been reading landed on the floor with a loud thud. Bre barged into my room like a merry child who had gotten a new toy for Christmas. "Holy shit! You won't believe it!"

She gripped my shoulders with both hands. She had gone out to meet Yuv's parents for lunch. I'm guessing that it had gone well.

"They liked you," I grinned.

She shook her head, for a moment my heart fell. "THEY LOVED ME!"

"I told you,"

"I was fretting for nothing. I mean they're so nice and his mom thought my tattoos were cool. She even asked me from where I got my haircut." Bre pointed at her short cut hair that barely went past the nape of her neck.

"She's sounds amazing," I watched Bre twirl a strand of hair around her index finger. "I have another good news for you,"

"What is it?"

"I cleared all my exams," The results had come this morning, just after Bre had left with Yuv. It was uploaded on my school account online. I got 83% in communication applications, 75% in botany, and 98% in human health science. It was more than what I could've hoped for. My hard work had finally paid off.

There was radiant smile on Bre's face.

"You know what this calls for?" There was a look on her face that told me whatever was running around in her mind wasn't good. "A party,"

"I'm not the party type..." I started out but she was quick to interrupt me.

"First, I'm going to change into my pajamas... this dress is too chocking the shit outta me," She pointed at her tight-fitted maroon dress. I furrowed my eyebrows together in confusion. "Oh! Come on, I'm not talking about a hardcore party. Devlin would kill me. Just a small get together. Brandon and Yuv are downstairs. Bear with them until come down and beat them up,"

"You aren't gonna beat up your boyfriend, are you?" I asked, skeptically.

A sinister smile over took Bre's features. "You have no idea,"

The lounge in Bre's mansion was a serenely calm room. Warm, red curtains covered the walls and the windows, suspending the place into a murky darkness. Yuv was sitting by the fireplace when I arrived and Brandon had hoisted himself up on a metal stool by the bar. They were throwing their typical insults across the room.

I plopped myself down on the black, leather sofa in front of the fireplace.

Yuv shot me a smile. "Thanks for handling Bre,"

I shrugged my shoulders. "It isn't a big deal,"

Brandon grunted, crossing his muscular arms. It actually made him look really intimidating. "Bre this, Bre that. I get it, dude. You wrecked my gamer girl into this frilly princess,"

Yuv rose from the armchair and stretched him arms whilst stifling a yawn. "Bud, if she heard you..." He left his words hanging in the air.

Brandon stiffened at once, his piercing honey eyes widened. I bit down on lip so I wouldn't laugh. "Crap, crap," Brandon literally leaped off the metal stool and ran across the mustard yellow rugs. "Swear to me." He gripped Yuv by the collar of his light pink t-shirt. "You won't tell her about this,"

"She's my girlfriend and my would-be wife." I could tell Yuv was deeply enjoying himself. "I can't really hide anything from her. It's kinda an unwritten rule,"

"She'll kill me. She'll skin me alive. I'm your best-friend. Don't do this to me," Oh my, what had Bre done to them? She had a full grown man crying for mercy.

I began laughing. Brandon stared at me, his skin pale. "Alice, you have no idea. She hits like professional two hundred pound wrestler,"

Before I could reply, Bre had walked in, wearing black plush pajamas and a t-shirt with a skull painted on it. "Well, thanks for compliment. I suppose you were talking about me." She moved towards Yuv, a different kind radiance on her face. Does love really do that to people? It changes literally everything about them.

Brandon's hold on Yuv shirt slackened. He gave Yuv a look that said 'you better not.'

"Seriously though, Brandon get your hands off my boyfriend. I'm seriously having my doubts about you two," Bre smirked. In flash, Brandon withdrew hands and made a face like he was going to vomit any moment now.

Yuv chuckled. "I'm as straight as a man can get. Especially when I've got you," He learned down slightly since Bre was few inches shorter than him and planted a soft kiss on her cheek. Maybe it was the glow of the fire crackling in the fireplace or maybe Bre was really blushing into different shades of pink.

I couldn't help myself and smiled at them. "You guys are can't be real. You're too cute,"

Bre buried her head into Yuv's shoulder, black strands of her hair curtaining her face. "Shut up!"

Brandon, Yuv, and I burst into fit laughter which was a really bad move because each one of us earned a sharp punch. It was true. The girl hit harder than any living wrestler, not that I've been beaten by one to know but the purple bruises adorning our arms was enough to seriously shut us up.

It was around nine in the evening. We sat on the mustard colored rugs, all the furniture had been pushed against the wall. A simple, wooden center table was set between all four of us. Bre had some vibrant indie pop band playing on the stereo above brick fireplace. We were played few boards, made some jokes, and probably laughed more than we actually talked.

It was my turn to roll the dice when Bre announced something that literally caused my heart to jump out my ribcage.

"I know how to prove that he really does love you," She whispered, looking thoughtfully at the flames licking the wood, rising and soaring like a bird's wings, cutting through the wind and sky.

I felt blood rise up to my face. Why did Bre have bring this up now when I was beginning to forget everything?

Yuv quirked an eyebrow. "Are you talking about Deva by any chance?"

Brandon shook his head, wearily. "There's no point, Bre. He won't budge."

"Hey," Yuv clicked his tongue and ran a hand across the rough stubble forming on his sharp jaw. "Let's atleast try,"

I sighed and buried my head into the maze of my arms. The last time I saw him was a week ago. What if he's already forgotten me? Words couldn't describe how much I wanted to see him, to see his lips curve into a smile, watch his warm eyes lure my heart away, to hear him laugh, to feel the gentle warmth of his hand against my skin.

"Alice, I promised-" Bre began, hesitantly.

"It's okay. You don't to do anything. None of you have to do anything,"

Brandon squeezed my shoulder. "No, it's not like that. We really want to see both of you happy,"

Yuv who sat on my opposite side met my gaze. "You can't give up on him," He held up his and Bre's adjoined hands. "Believe me, it's worth it in the end,"

I nodded my head and looked at Bre. "What's the plan?"

"You'll do whatever I say, right?" I was getting an ominous feeling about this but I ignored it.

"Anything for him,"

Bre dug her hands into the pocket and pulled out her phone. Without even waiting, she snapped it open, dialed someone's number.

"I'm putting him on speaker so no sounds whatsoever,"

Yuv placed a finger on his lips, pretending to be a kindergartener stuck in the morning assembly. Brandon simply rolled his eyes.

"Bre? What's up?" Devlin spoke from the other end. His voice had a slight rough edge to it as though he were in terrible mood. I clenched my fist together, tightly, nails dug deep into my flesh. Did he not miss me at all?

Bre was watching me, a slight frown pulling her lips down like she knew exactly what I was thinking. "Nothing much," I raised my eyebrow at Bre's mischievous tone. Was she doing this on purpose?

"Whenever you say nothing, there is always some trouble. What did you do this time? What police station do I need to bail you out from?"

If my pulse wasn't skyrocketing and my stomach wasn't turning into a flustering mess, I would have laughed at Bre's offended expression.

"Actually, I'm partying at my place with Yuv, Brandon, and Alice. For your very kind information, Alice has aced her exams,"

"I knew she could do it," I smiled, actually it was my first full-blow my smile after so many days. Then suddenly a panicked Devlin exclaimed. "Wait! Did you say partying? There better not be any alcohol-"

Bre winked at me. "Oh, sorry. I can't really hear you. The music's too loud. Alice, you go girl! Damn, Devlin you should have been here Alice just drowned ten shots in one go,"

My mouth fell open. No-way, not in million years. Bre can't be serious.

I heard Devlin shout a mouthful of curses. "I'm coming there right now!"

The phone's line went dead. I stared at Bre. My voice seemed to have gone for a vacation to Hawaii.

"Babe, I sure hope you know how to act drunk," Bre grinned.

"That was genius," Yuv spoke up. "Deva won't ever tell the somber Alice that he loves her,"

"But he'll definitely let his guard down in front of the drunk Alice," Brandon added, blown away by Bre's ingenious plan. "No wonder you always beat me in COD,"

"There's one problem," Bre was now paling slightly. "He'll slaughter me for letting Alice get drunk,"

Yuv wrapped his arms around Bre's waist and pulled her closer to himself. "How about we get away from here and leave them to solve their problems?"

"Well, I'm hitting the books, guys." Brandon got from his spot. "I have test in immunology,"

My breathing became shallow, the idea of being alone with a rage blinded Devlin was scaring the living daylights out of me. "No, no. I can't do this,"

"You'll be fine," Bre patted my hand.

"What if he finds out I'm not actually drunk?"

"Well less trouble for us then," Yuv smiled, kindly.

Bre in her sort of persuading voice began. "It's up to you to get him to confess, Alice. I know you can do it. Just pretend to be drunk long enough for him to spill the beans,"

"What if there is nothing to confess?"

"You don't know that yet" Brandon replied. "We've known him for a long time and I'm pretty sure we can tell when he likes someone,"

In all their eyes, I saw hope. For them, this war was already won. Who was the winner? I don't know. Will my love win? Or will the reality prevail?

I nodded my head. In the end, it was their love, their friendship, and bond we all shared had pushed me this far. Hopefully, I won't regret this.

The lounge that had been bustling with laughter and noise minutes ago, now lay deserted. I sat on the metal stool by the bar, empty bottles of vodka and shot glasses laid out like an elegant charade.

My face was buried in the maze of my arms, the cold granite counter didn't faze the sweltering heat inside me.

I know why he was worried. Being a diabetic patient, I'm supposed stay away from any form of alcohol. My doctor had warned me about it, taking me for a stereotypical teenager who spent their Fridays nights drowning beer cans. She had told me that if I were ever to drink alcohol that I took do it with extreme caution because drinking alcohol would cause my blood sugar to drop significantly.

I just avoided alcohol in general. It's not like there were any crazy parties in our high-school anyways. People always mistook the fictional movies for reality. Teenagers weren't as screwed up as on the screen. Most of us were actually concerned about careers and impending college tuitions.

The digital clock behind the counter was flashing 9:33 p.m. in red light.

There were footsteps, soles of shoes clacking against the floor. Someone was approaching the lounge. I closed my eyes and loosened my fear-stricken limbs. Here he comes, running towards me.

Breaths were leaving me in a rapidly drag, my lungs ached inside me while cold blood soared through my veins. There was beast inside my stomach, it was crawling up my throat, gnawing everything in its path.

A hurricane of light swept the lounge. In long strides, he advanced, the distance between us vanishing. He was dressed in a tight, tailored gray suit. Few buttons of his plain white had been set free. A black tie was dangling from his neck. Black strands of hair were sticking at odd angles like he had run his hand through them numerous times.

His golden brown eyes stared hard at me. At a gap of few inches, he stopped. A vein was protruding out of his neck. He held his jaw in a tensed position.

Bre's plan seemed easier said than done. Especially when his strong scent surrounded me, when his eyes held mine, when he was actually here and acknowledging my presence.

I got off the stool, swaying on my feet. No, I wasn't acting my part out. His presence which used calm me down now had me agitated and intoxicated. He grabbed my arms, steading me. His warm breath cascaded down my cheek, treacherous Goosebumps trailed my arms.

"How much did you drink?" He exhaled.

I inhaled. Would my voice give it away? Bre's words were looping inside my mind like circles. 'Do things you would never do,' was the only piece of advice she had left for me.

I looped my arms around his neck. Mother of all things chocolate, if he ever finds out that I'm not drunk, this will be so embarrassing. My lips traced his collarbone, they skimmed above his warm skin. Instantly, Devlin stiffened. His hands were slack against my arms.

"I...(intake of air)...don't... know," I mumbled against his neck.

There was parade inside my body, the marching of my heart, the dancing of my stomach, and bursting of my sense.

"Whe-where is Bre?" Devlin stammered. I placed my hand on his chest, there was something thumping wildly against my cold fingers.

"I dunno," I whispered.

He lifted me off the ground. My feet were dangling in the air as he cradled me into his arms. "Promise me, you won't get drunk again," He kissed my forehead, his lips lingered there for some time. "I love you just the way you are,"

To my hide, my shallow breaths and ghastly expression, I buried my face in his chest. Shiver shook my body, hopefully, he didn't notice. He carried me upstairs and set off towards my room.

I thought I would be happy if he loved me the same way I loved him but I wasn't. Because he thought it was okay to love me and make me think that he didn't. What was he playing at?

# Chapter 30

Devlin carried me into my dark room. He didn't bother turning on the lights. My stomach lurched in an ominous manner. This wasn't right. My hands became clammy and my heart began racing. He wouldn't do this. I know him. Maybe he didn't turn on the lights because he thought I was asleep.

I trust him. To some people, this might sound ridiculous. Liza would probably laugh at me for believing him the way I did. My Devlin had a heart of gold. He thought of others before he thought about himself. A man like that can't possibly hurt me or anyone as a matter of fact.

The soft, plush blanket brushed against my bare legs, the mattresses sunk with my weight. The familiar, nostalgic smell of his cologne surrounded me. In the faint light of the moon, I saw him sit next to me, he tucked a strand of hair behind my ear, his fingers trailing down the side of my face. The windows were open as the draperies flew with the wind letting more light flee into the room.

I still couldn't see his face, all I could see was a faint outline of his jaw. The swaying trees cast a flickering shadow upon him. I could hear the wind howl outside, I could hear his slow, calm breaths trickling down cheek, and I could smell the coffee in his breath. I wonder how many cups he drowned today.

His weight shifted slightly, I felt the mattress lift upward. He was leaving me alone again. If I were corpse, he would be my life. If I were body, he would be my soul. I was drowning again, the enormous waves of the sea began pulling me under. He was my shore. The same breathlessness filled me from the time I was a kid and nearly drowned in a lake.

Without thinking because love doesn't think before it fills your heart till the brim, I lifted myself off the bed and ran towards him. His bony fingers were about to take hold of the door's knob. I grabbed his arm, forcefully. We tumbled into each other, collapsing onto the bed. He lay onto top of me, his arms pressed on either side of my waist to prevent his weight from crushing me. My breaths were ragged, my eyes were hazy, and my thoughts weren't making any sense.

Moonlight flashed on his face. He was staring at me, his eyes were a feverish red- a red that reminded me of someone who had been crying through the night. My finger's traced the hollows under his eyes, my thumb ran over his lashes, stars shined upon them. A tear fell onto my face.

"Why are you crying?" I whispered, knives digging inside me, deeper and deeper they went with each passing second.

The light vanished as the curtains fell back into place.

My hands roamed around his face. I could feel the moisture sticking to my skin. I felt his jaw, I could feel the tension in it, I could feel the rough stubble on his face. I took deep breath in, my lungs aching inside me, somehow his pain had become my own. Why was he sad? I never wanted him to be sad.

Feeling for his lips, I lifted my head and pressed my lips against his. I felt his chest rise under my hands. The strong taste of coffee filled my mouth. He didn't push me away like I expected him to, maybe he didn't have the strength to do so.

A bitter winter storm collided against my rib-cage. There were stars, galaxies swirling inside me yet there were these strange flames rising and dying. The wings of a phoenix soared, cutting the winter storm of pain. The tears had stopped, I felt a smile playing like the sweet of melody of a flute, dancing on his lips. There was light, behind my closed eyes, I could sense the gentle moonlight once again surround us. The wind washed over our skins almost like rain falling upon an unsuspecting traveler. This new land was foreign to me. It had a language I didn't understand, words that made no sense, gestures that confused me.

He broke the kiss. In a swift motion, my hands were pinned above my head. There was a glint in his warm browns eyes, a kind that often reminded me of a deceitful magician.

He peppered soft kisses along my jaw. "I know you're not drunk," He spoke in between kisses, my hands were still above my head. "That means I won't feel guilty about taking advantage of you," He removed his mouth from my neck and stared into my eyes.

I should have felt scared. Maybe even embarrassment but I wasn't. I watched him, calmly, a serene peace running through all veins and vessels.

"You keeping forgetting that I'm a man. I can do anything I want with you," The tone in which he spoke didn't seem to be a threat. "The mansion is empty. No-one is here. It's just you and me," He held my arms more tightly than before. "You're too naïve, Alice." Fear clouded his eyes not mine. He was the one who was scared, not me.

"My life is yours. Do whatever you like," Men do not understand how much courage takes for a woman to say something like that. He had won me over and over again. He was the only reason my heart was beating today. He was the reason my father and sister weren't sitting near my grave.

The hold of his hands on my arms loosened. I don't think I've ever seen Devlin look so afraid. The usual color in his skin turned into ash. He bolted upright in bed, his face buried into the nest of his palms.

In a dreamlike cloudiness, I too followed his lead. Edging towards him, I kneeled beside him and carefully peeled his hand off his face. His face was warm in my numb fingers. He had a defeated expression, his eyes were dull, and his mouth was pulled into a sad smile.

"I'm sorry. This wasn't supposed to happen," There was an alluring softness in his voice. He were a flame and I were a moth, drawn towards him. I rested my hand on his knee, the gap was disappearing between us as he slowly lowered his head to meet gaze. "I'm sorry,"

I understood what he was trying to say. He was sorry that I had fallen for him.

I pressed a hand on his mouth, afraid that he would try to stop me from saying what I had been meaning to say the last time. Then again my heart sped away, again my pulse soared, today would be the day.

"You can't change that. I love you and will keep loving you till my last breath. I'm a one man woman, Devlin. It's either you or it's no-one"

"Why do you love me so much?" His hand was wrapped around mine as he lowered my hand from his mouth. "Honestly, tell me why do you love me?" He had his eyebrows furrowed together as though he were trying unravel me piece by piece and make sense of the shattered puzzle I was.

"Because I saved your life," The tight hold of his hand around mine now felt repulsive. I closed my eyes, wanting to block out his mocking voice.  "Because I cared for you, because I let you stay with me. My love, that is called infatuation, not love."

There was silence. His words weren't sinking in. I don't know how long it would take for them to.

# Chapter 31

I took a deep breath in, hoping it would unravel the tangled knots inside my chest.

In a dark haze, I lifted myself off the bed, his hand slipping away from mine. My hands feel the walls for the light switch. Light fled the room.

My eyes are closed, my breaths are rapid. "You're right. I do not love you,"

I hear the shuffle of bed sheets, the heel of his shoes mocking me as he stands up to leave. Devlin would have left. Almost.

I grab his wrist and push him against the wall, right beside the closed door. He should have been be shocked. Maybe he was but damn, was he a good actor.

"Mr. Impatient, what's the hurry?" I laugh. "Oh, wait. Do you have another meeting planned? Oh my, Mr. Perfect. I don't think anyone will mind if you're a minute or two late,"

I tightened my hold on his shoulders, my fingers were buried in his flesh. There was a slight smirk, a confident smirk twisting his lips upwards. I know he was angry. I could feel his fist against my thighs, I could see the vein throbbing in his neck.

My eyes begin to water, I can't look at him. I don't want to look at him. I don't want see that beautiful light in his warm brown eyes, the eyes that had watched me fall, laugh, and fall in love.

"You're right. You're not the man I love. He's nothing like you. He would never hurt me," I let go of Devlin and turned my back towards him.

The wind flew from the open window and twirled around my skin, hanging there like a gymnastic spinning through hoops. My heart felt like a circus, a circus without light. My senses were turning my insides out but they weren't amazing me. They weren't of any importance anymore.

"I've seen his soul that beautiful soul which can't possibly hurt anyone. I've seen his tears, his fears which he hides constantly. His father scares him yet he stood up to him for my sake. I've seen the fear crawling under his skin when he held my hand in front of his father. He has his own scars but he'll never let you know he's hurt. With a bleeding heart, he'll fight for you, he'll fight to bring a smile on your face. That is the man I love,"

The first tear left my eyes. I know the storm wasn't far. It was approaching, the tsunami of emotions I had bottled up for the past four years were barricading against the dam I had built. Cracks were beginning to form, more tears left my eyes. Another piece broke, the flood was almost here.

"Every night, in the flames that consumed my mother, I see you. You are my phoenix, Devlin. They say if God stole something from you, he'll give it back eventually. He has a strange way of repaying us, doesn't he? He brought you into my life,"

The room was spinning, maybe just maybe, I was the one who was actually spinning. I could feel my knees give up on me.

"Alice!" Devlin exclaimed. I felt his arms wrap themselves around waist, steadying the tumbling the tower.

"I'm fine," I pushed his chest. "I'm fine."

"You're not," Instead of removing his arms, he tightened his hold.

I laughed. "You're right, once again. I've never been fine."

"What happened to your mom?" He whispered. I met his concerned gaze and smiled.

"Burnt Alive. Murdered. By me."

"It was an accident, your dad told me." Devlin held me close to his chest. I closed my eyes, fire had been ignited.

"It wasn't. It was my fault that she died. My mom and I had gone to visit my aunt's labotartory. My aunt was testing out some new chemicals and their reactivity. Mom was always fascinated by chemistry but she had never had the chance to purse it as career because of me. I've always been a problem, you see. She had me when she was twenty and had to drop-out of college to take care of me."

I buried my head into his shirt as though he could shield from the memories. "My mom and aunt were discussing the newly discovered element. I snuck off into the supply room." Images were beginning to form inside my head, clear and sharp, not a single color had faded in my memories.

My mother's face was lit with an intrigued expression as she watched my aunt wave her arms and explain something I didn't understand. This was my chance. Aunt Julie never let me go the supply rooms. I was clever and quick on my feet. Carefully, dodging the workers, I snuck in the supply closet. There were large silver cylinders in the closet. A strange blue knob was on top of each cylinder. Curious, I reached for the knobs.

I was trembling. My vision was filled with red, orange flames. "The gases in the cylinder weren't supposed to come in contact with air because the instant they do, they catch fire. I was the one who started the fire that burned down the entire laboratory. I was the one who started the fire that stole everything I had,"

There were screams; petrifying screams that made my heartbeats halt. I ran, deeper and deeper into the fire. My breaths were raspy, the soot was chocking me. I couldn't breathe. My feet were bleeding but no, I had to be strong. I have to save her.

The smoke was burning tears down my cheeks, I couldn't see anything. She must be here, somewhere here. A door collapsed, burning the skin on my back, I could feel the fire scorching my skin but it didn't hurt. It was as if someone had poured a bucket of icy water on top of me.

Then there was a scream but unlike the other screams I recognized the voice. Dread choked my throat. I felt my body go numb. A woman emerged through the door. Her entire body was lighted by fire. She was screaming. All I could hear was her screams, nothing else-not even the voice calling out my name, not even the sound of the building collapsing.

The flames weren't letting go, they were stubborn. The women stopped fighting. She stood still, the fire eating her away, the red flames swallowing her whole. She reached out for me, I backed away. My head dizzy, everything was fading into white.

The women didn't move, her body collapsed- the fire had burned her down. But before she collapsed, she raised her hand in farewell.

All that was left of the woman was a charred body of black. She was dead. My mother was dead.

I could have saved her but I didn't.

"I didn't even try to save her. I could have done something, anything. Why am I such a coward? I had everything, Devlin, everything. I burned down my life with very own hands. I killed my mother. She didn't deserve to die. She deserved to be happy. She deserved to be with Liza and dad. I should have died that day not her,"

"Alice!" My heart leapt inside my rib-cage at Devlin's loud tone. He was breathing hard, the anger was clear as crystal now. A wine red stained the whites in his eyes. "Don't. Ever. Say. That."

The expression on his face softened. "It wasn't your fault. Everyone makes mistake,"

"My mom died because of me. My aunt lost her job because of me. She took the blame for everything. Everyone thinks my mother died because of my aunt's careless mistake. They're...(sob)... so..(sob)... wrong,"

Devlin didn't say anything. Maybe that was exactly what I needed for once, to be able cry my heart out, to be able to lay my head against theirs and know that someone was here to hold my broken pieces together as I fell apart.

I will always love him for this.

# Chapter 32

----------------------------------------------------------------

After silence was exchanged, Devlin left and I didn't have a reason to make him stay.  I stared at my laptop's screen as it flickered in the darkness of the room. The cream curtain's had been parted. City lights were beginning to come to life while the sun died away behind the horizon.

A nostalgic euphoria filled my bones, the kind one feels after someone takes the load off your back. Breaths filled my lungs easily. It wasn't a lie, talking to someone is the greatest cure.

There was still one problem I needed to solve and that was to find a college to go to. I was thinking of joining a community college since I didn't really apply for any colleges. I could transfer into a regular college after some credit in the community.

A small mail icon appeared on the upper right column of the screen. It's probably some advert or spam mail. I clicked it nevertheless.

To my very surprise, it was mail from Reilen University.

Dear Alice Brown,

It is my greatest pleasure to inform you that you have been accepted to our university. We offer a wide variety of art-related majors. Surprised as you may be, I have would really be honored if you decide to join Reilen University. Your portfolio has impressed our scouts and we would like to offer you admission at zero tuition for the first year. If you can decide to join us, this scholarship will proceed into the following semesters based on your GPA. Our fall semester begins from 3rd September. Be sure to register for classes by the end of the following week.

Eagerly waiting for your reply!

A⊠⊠⊠⊠⊠ B⊠⊠⊠⊠⊠⊠

The Senior Dean

It took me a good five to ten minutes to register the contents of the letter. Abelard- that guy in the sweatshirt was the dean of Reilen University. Chocolate Fudge!

This was a miracle and miracles never happen to me. I slapped myself, twice.

It was real.

A slow, overjoyed smile began forming on my lips. Miracles do happen. A warm glow of the rising sun encased the room. The walls were yellow, the white bed sheets were now golden, and so was my future. After the dark night, the sun finally had risen for me. Maybe, just maybe this is what God wanted. He wanted me to adore life before a miracle was gifted.

Sandy, Oliver, and I sat outside on the bleachers, watching our school football team practice for the last game of the season. The sun was looming high above our head in the cloudless sky. The wind was gentle and the weather was warm. It was a perfect last day of my school life. Oliver was laughing at a joke Sandy had just cracked.

Sandy, I stared at her for a moment, her eyes glowed in the light, her pigtails swung back forth every time she twisted her neck to meet my gaze, the freckles on her cheeks turned brighter whenever Oliver's hand brushed against hers. Oliver, his dirty blonde hair was pasted against his forehead, as he moved- the slight smell of chlorine drifted through the air, and his stormy eyes would disappear behind his eyelids whenever he sighed.

Words cannot describe how I was going to miss them. In few months, Sandy will be leaving town to settle down in her dorm and so was Oliver. He was going to stay with his dad down in Florida. I supposed nothing lasts forever, not even this. Life is like long, winding highway where on the intersections you meet new people and when their exit comes, they have to leave.

"You should come to the dance tonight," Sandy bumped her shoulder against mine.

"We could all go together," Oliver suggested, grinning.

"Not in the mood, guys" I sighed. "Plus I have to pack my bags and head home," The mere thought made my feet cold. I wonder how Liza and Dad will react.

"Aw, bummer," Sandy gave me a sad smile. "It's our last-"night together- She didn't complete her sentence as she stared off at the field where the football players wrestled each other.

"We'll keep in touch. You know like through e-mails and stuff," Oliver tried breaking the strange ice settling between us. My chest became heavy. Keep in touch that never works eventually one of us will stop replying and the other will forget about the friend they ever had.

We'll make new friends and the old ones will diminish in our memories.

"Sure." I whispered, wrapping my hands around my arms. "We'll keep in touch,"

"Yah," Sandy replied, her eyes meet mine half-way. I could see the realization settle inside her eyes. She and I both knew that this was goodbye.

"So?" I could hear the sly smile on Bre's face as she folded my t-shirt and placed it inside the bright blue duffle bag. "How did everything go?"

After stuffing a handful of books inside my rucksack, I buckled its sequin front and turned to face her. "You're not making any sense,"

She collapsed on the bed. "Seriously? I'm talking about my idiotic cousin. Ring a bell,"

If only she wouldn't take me there. I did not want to talk about Devlin at this moment, not when I was grieving about goodbyes and was scared about meeting my family.

How did everything go? I considered her question for a moment, shifting the weight from one foot to another.  I watch the crystal skies whirl about outside the French windows.

How did everything go?

I felt his lips linger down my neck, I could feel his hands around my waist, I could see the fire, and I could hear my voice betraying all the secrets.  There were stars on his lashes and the universe inside my body.

Yet I did not know how everything went.

It was like I was child lost in the world. I did not know where to go from here and what to do. I really hoped that he knew everything, everywhere we had to go.

"It's was..." I couldn't find the words to say. Bre smiled as though she knew exactly what I was thinking.

"Did he confess?"

"I love you just the way you are," His eyes glowed with something I couldn't decipher as he whispered the words in my ear.

I shook my head. "No, he knew I wasn't drunk."

"Damn it," Bre punched the air. "No wonder he didn't yell at me,"

Bre suddenly shot up in bed, her haunting grey eyes wide. "You guys did solve your problems. Right?"

"Well," I curled a strand of hair around my finger. "We didn't get to the  solving our problems part,"

"Then what did you guys do all night long?"

"He was only here for an hour," I muttered, red coloring my skin.

"Alice!" Bre sighed, exasperated.

"Why are being so hyper about it? We've got plenty of time,"

She took hold of both my shoulders. "Has he not told you any-thing?"

I furrowed my eyebrows together. "About what?"

"He's  leaving for Nepal tonight,"

# Chapter 33

----------------------------------------

There was a wild frenzy of last minute preparation inside the humble apartment 303. A woman was rushing between the two lighted stoves, cooking potato gravy for her brother and soup for her husband. There was a sizzle as she tossed garlic and cloves into the hot saucepan.

"Akihiro," The woman spoke over the smoke, coughing and spluttering as the garlic began burning. "Will go check on Devlin and see if he's done packing?"

A jet black haired man with rectangle framed glasses peaked from underneath the plastic wrapped sofa. "I can't, I'm kind of occupied,"

"You just have to cover the furniture. Don't wrap it. Sheesh, he's going to Nepal for three month's not a decade,"

"What if there is termite attack?" The glasses were beginning to fall off Akihiro's nose while a droplet of sweat trickled down his forehead. "Sarah, you don't understand the seriousness of this"

Sarah gave him an incredulous look, not before turning her back towards him. She began chopping the cilantro. "You're such a perfectionist," She spoke under her breath. "Didn't you already spray every inch of wood in here with termicides?"

"Well," His whispered in her ear. Sarah felt pressure against her back as Akihiro wound his arms around her waist. "Isn't that the reason you married me?"

"True," She smiled to herself, twisting her body so she could face him. "But you seriously need to take a shower, you reek of termicide."

He kissed her cheek. "I'm sure you don't mind though,"

"I don't." She pushed his chest lightly. "I'll go check on Devlin. Keep an eye on the food,"

"Of-course," He smiled.

Devlin lay on his back, blinking, watching, and breathing in the cold air swimming from the outside. His American touristers were zipped and ready to go. But he wasn't ready to go, not yet. Something felt wrong.

He couldn't believe his mother, his life's strength, his anchor would do this to him. He lifted himself off the bed, like a wounded tiger, he groaned- as if there were knives and swords digging inside him.

His ebony fingers ran over the letter his mother had left him. The paper was slightly yellow and age-worn. Its corners were rough like the letter had survived many battles.

This was the last war the letter had to fight, the very last.

My Dear Devlin,

I'm sorry, baby, I know by now you've been through hell and back. I'm sorry that I'm doing this to you but I have my reasons.

He began crying again, stars landed on the paper, smearing the ink, making a river of blue flow down the page.

If the doctors have given you this letter then it only means one thing, I've gotten worse and my Alzheimer's had progressed into its final days. I don't want to live a life as ghost, darling, I want to die in your memory as the mother who used laugh with you, not the one who doesn't remember her own son, her own family. I want to die with the little dignity I have left.

Why Nepal? You've must be asking yourself. Why does my mother want to die in Nepal? There are so many things I haven't told, there so many tales about my youth I want to tell you but I've run out of time like all of us do.

Before you and Sarah were born, before I met your dad, I was a mountaineer. A God damn, good one!

Devlin laughed through the tears.

Mt. Everest was my last mission. Ambitious as it was, I was never able to reach the summit. It was a beautiful journey though and I have no qualms or regrets about it.  Devlin, that mountain taught me so many things. Lessons I failed to learned from humans. It would free my soul to die in the air of Nepal.

This is my last wish before I do die, my son, to die in the lap of my spirit, the spirit of Mt. Everest.

My love, look after your father- I know he scares you but he's doesn't have a bad heart. There is only love for you inside him, he loved more than I've ever loved you. He's lacking in the prospect of showing affection and so are you, maybe that's why you two never got along...

...Always stay by your older sister's side.  She can be selfish, that girl, but Devlin, you know her more than I do and you know how much she's done for all of us. You were always the pillar she could rest her head upon. I just fear you might hinder her from reaching her full potential. Sometimes we have to the bird fly on its own rather than carry it on our back.

And last of all, Devlin, take care of yourself. I've always been worried for you. My dear, you're too soft-hearted and honest. Go so much after your father. He used to be like you until some people betrayed his trust. In this world, there are many kinds of people, some who take advantage of good people. Remember dear, there's a thin line between being foolish and being good.

Life gives us many scars. A true human being is the one that carries his scars and does not let them pull him down. I know my death will be hard on you, your father, and your sister. Remember, love, I will always be alive in your memories. All of us have to leave this world one day. It's just that some of us have to leave earlier than others.

I know you must be crying right now. Trust me when I write this, I can feel the wetness of your tears on my bosom. Dear, I don't want you to cry. I want to smile and be happy. You always used to say that I'm the funniest mum a boy can have. For your funny mama, laugh dear, give me a joyful farewell.

Your mother,

Dorothy Hutchins

The letter slipped out of his hand and landed on the floor, next to Sarah's feet. With frowning eyes, a downturn on her lips-Sarah whispered "Are you crying?"

Devlin quickly swept the tears from his eyes. "I was thinking about Alice," It seemed like a good enough excuse for everything these days. No-one doubted him when he said so, not even for a second.

"You should tell her how you feel," She was about to walk over to her brother's side, when her foot collided with the letter. "What is this?" She spoke, reaching for the worn piece of paper.

Her brother, always the quicker one, acted on his reflexes and swooped the letter from her feet. "Nothing important,"

Sarah, being the carefree one, shrugged her shoulders. "As you say. Get ready, we need to head out for dad's party. Apparently we've got new clients. Hooray!"

"Yah," Devlin swallowed the lump in his throat.

"Wear that black suit I bought for you last Christmas along with that brown-striped shirt." Sarah smiled, her rare smiles. There was a bright, happy light in her eyes. "It looks really good on you,"

"Okay,"

She was half-way out of the door when she spun around to face her beloved brother. "It's a really nice thing you're doing. Taking mum with you on your charity trip. Maybe her condition will start improving. God knows what can happen, maybe some kind of miracle,"

Devlin couldn't form any coherent words on his tongue. If she only the truth, he was going to Nepal not to save his mother but to fulfil her death wish.

# Chapter 34

----------------------------------------------------------------

Somehow half an hour later, I find myself in a red dress, standing outside a star-studded banquet. There were people standing in small, formal groups, some were dancing in the middle. A man was playing a sad tune on his violin, the melody hung in the air before drowning in the noise of the chatter.

I clung to Yuv's side as he led me through the masses of people. Dressed like the next James Bonds, he gave me a cheeky grin. "We'll find him. Don't worry,"

"That's not what I'm worried about," I muttered as my eyes scanned the simple, lilac filled ground. There were few cream colored silk drapes tied upside down into a small canopy. All the office staff of Enlighten was here. I feared for my dear life.

I didn't want to bump into Mr. Hutchins, better yet into Sarah.

What am I doing here anyways? I wasn't here at this beautiful party to ask for explanations. I just wanted to see him before he left for Nepal. Maybe this will be the last chance I have.

I recognized some of my father's colleagues by the buffet. Is he here too? Unfamiliar faces surrounded me, they blur under the yellow lights.

Yuv pointed a finger at the center of the trimmed grass ground where Devlin was dancing, in confident strides, he held a woman in a bold, gold dress by the waist. They moved through the strings of dancers. There were dark hollows under his eyes, even though he stood amongst a merry crowd, not a single ounce of cheer filled him. My arms were aching to go and breathe life into his lifeless self. I hated when he was sad. It was like dying a thousand every second.

"I'll go bring him," Yuv's eyes flickered from Devlin to me. "Stay here,"

I wanted to tell him that I wasn't here to talk to him. I just wanted to watch him, watch him become less and less the man I knew.

"There's no need," Sarah approached us, her blue eyes narrowed on my face. "You should be the one going to him, not the other way around,"

Yuv clenched and unclenched his fist. "Sarah, you know nothing so stay out of this,"

She curled her hands around my wrist, the diamond bracelet on her wrist felt cold against my skin. "What did you do to him?"

I couldn't reply. My eyes had been caught by her brother.

I could distantly hear Yuv. "... he didn't even tell her..."

Devlin's hand slackened from the woman's waist. He half-ran, half-walked towards me, quite breathlessly. It was like he was running away from death -that was the kind of desperation in his expression.

"Alice, Alice..." his lips read.

Seconds later I was wrapped in his arms. He held me as a lifeless soul clenching to the last air of life. Everyone was watching us, even Mr. Hutchins. To my surprise, he wasn't angry. There was a misty look glazing his eyes. He smiled at me, a wavering smile.

I felt Devlin's breath fall over my neck. "Please, take me away from here. I can't take it anymore."

I drove us far from the party, far from the prying eyes to the place where it all had begun. All the time I drove the car, he cried. Silent tears dripped down his face, flowing down his neck and staining the brown shirt he was wearing.

I had to lift him up the stairs. There was barely any energy left inside him.

We sat on the floor of his apartment, two bodied molded into one. He told me everything: from his mother wanting voluntary euthanasia till the point of loving me so desperately that it physically pained him.

I listened, not saying a word when he spoke. My desire for wanting him to confess his love seemed selfish and childish now.

"One moment I have everything sorted out. I know what I want to do and who I want to be. Suddenly it all vanishes into thin air and life doesn't have meaning anymore,"

Have you ever had a needle prickle your finger? In this moment, seeing him like this felt like there were thousands of needles skimming above my skin. He sat there like a broken glass figure, his eyes red, and tears frozen on his cheeks. A lost look haunted his eyes.

"She always begged me to take her home. She didn't like the hospital. It made her sick. I always thought let me completed my MD then I'll be capable to take care of her but God!"

He sobbed. "I didn't know she had other plans. I don't know what to do without her,"

"Yes, you do." I whispered. Devlin looked at me. "She was proud of you for chasing your dream,"

"I don't understand,"

"You should chase the dream you abandoned for your family," I wiped the tears from under his eyes. "It's time you stopped thinking about others. You need to live for yourself." I smiled, as I repeated the words he had once said to me.

"Look at you," Slowly a smile, flickering as an open flame, began forming on his lips. "You've grown so much,"

"What can I say?" I sighed. "You've rubbed off on me,"

He laughed, a throaty laugh. It made my cold toes warm up.

"You will though, right?" I entangled our fingers together so our hands looked as though they were one. "Learn to live again and try reaching for your dream,"

We stared into each other's eyes, trying not to get lost as storms whirled around us. "I will, my angel"

# Epilogue

----------------------------------------------------------------

8 3 days later

Cooking classes weren't as hard as I thought they would be (well most of the time). Bre and I finally had started attending these classes for the past month or so. Strangely enough, Sarah had tagged along with us. I really doubt that she needed any help with her culinary skills. She was killing the class with an A plus (not that we were getting graded but if we had been, she would get an A).

We were making bread today and I had accidently had too much water to my mixture. Strings of dough hung from my fingers.

Sarah clicked her tongue. "This is supposed to the easiest bread recipe ever,"

Bre glared at her. It was enough to make Sarah shut up.

Coincidentally, we shared the same counter so whatever mess or mistake I made didn't miss Sarah for a second.

Our instructor was just about to reach our table. If he caught this mess today, he'll turn me into the laughing stock of the class. That man was always looking for a reason to laugh.

Before I could even blink an eye, Sarah took my mixing bowl and replaced it with hers.

"Use my dough. I'll fix this," She muttered under breath. She added more flour to the mixture and began kneading it with both hands.

I smiled. "Thanks,"

"Just promise me one thing," I could tell Sarah was trying to bite off the mischievous smile.

"What?"

"When you two do get married, you'll let my brother do the cooking."

Bre coughed up a laugh while I tried really hard not to die out of mortification.

Sarah jabbed an elbow into Bre's ribs. "I trained him well, you know,"

"I want to go visit mom," I whispered as I helped Liza carry the laundry basket upstairs. "You know before I start college, I just want to..."

Liza gave me a soft, understanding smile. "I know what you mean. We'll go together after lunch,"

"Okay,"

"Liza, go grab the car keys," I spoke, getting from up from the table.

Dad set his fork down. "Going out somewhere girls?"

Liza gave me a cautious glare. I knew well what she was trying to hint at. Dad never liked it when we brought up mom's death or anything related to our mother.

"We were going to visit mom's grave" I spoke, hesitantly. Dad and I had just mended our relationship. I don't think it was a good idea to put strain on it so soon.

He got up from his chair, a grave expression on his face. "I'll come too,"

Liza and I exchanged surprised looks.

"I think my daughters have had enough. It's about time their father took some of his responsibility. Don't you think?"

Liza and I ran to dad and hugged him as tightly we could.

He tried inconspicuously wiping the tears from his eyes. "I'll be in the car. Hurry up. We can't keep your mom waiting."

He left us alone and staggered outside.

"This is great!" Liza grinned from ear to ear.

I nodded.

Suddenly, my phone began blaring. A flustering sensation erupted in my stomach when I read the caller id.

Liza smirked. "I'll clean table," She winked before leaving me standing in the dining room. That girl, seriously, is it me or is she becoming naughtier by the day?

I pressed the phone against my ear. Even before I could say hello, Devlin's voice greeted me. "I'm coming home, love,"

I closed my eyes as relief filled my bones. "I'll be waiting".

www.ingramcontent.com/pod-product-compliance
Lightning Source LLC
Chambersburg PA
CBHW071723190726
48292CB00003B/585